THE PRIVATE REHEARSAL

LAUREN BLAKELY

ALSO BY LAUREN BLAKELY

Big Rock Series

Big Rock

Mister O

Well Hung

Full Package

Joy Ride

Hard Wood

The Gift Series

The Engagement Gift

The Virgin Gift

The Decadent Gift (coming soon)

The Heartbreakers Series

Once Upon a Real Good Time

Once Upon a Sure Thing

Once Upon a Wild Fling

Boyfriend Material

Asking For a Friend

Sex and Other Shiny Objects

One Night Stand-In

Lucky In Love Series

Best Laid Plans

The Feel Good Factor

Nobody Does It Better

Unzipped

Always Satisfied Series

Satisfaction Guaranteed

Instant Gratification

Overnight Service

Never Have I Ever

Special Delivery

The Sexy Suit Series

Lucky Suit

Birthday Suit

From Paris With Love

Wanderlust

Part-Time Lover

One Love Series

The Sexy One

The Only One

The Hot One

The Knocked Up Plan

The No Regrets Series

The Thrill of It

The Start of Us

Every Second With You

The Seductive Nights Series

First Night (Julia and Clay, prequel novella)

Night After Night (Julia and Clay, book one)

After This Night (Julia and Clay, book two)

One More Night (Julia and Clay, book three)

A Wildly Seductive Night (Julia and Clay novella, book 3.5)

The Joy Delivered Duet

Nights With Him (A standalone novel about Michelle and Jack)

Forbidden Nights (A standalone novel about Nate and Casey)

The Sinful Nights Series

Sweet Sinful Nights

Sinful Desire

Sinful Longing

Sinful Love

The Fighting Fire Series

Burn For Me (Smith and Jamie)

Melt for Him (Megan and Becker)

Consumed By You (Travis and Cara)

The Jewel Series

A two-book sexy contemporary romance series

The Sapphire Affair

The Sapphire Heist

ABOUT

From #1 *New York Times* bestselling author Lauren Blakely comes a scintillating forbidden romance between a director and his actress...

The first rule of directing is simple: Never fall for your leading lady.

The second? Don't let it get to you when she stage kisses another man.

Looks like I've already broken both. Now my jealous, possessive heart wants all of her – the ingenue who's the star of my next show. I'm captivated by her raw talent, her addictive charm, and her desperate need for me.

Soon we're staying late in the empty theater, our private rehearsals spiraling into forbidden territory.

Exactly where I can't go. Because then I'd break the most dangerous rule of all.

Don't give her your heart.

Because how can I be sure that what she feels is real and not a part of the play?

Author's Note: The Private Rehearsal was previously titled Playing With Her Heart. It has been significantly revised and updated. I hope you enjoy this new edition of one of my first novels!

THE PRIVATE REHEARSAL

By Lauren Blakely

Want to be the first to learn of sales, new releases, preorders and special freebies? Sign up for my VIP mailing list here!

PROLOGUE

JILL

There's a magic moment in the theater, when the lights go down and you know that when they come up, you'll be a different person. I leave my past backstage and enter the scene as my character, and I'm self-assured and brave. I share a lingering look with the handsome man across the crowded room, then I turn away to mingle with the other guests. I don't go far before a hand brushes my shoulder. I shudder. Close my eyes. Feel him near me. Everything else fades away, and we're the only ones there. He kisses me. I kiss him back, feeling the kiss in every cell—deep, and fevered, and possessive. My head spins because my character is falling head-over-heels. I am that woman on the stage, and I can have what she has, know what she knows. Love without reason. Love without fear.

For two hours, in that world under the spotlights, I'm living someone else's life.

Then the play ends, the curtain falls, and I am back to being me. I come down from my high still wanting, missing something that was only pretend. I'll need another play, another character to become before I feel this way again.

The curtain rises to applause, and I take my bow, saying goodbye to the character, to the kiss, to love that only happens in stories and make-believe.

At least, I've always thought so.

1

DAVIS

She has my attention the moment she steps onto the stage at the St. James Theater, but when I hear her sing, I know she's my Ava.

After the opening bars from the accompanist, she doesn't launch into the solo—she floats into it with a tremulous, vulnerable quality that gives me chills. Her voice strengthens as emotions swell to match the lyrics, playing out the story in the music: a young woman on her own, searching for the way to reach her dream and finally finding it through pain and patience and heartache.

When she builds to the final chorus, I don't think—I only *feel*. Her voice has arms that stretch to encompass the empty house and fingertips that tendril far up to the balcony. It mesmerizes with color and texture, with layers of hope and hurt. So does this actress as she embodies the song and story, pouring out the character's emotions.

I rest my elbows on my thighs, my hands clasped

together, seeing only her from my seat in the second row. I want to hold on to this moment, this feeling of being the director who discovers the next big star, because it comes around so rarely.

She has it all, everything I want, and something more. It's in the way she carries herself on stage, unaware of her own sex appeal. At first glance, she's all innocent blonde, but catch her eye and there's a torch singer sensuality in her gaze. That's what I need. That's what I want.

She's going to bring down the house. She's going to make the audience cry and cheer. She's going to make them *want* her.

And she's absolutely fucking beautiful, which sure as hell doesn't hurt.

When she finishes, I want to stand up, clap, and announce to everyone else here that she's been cast in this love story. But I restrain myself. "Thank you. Now, the scene and song with Mr. Carlson."

Patrick Carlson, already cast as the lead in *Crash the Moon*, jumps from the red upholstered chair next to me. He's here at the final auditions, along with the producer and Frederick Stillman himself, the most revered composer in the last quarter-century. Stillman's collected armfuls of awards for Best Musical. Actors fall all over themselves to star in his shows, and directors fawn at his feet.

I would have prostrated myself for the chance too, if I'd had to.

I've won three Tonys, received an Oscar for my only film, and—maybe more to the point—my Broadway shows have all made a return on their investors' dollars. But it felt like the pinnacle of success when, six months ago, Stillman called my cell one fine afternoon and said he was offering the directing job to me, only me, and no one but me.

I said yes on the spot.

Now I want to say yes to her.

2

JILL

The floorboards creak at center stage in the St. James Theater. I didn't notice while I sang, but now I focus on that surreal detail so that I stay in the moment.

This moment is all I want.

Everything I've done in my twenty-three years has led me to this gem of a Broadway house.

Every vocal lesson and every acting class.

Every script I learned and every memory I plumbed for authentic emotion to pour into a scene.

But more than anything, it's the five marathons I've finished. That discipline keeps me from freaking out as Patrick Carlson joins me under the spotlights. With the stage lit and the house down, I can barely make out the powers-that-be in their seats. There's the silhouette of the hotshot director Davis Milo in the second row, along with the producer, and, beside him, Frederick Stillman himself, who composed this anthemic musical. I'd volunteer for the Hunger Games to get a role in something he's created, but fortunately all I have to do is nail this scene with the male lead.

Who is Patrick Carlson, the man I've loved from afar the last six years.

So, I draw on the same stores of willpower that keep me focused for twenty-six miles—blinders on so I can ignore how Patrick is the most beautiful man I've ever seen. It's his magnetic stage presence as much as his looks. In college, when I skipped class to catch a matinee of *Rent* to watch him play Roger, or *Wicked* to see him as Fiyero, he'd mesmerized me all the way up in the cheap seats, and now, close up . . .

I am a professional, for God's sake. And when I take a deep, diaphragm-stretching breath and let it out, I'm not even that.

I'm not Jill, working actress, auditioning for her first Broadway role, and he is not Patrick, slaying audiences with talent and charisma six nights a week. This is not a brightly lit stage in an antique gold auditorium, surrounded by high-flying balconies and almost 1,600 empty seats.

This is the best art school in the country. I am Ava, a twenty-two-year-old painter without a family, and my teacher, Paolo, is a mercurial and world-renowned artist.

He steps behind me, wordlessly studying the work Ava has just finished. My shoulders are tense; Paolo's critique could crush her. He breathes a thoughtful *hmm* as he moves his attention from the art to the artist. He places his hands on my arms then runs his palms sensuously from my wrists to my shoulders.

"You must let go, Ava. You try too hard to make your paintings perfect. You need to make them *you*."

I nod, breathless, speechless, because this man Ava has admired, looked up to, is touching her. He brushes my hair away from my neck, and I tilt my head, letting him trace a fingertip along the vein in my neck. Then, before my eyes drift closed, I remember that I'm a good girl, that I don't do this, and I jerk away.

"I am only here to learn," I say primly.

He narrows his eyes. "I am teaching you."

Ava knows he's not, wants to say he's out of line, even though his touch feels so good to this young woman who has known too little good in her life. Ava's not ready for this, and the accompaniment comes in as Ava wheels on Paolo, fire in her eyes, and lashes out with the first sung line in a heated duet.

"You don't have permission to lay your hands on me."

He plays the gentleman, surrendering, but with a mocking half-bow. "Forgive me. I only touch you as your teacher," he sings, in a soft but powerful tenor that could melt igloos.

"That's not teaching."

"Then find your own way to paint."

He stalks off and Ava breaks away and sings roughly of how this man makes her crazy with his demands— her brushstrokes are too controlled, her head is too much in the way, she needs to throw her body into the act of painting. And I hate it, and him, because he feels like the one thing that stands between true creativity and me.

I sing an angry lament, a furious plea to the universe to show me a way to leave. But there is no place else, no one else. All I have is my art, and he's the only one who can make it better.

Make me better.

And he is leaving.

Ava detests solitude, even though it's the thing she knows best. I rush across the empty classroom after him. He's nearly off-stage, and I grab his shirt. He stops and gives me a *look*—satisfaction and curiosity.

"I see you've changed your mind . . ."

I drop my squared shoulders in resignation to Ava's reality. I was born to be an artist and will only succeed with him. "I need you, Professor."

"Don't call me professor."

"What should I call you?"

He casually runs a strand of my hair through his fingers. "Don't call me. Kiss me."

He lets the strand fall and I grab him, bestowing a hard, wet kiss on his lips.

Patrick's lips. Paolo's lips.

He tastes divine. Paolo. Patrick. My teacher. The actor I idolize. They all collide—reality, make-believe, years of crushing, a moment of pretending. I don't know if the way I feel right now comes from me or from Ava, but before I open my eyes, before I hear "end scene," I know we have crazy chemistry, the kind that can't be faked.

The kind that leaves me with a buzz when I break the kiss and step back. I blink in the harsh light, trying to reorient myself. St. James Theater? Yes. Done with my audition? Yes. Desperate to get where I can unpack some of this? Hell, yes.

I blurt the compulsory, "Thank you for your time," and dash offstage, where I slam into Alexis Carbone—all bleached blonde hair, bosoms, and pipes like nobody's business.

She's a certifiable star, so I guess the next thing I can kiss is this role goodbye.

"Watch where you're going!" Alexis has a sweet soprano voice, so pure and lovely I almost think she means "Take care you don't hurt yourself," instead of "Walk where you want as long as it's nowhere near me." Still dazed from the kiss to end all kisses, I mutter a quick, "I'm sorry," and edge past her in the wings. Or try.

"I'm sure you are," she says as she tugs down her jacket and makes sure her breasts look good. They do. "Too bad, your being scheduled just before A-List arrives. Must be so disappointing."

That stings. "I'm sorry—Yes, you are," is grade-school level burn, but I am one raw nerve after laying it all out there on the stage. And what have I ever done to her? I know not to take the bait, but in a breathy, ingenue voice, heavy on the Southern Belle, I gush, "But it's such a pleasure to meet you, Ms. Carbone. I've been a fan of yours since I was in high school." I twinkle at her, chirrup, "Break a leg!" then split backstage before she can completely ruin my Patrick Carlson buzz.

I head past the dressing rooms, exchanging friendly goodbyes with a stagehand wheeling a dolly in the cramped hallway. At the stage door, I push it open and step into the alleyway behind the theater.

A snap of cold air greets me, and I lean against the brick wall, drop my bag, and run a finger across my lips as if I can reactivate that kiss like a loop of a hologram. Closing my eyes, I replay everything—Patrick's breath, so soft. The slightest bit of stubble on his jawline. The way he tasted faintly of cinnamon.

Even staged, kissing the real man is so much more potent than anything I imagined as a seventeen-year-old, when he was Fiyero. How is that for a theater geek, dreaming of kisses from a stage actor?

Now I've sampled the real thing, and I want to hold on to the details. Not many men could outclass an idealized version of themselves.

Sharing the stage with the actual Patrick Carlson couldn't make me want this part any more than I already do. It's a terrific role. A dramatic, marvelous, career-making role. Acting with someone I admired —*mostly* just professionally—would be a bonus, though.

Now I need to get on with my day before anyone calls the NYPD about the crazy stalker actress outside the theater.

I'm meeting my friend Reeve nearby, at Bryant Park. He's an actor too, and when I get there, he's lounging at one of the metal tables, reading the script for the movie he's working on. He has his girlfriend's dog with him. The little brown and tan Chihuahua/Min Pin curls up in his lap. It's adorable how when Reeve fell hard for Sutton, he fell for her dog too.

He puts the dog on the ground and the pages on the table, then stands and holds out his arms with a wide, expectant grin. "So, do we have a reason to celebrate? Are you the new ingénue of old Broadway?"

When I start to tell him, reality comes crashing down. Alexis was right—there was no point in hoping after she showed up, and yes, it was damned disappointing after I'd nailed that audition scene. "I highly doubt it," I tell Reeve. "Alexis Carbone showed up right after me."

He makes a face as if I just breathed last night's onions on him. "Can I hope that Ava has an evil sister and they want Alexis for that role?"

"Ha. I wish." I lean my hip against the table, shoulders slumping. The high of performing—not to mention the stage kiss—is dropping off fast. "But you know it's going to be her. She has an insane following. Her fans love her and would line up for blocks to see her."

"Yeah, but you never know." Reeve nudges me with his elbow. "Every star was the new kid once. Even Alexis Carbone."

But already there's a hitch in my throat and the sting of tears. I don't want to cry over a role, but I worked so hard on this audition and it felt like the chance of a lifetime. "I felt so thoroughly Ava, almost as if the character had possessed me. I swear I could read it on the director's face too, even after my first piece. He stood up and I could have sworn he was going to say, 'You're it. You're my Ava.' And then she walked in."

"Hey . . ." He pulls me in for a quick hug, and I let one more tear fall against his shirt as he pats my hair. "Sometimes you nail an audition and lose out. Sometimes you flub one and still get a role. You never know. The only thing you can do is leave it all on the stage, and I know you did. You've never given less than a hundred percent of your heart and soul in any rehearsal, let alone a performance."

I grab a deep, steadying breath and nod, then I rummage in my purse for a tissue to swipe the errant tears on my face.

"C'mon. Let me buy you a coffee," he says, bumping my shoulder with his.

"Sure." I let myself be cajoled. "Since you're the bigtime film actor now."

"From your mouth to God's ears." He's just landed his first starring role, and being Reeve, he's not even obnoxious about it. He leashes the dog, and we wander over to a pretzel vendor who's hawking espressos, lattes, and coffees too, and order some hot beverages to stay warm on this chilly day. I try to stay upbeat, even though I'm braced for the "Better luck next time" call from my agent.

Reeve breaks off a piece of the pretzel for the dog, who stands on his tiny back legs to snag the bite.

"Are you a full-time dog nanny for the Artful Dodger now?"

Reeve laughs. "What can I say? He's kind of an

awesome dog, so I like hanging out with him. And it makes Sutton happy to know he's with me."

"You're so in love with her, next thing you know, you'll be raising a whole pack of min pins together," I tease. But I think it's awesome that Reeve and Sutton are in love and *official*.

I glance at my watch, thinking I should head home. "We're still running tomorrow, right?"

"Of course. I have to kick your ass."

"You wish."

I set off, thinking of Reeve paired up with Sutton, and my roomie, Kat, now happily engaged to her long-time love, Bryan. Funny, how my singleness has become more, not less, obvious by my friends not mentioning it. It's been a long time since I've been with anyone—much longer than I let on. Long enough that they'll want to know why, and that's not part of the story I want to tell.

Acting isn't just my job. It's my whole damn life.

3

DAVIS

"I agree. She was brilliant, but it's irrelevant."

I press my thumb and forefinger against the bridge of my nose. I cannot believe I am having this debate. I cannot believe this suit is being such a . . . suit.

"How can her acting be irrelevant?" I demand. "She's an actress."

The suit in question is the show's executive producer, Don Kraftig, sitting across the aisle from me in a pinstriped, double-breasted number that could have walked out of wardrobe for *Guys and Dolls*. The auditions are over. The callbacks are done. Patrick Carlson has left for the day, and we are sliding into the early evening. There's just Don, Stillman, and me in the seats of the St. James. At least until they open the house for the audience of *The King and I*, in the final week of its run before we take over the theater.

Their curtain is at eight, and I'd like to be out of here by then, so I try—I really try—for a reasonable tone. "Look, Don. She's tailor-fucking-made for this part. She *is* Ava. How can there be any question?"

The producer shrugs. "She was amazing," he concedes. He has a voice like gravel in a tin can, and I hated it even before he wanted to run this production like an accountant. "But she's not Alexis Carbone."

"Exactly. I don't want Alexis Carbone. Alexis Carbone is a classic, grade-A diva and a half. She misses shows if she has so much as a sniffle."

"She should rest her voice if she's ill." Now he sounds prissy, and I want to reach over and shake him even more.

Instead, I switch to Don's native tongue—dollars. "She missed *one-third* of her performances in *Fate Can Wait*. How many ticketholders was it, who called asking for refunds because they'd paid to see Alexis Carbone and not her understudy?"

"We are not the Logan Theater Company." He folds his arms, on the defensive, distancing himself from Alexis's one Broadway flop. "That show was a mess. It had an awful title."

"But our show is not a mess. We have a show with a fantastic title, moving script, haunting score, and a sexy-as-hell storyline about love and loss and sex and art."

"Alexis can open a show." Talking to him is as productive as banging my head against the wall and about that painful. "She has her own album, her solo concerts sell out, she was on that TV show, and she's still regarded as the best damn Velma Kelly in the last five years."

On my last nerve, I push out of my chair and pace the aisle until the worst of the temptation to strangle him burns off. Don looks over at Stillman, who still doesn't speak. He lets his work do his talking. He's also, I've learned, passive-aggressive as fuck.

When I have a hold of myself, I come back and lay it out there. "Here's the thing. I don't want to work with her. I want someone who is fresh and amazing and who is going to blow the audience away. That woman. Jill McCormick. I want to read in Playbills for years to come that she got her first big break as Ava in *our* show. She is going to be a star. I want to be the one who discovered her."

Don digs in his heels. "I want someone who is already a star."

"We have one." I gesture to the bald, bespectacled theatrical genius next to me. "Book and score by Frederick Stillman."

The stony look on the composer's face gives nothing away. I respect Stillman far too much to talk to him as I talk to Don. "Mr. Stillman, you wrote this living, breathing, beautiful show. Who do *you* picture as your Ava?"

Stillman crosses then uncrosses his legs. He closes his eyes and taps his fingers on his thigh as if playing the piano—his way of remembering actors and their performances.

He opens his eyes. "I want the Ava who will move the audience."

You're killing me, Stillman. I respect him, but his avoidance is killing me.

I try again. I need an ally here. "So, who would that be? Is that Alexis or Jill?"

Stillman stands up, smoothing his pants legs. "I need to go to the little boys' room."

Then he walks out.

The composer may have a problem with confrontations, but I don't, so I turn back to Don. "We need to start rehearsals in four weeks, the day after New Year's. I would really like them to blow me away."

Don rises, reaches inside his jacket pocket, and removes a checkbook. "Does the name Julie Taymor mean anything to you?"

I don't answer. He knows I would recognize a fellow director's name, even if her involuntary departure wasn't a notorious Broadway debacle. And *I* know a threat when I hear it.

"The *Spiderman* producers were happy to let their director go once upon a time," Don says, making the expected play. "I have no problem paying your exit clause. How much was it?"

The man knows about brinksmanship, and he's got the upper hand. Because he'll walk and I won't. I want this job too much. "Fine. Call Alexis's agent and give her the good news. But I choose the understudy, and my choice will be final. Is that clear?"

Don nods, and the deal is made. It's hardly a compromise, but if I'm lucky Alexis will have a whole lot of head colds.

4

JILL

As I head for the subway, I check my phone out of habit. No missed calls from my agent, so I swipe to my to-do list: email the ladies in my running group, new training regimen for their upcoming breast cancer awareness 10K. With *Crash the Moon* out of the frame, I suppose I'll devote more time to coaching, maybe find some gals who want to train for marathons and other distance races. And there will be other auditions, other shows.

I pocket my phone and head down the stairs into the busy Forty-Second Street station, full of rush-hour New Yorkers and tourists with bad timing. At the turnstile, I'm about to swipe my Metro Card when I spot a poster on the sooty wall opposite, advertising a limited run of *The King and I* right now at the St. James.

With a pang of longing, I wish this was my exit every night at six-thirty. The one for *that* theater, where I'd go through *that* stage door, drop my purse on the floor of a dressing room, and do my makeup in a mirror framed with naked lightbulbs.

"C'mon," a man growls from behind me. "Go or get outta the way. We're trying to get through."

I can't make myself wedge onto a packed train and go home to stew in disappointment. I ditch the turnstiles and head above ground, joining the current of people streaming into the theater district.

Tomorrow I'll focus on what's next. Tonight, I want to walk past the St. James one more time, and say goodbye before moving on to the next project.

Night has fallen and the St. James is lit up, a beacon for young and old, tourists and residents, anyone who wants to suspend disbelief for the length of a show. A marquee like this, bright as day and framed by the night sky, stills my heart every time. I have loved the theater fiercely and deeply for my entire life, both as a spectator and as an actress.

"Someday," I whisper.

I turn to go and notice a man walking toward me, dressed in jeans and a button-down shirt, neat and tucked in, tailored to fit a trim waist and flat abs. I suspect washboard flat. Maybe chiseled.

He looks familiar—trim clothes, strong jawline, thick brown hair, and eyes as blue and dark as midnight. The pieces click together, and I realize he's *Crash the Moon's* director.

Davis Milo.

Oh heck, no. I can't think about his abs or anything else on his body. No tawdry thoughts at all. Delete, delete, delete.

I'd barely been able to see him out in the house with the stage lights blaring. I can see him now, looking incredibly intense as he pounds out a number on his cell phone, head down and walking toward me.

I wonder if I should say hi, if he'd remember me from the audition. I didn't interact with him much, but he's a legend. Barely thirty years old, a litany of hit shows on his résumé—he's got the Midas Touch, they say, and the best eye for talent in New York City. Insiders know, but he rarely takes credit publicly for the careers he's launched. I've seen his awards' acceptance speeches on TV, and they're gracious and generous. And, to top it off, he's heart-stoppingly handsome. In every picture I've seen, he has a brooding air, as if he rarely cracks a smile, so when he does you know it must be special.

Awkward uncertainty sweeps over me. My hands are cold and clammy. I don't know what to do or say in front of him—if anything. Should I act friendly or pretend I don't see him? This man decides fates and careers.

I chicken out and angle to walk by, eyes on the ground, when I hear him say, "I'm looking for M.J. Kim," and stop in my tracks. That's my agent's name.

Some sound of surprise—a word or a squeak or a bark, I don't know—comes out of my mouth. Davis looks up and, as if in slow motion, a grin curves his lips. They're nice lips, particularly when they smile.

Just an observation. Not tawdry at all.

"Hi," he says, and I think it's both to me and to my agent on the phone. I smile because that's funny, but I still don't know what to do. It would be weird to keep walking now—as if I could with him calling my agent at six p.m. That doesn't seem like the way you deliver a "no."

"Kim, it's Milo." His voice is commanding, deep and rich, and I wonder if he's ever been on stage or if he's always been behind it. "I'm standing on Forty-Fourth Street where I just bumped into the actress I want to cast in the chorus and, more importantly, as the understudy for my lead."

Jet fuel ignites in me, and I take off for the moon.

I clasp a hand over my mouth to hold in a squeal, and then I grab Davis Milo and hug him hard. His phone clatters to the ground, and I hear my agent say "Hello, hello," but I don't care, because Davis Milo has given me my biggest dream ever—and it's a double whammy of amazing. My first Broadway show and understudy for a role that feels made for me. I have zero ambivalence about learning a part with the risk I'll never get to perform it, because Alexis Carbone is notorious for flaking, and just rehearsing this amazing role with this gifted director and talented costar is closer to my dream than I've ever been.

There's something perfectly circular about it, because I don't know where I would be if I hadn't fallen in love with the theater and Patrick Carlson.

5

DAVIS

Her arms wrap all the way around me, gripping me as if she won't ever let go. For a moment—or two—I let myself notice how fantastic her body feels against mine. Then I peel myself away because that is the last thought I'll entertain about her that is anything but professional.

Cardinal rule of directing—do not fall for an actress in your cast.

Secondary rule of directing—do not fall for an actress, period.

But her hair smells ridiculously good, a pineapple scent that lingers in the cold December air as she breaks the embrace, and my hand twitches with a sudden impulse to twine my fingers through her dark blonde hair. But I broke rules of directing once before and have the battle-scarred heart to prove it. Scars and iron-clad resistance.

I pick up my phone from the sidewalk; Ms. Kim is still on the line, sounding worried. "Is everything OK?"

"My apologies. I'm here," I reassure her.

In front of me, Jill stands shaking. Or bouncing. Or bounce–shaking.

"Yes," I tell Ms. Kim, straight-faced, when she asks about the earlier noise. "That was her. I don't think you'll need to call her with the news." Eyes widening, she presses her hand tightly to her lips. "I'll be in touch about the details."

Signing off, I study my new actress. Those eyes are tearing up now, but when she drops her hand, she flashes a smile that could launch ships.

"This is the best thing that has ever happened to me professionally. Ever. Thank you, Mr. Milo."

"It's just Davis." I pocket my phone.

"Davis," she says, the way some women say "chocolate."

I don't know why I gave her my first name. Most actors I've worked with have called me Mr. Milo. You don't call your doctor by the first name, or your teacher, and the same applies to your director, as far as I'm concerned. But, from her, Davis sounds right.

"We've got a lot of work to do before the show opens. Rehearsals start in a month, and you'll be shadowing Alexis Carbone, who's been cast as Ava." I revert to cool professionalism, though her genuine joy at being the understudy melts a tiny piece of my icy heart. I see so much entitlement in this business. A little gratitude makes a nice change.

Another tear rolls down her cheek, and I amend, *A lot of gratitude.* Then I do something entirely out of character. I swipe the pad of my thumb across her cheek to wipe away a tear. Her skin is soft, and I could get used to this.

"Can I take you out for a drink or something?" She looks so sweetly hopeful. "A coffee, or a bagel, to say thank you?"

I want to say yes. But that would be a huge mistake. Maybe if it were daylight. Or I wasn't so attracted to her. As it's not and I am, she is absolutely off-limits.

"That's not necessary."

"Right. The bagel sounded really lame, didn't it? And where do you get a fresh bagel after six p.m.?" Her self-deprecating humor tests my resistance. "And coffee? Argh! When did coffee become such a cliché?"

"I don't know. But you can get it twenty-four/seven." I almost keep a straight face but give in to a grin, which she mirrors.

"Screw coffee. What if I bought you a drink to say thanks?"

"I swear you don't have to take me out for a drink, Jill. I'm just happy you're going to do the show."

She holds up a hand to say she's backing off, though she doesn't, really. "Then I'll go to Sardi's by my lonesome. I vowed if I ever landed a Broadway show, I'd go there to celebrate." She tips her head toward the restaurant, a Broadway institution. "And I'm already there. So, it's fate."

The neon green sign flashes, beckoning tourists and industry people as it has for decades. The place is venerable—it's the heart of the theater district and teems with history, having hosted theater royalty for dinner and drinks for nearly one hundred years.

She's clearly waiting for me to give in. A cab squeals by and stirs a quick, cold breeze that blows a few strands of blonde hair across her face. Brushing it away, she arches an eyebrow. "The breeze is blowing me to Sardi's."

Turning on her heel, she saunters to the door and then inside. It feels like a challenge. Maybe even a dare. I know better, but follow her anyway.

She's not easy to resist.

I find her at the hostess stand, telling the black-jacketed maître d' that it'll be just one for the bar, and I place a hand on her back so she knows I'm here. "Actually," I cut in, "that'll be two."

Her eyes meet mine as I touch her, but her gaze is steady, and she doesn't seem to mind the contact.

"Right this way, then." The maître d' guides us past tables full of theatergoers, men in jackets, and women in evening dresses, chatting about the shows they're about to see. There's a table with two guys who look like Wall Street types dining with their wives. Jill walks past them, and one of the guys lingers on her much longer than he should. The woman with him doesn't notice, but I do, and I give him a hard stare. He turns back to his plate of shrimp instantly.

At the bar, I pull out a stool for her. She thanks me then shucks off her coat and crosses her legs. They look as good in jeans as they probably do out of them. She has that kind of figure—athletic and trim. Probably flexible too. This woman might be all my weaknesses, dammit.

A caricature of James Gandolfini hanging above the

mirror behind the bar distracts me. I give the actor a salute to say thanks as I sit down.

The bartender comes over. "What can I get you tonight?"

I look at Jill, letting her go first. "Vodka and soda. Belvedere, please."

He nods. "And you sir?"

"Glenlivet on the rocks."

"Coming right up."

Then she turns to me, her blue eyes sparkling and full of happiness. "Do you have any idea how happy I am?"

"Yeah," I say, playfully. "It's kind of written all over your face."

"Well, I'm not going to hide it. I think I might light up Times Square tonight. And now I'm having drinks at Sardi's with my director!"

"Don't tell anyone. I don't want word to get out that I'm consorting with the talent."

She leans in with a pout and kind of shimmies her shoulders. "Oh, I get to keep your secrets already."

My breath hitches. I know it's the excitement of landing her first show that's making her so flirty, so playful. But that unconsciously sexy way she has about her spells trouble. She could reel me in before I know what's happened. Actresses are wonderful, and talented, and often too gorgeous to be real, like this one. Some are genuine, but a few are mostly attracted to what you can do for them, and you don't know which is which until it's too late.

"I have very few interesting secrets," I say, bowing

out of the banter. Thankfully, the bartender arrives with the drinks.

"One Glenlivet and one Belvedere."

"Thank you," I say. He nods and heads to take an order at the end of the bar.

I reach for my drink and see he's given me hers and vice versa. "I believe this is yours."

She takes the glass I offer, and her fingers brush mine. Such a quick touch, but it ignites something in me. When she bends to reach for her purse hanging on a hook under the bar, I watch her, memorizing the way she moves. I run my hand across my jaw. I need to get it together if I'm going to work with her.

She retrieves lip gloss from her purse and reapplies it, and now I wonder how her lips taste.

Finally, thank God, she tucks the tube away then holds up her vodka and soda.

"To your first show on the Great White Way," I offer, and we clink glasses. I need an easy, superficial question so I can collect myself. "What was the first musical you ever saw?"

"*Fiddler on the Roof*," she says and then hums a few bars from "If I Were a Rich Man."

"You make a good Tevye," I say dryly.

"You'll keep me in mind for that role if you ever direct a revival?"

"Absolutely. You'll be top of the list on my call sheet."

"Can you even imagine what the critics would say?" Jill gestures wide as if she's calling out a huge headline. "Hotshot director casts lady in iconic male role."

"Hotshot director?"

A blush floods her cheeks, and she waves her hand in front of her face. "I didn't mean anything . . ."

"It might strike you as crazy, but I'm one hundred percent fine with the hotshot title." I take a long swallow of my drink. "By the way. I saw you in *Les Mis*."

"You did?" She seems genuinely surprised.

I nod. "Yes. That's why I called you in."

"I thought it was the producer who saw me."

I laugh. "No. Though I'm sure he took credit for it. I don't think I will ever see that show again without picturing you as Eponine."

"Really?" Her blue eyes widen, and she seems so pleased with the compliment. I love that she's not jaded, not full of herself. She's still hopeful, and that's attractive. It's part of why I called her in after seeing that off-Broadway revival, where the show had been modernized into a rock opera. When she was on stage, I never doubted for one second that she was the character. That's a tough thing to nail, but it's what I want most in an actor. No, it's the thing I want to *feel*. I want the walls of the real world to collapse around me, so I can *believe* in the illusion.

"Every actress who can sing wants to play Eponine," I say. "But it's incredibly hard to pull off feisty Eponine, love-struck Eponine, and then be dying Eponine on top of it all. Most actresses can handle one of the personas, sometimes two. You'll see someone who can sing the hell out of 'On My Own' or fawn all over Marius and then do a damn good death scene. But they can't manage the playful side of her. But you, Jill . . ." She's looking at me with the glass held in one hand and her lips slightly parted as I talk about her. It's more intoxicating than the scotch and threatens to cloud my cool head in a haze of heat.

I didn't cast her because she's fuck-able. I cast her because she's fucking amazing. I need to keep it objective as I finish, "You were brilliant. You were stunning. You were everything and more."

Her face lights up. I've failed miserably at being professional, and the best thing I can do now is not let on—to her or to anyone.

* * *

We chat about *Fiddler*, and as soon as she finishes her drink, I pay and say goodnight. Then I head to the boxing gym near my home in Tribeca and work out my frustrations on a punching bag. On my way out an hour later, I run into my buddy Ryder, who is headed in. He doesn't box, but there's a weight room attached to the gym. That's his haunt, and he has the arms to show for it.

He lifts his chin in hello. "Hey, man. How's it going?"

"Better now," I grumble.

He smiles. He's an affable guy. Ryder hosts a radio show about sex and dating in the city. "Took things out on a punching bag, I take it?"

"That's my way."

He laughs and claps my shoulder. "Someday, man,

you're going to find a good woman and you won't spend nearly as much time pummeling the bag."

I roll my eyes. "Yes. That's my goal. I'll call into your show when I do."

He winks. "Can't wait for that day."

I flip him the bird as I leave. "You'll be waiting forever."

Because that just won't happen.

6

JILL

The next night Kat swirls her straw in a chocolate milkshake, looking at the drink with disdain. "These milkshakes are not the same as they are at Tino's Diner."

"We'll just have to keep trying all the diners in Chelsea and Midtown until we find a replacement," I say to Kat.

"Hopefully before we celebrate your Tony for Best Actress in a Musical."

Narrowing my eyes, I threaten her with a French fry. "I'm warning you, Kat . . ."

She is unimpressed. "You think I haven't learned by now how to avoid your projectile potatoes?"

I brandish another one, not backing down. "Don't. Jinx. Me. You know my rules."

"You mean superstitions. Like how you didn't even tell me you were auditioning until you got the callback. And now you've gone and won a role in a Broadway show."

"With Patrick Carlson," I say excitedly. Anybody would be thrilled.

"And in a Frederick Stillman show," she gushes back. "I know he's your fave."

"And Davis Milo directing." It seems important to mention him, give him his due, especially after our drinks last night. God knows what came over me, asking my director out for a drink. I was floating on cloud nine, and there he was, delivering the best news of my life, and there was Sardi's, saying "Stretch this moment out as long as possible."

Nothing to do with how the TV screen and glossy magazine pics don't do him justice. They don't capture his intensity. But in the bar with him last night, I understood why actresses (and some actors) go dreamy-eyed at the mention of him. Those are *undress me* eyes, the kind of gaze that holds yours as he walks across the room, all crazy possessive, and marks you with a territorial sort of kiss. The sort of kiss where he pushes you against the wall, cages you in with his arms, and claims you. I wonder what it would be like to be kissed like that.

"Do you think he'll bring his Oscar to a rehearsal?" Kat muses, breaking my naughty reverie. I have no business thinking of Davis that way. He's the director. Drinks, okay. Steamy kissing, no. "I love that movie he did where he won it. *Ransom.*"

"Want me to tell him you're a fan?"

"Oh, please do." She gives up on the milkshake, pushes it away, and rubs her hands together. "But what I really want to know are all the details about this audition scene with Patrick. What was it like to kiss the love of your life?" Her eyes widen dramatically. "Does he know you're the same gal who once sent flowers to him and asked him out?"

"God, I hope not." Fire rushes into my cheeks. "I hope he doesn't remember."

When I was seventeen, I saw a revival of *Wicked* at the Gershwin Theater. I'd just sung "Defying Gravity" in a high school concert, so I bought one nosebleed ticket and took the subway into Manhattan, happy to leave my real-life drama in Brooklyn and lose myself in dramatic romance for an afternoon.

In an act of Fate, or maybe Thespis, muse of the theater, I was there for one of those legendary Broadway moments—the lead actor had laryngitis, the understudy contracted a bronchial infection, and Patrick had been called in, stepping into the role with 48 hours' notice. I perched on the edge of my seat the entire time, mesmerized, sure he locked eyes with me when he sang that gorgeous duet I knew by heart, "As Long as You're Mine."

Ironic how much I loved that love song, even though love was what brought my world crashing down with Aaron. Loving too much. Not loving enough.

Enter Patrick Carlson—stage presence for days, playing that bold and romantic character the audience longs for.

At curtain call, I clapped and cheered, then shyly joined the crowd of fans at the stage door. I waited, smoothing the sky-blue dress I'd worn, which matched my eyes, and when Patrick had signed dozens of Playbills and the crowd thinned until there was only me, I said hello.

He flashed the warmest, kindest smile I'd ever seen, and I felt a rush like I did on stage. I felt like a person who deserved a smile like that, and oh so confident. "Hi. I wanted to say you were amazing. I'm so impressed with how you pulled off this performance in two days. You were simply breathtaking."

"That's lovely of you to say."

His hair was slightly damp, and his cheeks were red; he had a sort of glow about him. He looked like I felt after a great show, and it seemed like a kinship between us.

I held out a hand to shake. "I'm Jill. I'm an actor too." Not that there was a comparison. He was a Broadway star; I was merely a theater student with only a few high school productions to my name.

He took my hand into his warm, strong grasp, to shake and I wanted to preserve that perfect moment forever. "That's fantastic, Jill. How is it going? Tell me about some of the roles you've played."

My insides fluttered as he leaned against the stage door of the Gershwin Theater, looking so relaxed in his jeans and a gray V-neck T-shirt.

"Well . . . I sang some of Elphaba's songs in a concert last year in school."

With a grin, he launched into the opening notes of the duet from that show, wordlessly inviting me to join in, and there we were, outside the theater, singing together, and now *that* was the best moment of my life.

Soon, he said he needed to get some rest since he

had a matinee and an evening show the next day, but he walked me to the subway stop and I thanked him profusely, and he said he'd had a grand time.

Grand. Yes, that's how he said it. A *grand time*.

If I'd had a fainting couch instead of a subway seat, I would have swooned.

Emboldened, I sent him flowers by way of the Gershwin's stage door—so old-school theater, even though I ordered them online—and included a note: "Hi. It was so fun meeting you. Would you like to get coffee sometime?"

I never heard back.

Seventeen-year-old me decided the flowers had never arrived. Patrick wouldn't have ignored me like that, right? We were star-crossed, obviously. (Cue more swooning.)

Adult me isn't surprised. Maybe he thought I was a stalker. Maybe I was, but at least it was from the cheap seats.

But that's how I fell madly in love with Patrick Carlson. Not in a delusional way, but as a safe person to love when love had wrecked everything. The *possibility* of Patrick got me through so many days when I was shattered, nights when I felt cut off and alone. The fantasy of Patrick was damned good in bed—and still is, if I'm honest.

Which I should not be, or working with the real Patrick could get awkward.

"What if he does remember?" Kat asks, eerily on topic with my thoughts.

I shrug. "I'll improvise. Broadway actress,

remember."

* * *

The next morning I'm up before the sun and out on the West Side bike path, my ponytail swinging behind me as I take my surefire cure for when the past drags me down. I run off my regret. I picture it unspooling behind me, layers of remorse that I peel away. Someday, maybe even soon, I'll have let go of them all.

Reeve meets up with me after a few miles.

"Try to keep up," I shout as he joins me mid-stride.

He rolls his eyes and keeps pace with no problem. I like running with Reeve because he runs like I do. Full tilt. Nothing held back.

"Can I say I told you so?" he says after the first half-mile.

"About not being able to keep up?"

"No, doofus. About the show."

"By all means. Say it all day long."

"Get me good seats for opening night."

"I'll do my best." I smile, happy to see my friend. Happy to be out of my own head for a while, where I can escape from my thoughts.

I am happy, I am happy, I am happy. The more I say it the more I believe it. Lather, rinse, repeat.

* * *

On the way home from the run, my phone rings while I'm on the stairs to the second floor. I dig around in the pocket of my fleece jacket and pull it out to see my agent's name on the screen. My heart gallops off in irrational fear. I'm about to lose the job. It was all a mistake.

"Please don't tell me Davis Milo changed his mind," I say, stopping on the stairwell.

M.J. laughs. "No, darling. No worry there. The producers sent me the contract already, and I'm working on it."

I can breathe again, so I walk up the rest of the steps.

"But that's not why I'm calling," M.J. continues. "I just got off the phone with Milo. He wants to meet with you before rehearsals start."

"Oh. Why?" I have no clue if that's normal for a Broadway show, but M.J. wouldn't pass on a sketchy request. Davis doesn't seem like he'd make one, either.

"He likes to meet with understudies to set their expectations. We'll go together to his office on Friday at ten. Does that work?"

"I'll see if my schedule is clear."

Another laugh. "I'll email you the address."

After we hang up, I let myself into my apartment, pour a glass of water, and sink into my couch with my laptop and Google.

I quickly cycle through Davis Milo's résumé, though I memorized the key points before the audition. The *South Pacific* revival when he won his first Tony, then an original production called *Anything for You*, followed by the play *The Saying Goes*. He's worked on the West Coast too, and three years ago, directed a production in San Diego at the La Jolla Playhouse called *World*

Enough and Time, inspired by a line from an Andrew Marvelle poem. Lots of accolades for that, and rumors it would become a movie.

I find a photo of him with Madeline Blaine, the young actress who played the lead in that show and then landed a romantic comedy movie that made millions at the box office and sent her career soaring like a rocket. She now commands top dollar for her roles.

After that, I can't resist looking up more pictures of him. From last year's Tony Awards, a photo of him with his arm draped around a stunning redhead. The caption reads: *Award-winning director Davis Milo and publicist Amber Surratt*. In a pic from the year before, his hand clasps the waist of a black-haired beauty in a slinky gold dress. I recognize her as a talent agent for many of Broadway's top stars. Then, at a Broadway Cares event last year, he's snapped with a well-known choreographer, guiding her through a crowd with his hand on her back.

I touch my lower back briefly, remembering when he laid his hand there as he caught up with me in Sardi's.

I sink into my couch pillow and conclude two things. One, except for Madeline Blaine, he seems to prefer the company of women who work in the business behind the scenes. Two, he and formalwear are made for each other. He wears a tuxedo with understated elegance that seems effortless, rather than the tux wearing him. I run my index finger across a photo, absently tracing his outline, and arrive at a third conclusion: I bet he looks best viewed from close beside him, on his arm for the evening.

I close my laptop and head to my bedroom, opening my tiny closet to pick out something classy for our meeting Friday. A pencil skirt, I think, and my favorite emerald green sweater. Then I knock on Kat's door.

"Come in," she says sleepily.

"Rise and shine."

"Some of us don't care to wake up at the crack of dawn, you know." She rolls onto her side, bringing her purple comforter snug around her neck.

"Hate to break it to you, but it's the crack of ten. Can I borrow your black pumps for a meeting later this week?"

"You know I have huge feet."

I laugh. "You're an eight. I'm a seven and a half. I'd hardly call that huge."

"Bottom shelf in my shoe rack. But be careful. They're true to size, and I don't want you to stumble."

"Ha. I'm like a cat. I always land on my feet."

"Then my Louboutins are your Louboutins."

"Your generosity is one of the many reasons I love you."

I find the black beauties and return to my room, placing them next to the skirt and sweater. There. It's the perfect ensemble.

Then I find myself wishing it were Friday.

Because I'm eager to learn about the job, anxious to get started.

Because I want to impress Davis Milo as an actress.

No other reason at all.

7

JILL

Davis's office is in a red brick building with a gleaming glass door in a Tribeca neighborhood teeming with industrial spaces, lofts, and celebrities. I've pictured him in a sleek, black office building in the middle of Times Square. But then, Tribeca is the epicenter of New York cool and has claimed people like Beyoncé, Justin Timberlake, and Leonardo DiCaprio as its residents, so I suppose it's fitting that Davis keeps an office among the glitterati.

I adjust my purse strap, walk a little way from the building so I can't be seen from the lobby, and check my makeup in the side mirror of a parked car. Good. No smudged eyeliner. No lipstick on my teeth. Just so much anxiety in my belly. The initial excitement has worn off, and I'm glad M.J. will be here too.

I scan the block, hoping to spot her marching my way, looking tough and agent-y with her shoulder-length brown bob and kick-ass attitude. When I check the time on my phone, though, I see a text message from her marked as urgent.

Jill darling!! I'm so sorry. I'm stuck on the Metro-North, and my train is delayed a whole hour. But you'll be fine!! You're there, right?

Well. That's a kink in my plans. But there's nothing we can do about it, so I type back: *Yes, don't worry about me.*

Sure, I'll be fine. If I'm not, I'll fake it.

My nerves ignore the pep talk, and as I turn the phone off and head inside, I try again. I've got the part, I've already had a drink with him, and we got along swimmingly. These are first job jitters I'm going to ignore.

There. Done. Ignored.

I am confident. I am bold.

The lobby has an unfinished vibe and continues the eclectic mix of materials from outside with huge potted plants, exposed pipes, and concrete walls painted a bright white. I check in with a security guard behind a counter then take the stairs to the second floor. Davis's office is at the end of a long, quiet hallway, and the door is slightly ajar, so I knock.

"Come in."

His voice is strong and deep and oddly calming. It

brings to mind the other night—this is the man I teased about casting me as Tevye. I'll be fine.

I peer in and see him seated behind a large oak desk. It's surprisingly untidy, spilling over with scripts and sheet music. I would have pegged him as a neat freak from the impeccable way he dresses. Today, his navy-blue shirt looks crisp and freshly laundered, but his dark brown hair is slightly messy, as if he ran a hand through it right before I walked in. What's most unexpected, though, is the music playing from his computer. Not Rodgers and Hammerstein, not Sondheim—he's listening to Muse. "Madness," specifically. I could sing along, I know it so well.

When he looks up from his screen, he seems about to smile, but then he makes his face impassive and simply nods in greeting.

Neither one of us says anything. The only sound is the music.

"I love this song," I say. *Someone* has to break the silence.

He hits a button on his keyboard and turns the music down.

I'm even more nervous than before, plus really confused.

Did I do something wrong?

Finally, he rises and walks over to me, offering a hand.

I take it, and it's awkward. I mean, I half tackled the man on the street when he told me I'd been cast. This ultra-professionalism feels stilted and weird.

"Good to see you again, Ms. McCormick."

Ms. McCormick?

Oh. I get it. We've done the celebratory drinks, and now we're all business. "And you as well, Mr. Milo."

I wait for him to correct me. To tell me I can call him Davis. Instead, he peers down the hall, seeming annoyed that I'm alone. "Where's M.J.?"

"She's stuck on the train. She can't make it."

"You and I can chat for a few minutes, then. There's a hook on the door for your jacket."

I take off my coat and hang it up. He gestures to a beige couch, and I sit, crossing my legs. The natural place for him to sit is a chair angled toward the couch, but he gives his desk a pained look, as if the seating arrangements are life and death business.

He finally settles on the chair. "I wanted to speak with you before rehearsals start because you might have the most difficult job in the show—you and Braydon, Patrick's understudy, that is."

I lean forward and listen eagerly. Whatever weirdness might be going on doesn't matter anymore. This is what I'm here for.

"Being an understudy might be the toughest job on Broadway. You're essentially learning and rehearsing two parts. You'll be in nearly all the chorus scenes and songs, but you also need to know Ava cold—and you might not ever go on."

I nod. Some understudies warm the benches for an entire run. "Right."

"Or you might have to go on at a moment's notice. A moment that can make your career." There's intensity now in his voice. He leans in slightly, his body language loosening up. "And I'm going to expect that of you. You're going to need to know all the lines backward and forward, all the songs inside and out, and all the blocking, top to bottom."

His dark blue eyes lock onto mine. He's so passionate with the instructions. It's the complete opposite of his earlier coldness, and I see how much he must love directing.

"Whatever it takes." I'm absolutely serious as I match his stare. Then I add, almost mischievously, "Mr. Milo."

Because I want to get back to where we were.

He turns to stare out the window, but the slightest of grins tugs at the corner of his lips. He wins the struggle not to smile, though, and returns to the task. "Take the script home and work on it over the holidays. You should be off-book when we start rehearsals."

"Absolutely." This is what I've lived for. I'm not going to complain because it's hard.

"I'm going to ask a lot of you, Jill. I have ridiculously high expectations for the show and everyone in it, and that includes the understudy for the leading role."

"I won't disappoint you."

He leans forward again, his elbows resting on his thighs, his hands clasped together. "Do more than that. Exceed my expectations."

The room seems to compress, to tighten into one tense line connecting my gaze to his. Whatever mine might say, his dark eyes give nothing away. Is he trying to break me, or test how I withstand pressure? "I will give you everything, Mr. Milo."

At last, his frown softens. Then, he whispers in a low voice that makes me dizzy, "It's Davis. Just call me Davis."

"Okay." Trying it on for size, I say, "Davis."

He shakes his head and breathes out hard. I like that reaction—like he's resettling something that was knocked loose.

He walks over to his desk, and I look at the walls, at the table, at the floor—but I still come back to his broad shoulders and his deliciously sculpted ass. Things I should not, under any circumstances, be looking at. Then he grabs a thick book of spiral-bound pages, and even that ass goes out of my mind.

The script.

The book and music for the newest Stillman musical, and he holds it like the treasure it is. I've only seen the pages from the audition scene. Now I'm about to dive into the whole story. I cannot wait, and when he hands it to me, I take it reverently.

"Spend the next few weeks immersing yourself in it." He's still standing, so it's clear the meeting is over. I stand too, then tuck the script into my purse and loop the strap over my shoulder. He walks with me to the door, and as I'm reaching for my coat, I wobble in the too-big heels.

Because Kat jinxed me, dammit.

He moves fast, hand on my elbow to steady me. It makes him the closest thing to grab onto so I don't fall. When I look up at him, I feel the flush of embarrassment in my cheeks and decide to make light of it.

"That's what I get for borrowing my roommate's shoes. I room with Bigfoot, you see."

Lips twitching, he glances down at the black pumps. "Nice shoes, though."

I realize my hand is on his shirt, my fingers fisted around the cloth, wrinkling it. I should let go. But I don't. He smells clean and freshly showered, and I don't want to move unless it's to get closer.

Kissing my director is a terrible idea. A Bad Idea straight from the Top Ten List of Bad Ideas.

I relax my clenched hand and smooth the fabric. "Nice shirt," I say softly and glance up.

His dark blue eyes aren't cold. They're not freezing me out. They're heated, searching mine.

It's hypnotic, the way he looks at me. The room goes quiet, the air between us charged.

I bite the corner of my lower lip, and my heart pounds wildly, insistently. I feel like Ava. And Ava is bold. She voices what she wants, and so do I, whispering, "Kiss me."

There's a flash in his eyes, and they drop to my mouth. My words are permission, but he still bends his head so slowly, until our lips are as close as can be without touching.

My breath catches, everything in me poised and waiting. The heat of his lips is almost a kiss, but it isn't enough. I want his mouth on mine and his hands in my hair, winding his fingers through the strands to grip tight. I want a kiss so deep and hot that I feel it in every cell of my body like a fever I don't want to get over.

I want all those things, and I shouldn't.

I want *him*.

"Davis ..."

Just like that, he is claiming me, first tracing his tongue across my top lip, then nipping at the bottom one, then kissing me so fiercely that I shudder and everything else falls away. His lips own me, his hands want to know me, and I swear I might combust from this electric contact.

When he breaks the kiss abruptly, I'm reeling, and I look at Davis through a haze. I don't know what to say, and he seems robbed of words too. As if he doesn't know how the kiss happened, either.

After a moment, he exhales deeply, collecting himself.

"I'm sorry," he says, then steps back. He looks away, staring at some distant point on the wall. "That was a mistake," he says quietly.

A mistake? I blink. That was a kiss that begged to become so much more.

The haze finally clears, and all that's left is embarrassment. That seems like too mild a word for kissing the director—my first *Broadway* director of my first Broadway job.

God. All I can do is what he hired me for. *Act.*

"Yes." I nod in confident agreement. "A mistake."

"It won't happen again." His gaze turns back to me, cold once more, stripped of the longing there just seconds ago.

"Of course not," I say. "Thank you for the script. I'll see you when rehearsals start."

"Yes." He returns to his desk, and I grab my coat, my head still spinning, body still wanting.

I let myself out and walk away. My lips feel bruised and so does my heart, especially when I hear him turn up the music now that I'm gone.

8

DAVIS

The cast gathers on metal folding chairs in the Midtown rehearsal studio, not far from the theater district. The windows look out over Broadway, five stories down, cars and cabs screaming by. I've rolled up my shirtsleeves, figuratively and literally. It's January, but it's hot in here, the heat already rasping through the radiators and the sun through the windows warming things even more.

"There will be no Broadway spectacle to fall back on. No dancing paintbrushes or flying monkeys. I'm not going to ask anyone to zip in on cables from the balcony and perform aerial sequences." This is the inspirational go-get-'em talk before football season starts, without the locker room. I stand at the baby grand rehearsal piano, the music director at the bench, the choreographer leaning against the wall across the room. I take a beat, survey the wide-eyed talent and the jaded veterans that fill the chairs. But even those with fat bios and long lists of credits have their eyes on me.

Except Jill. She's staring hard at a point behind my head, hasn't once made eye contact.

That's fine. I've haunted the boxing gym, and an hour-plus of hard-hitting every day has smoothed over the memory of that surreal day in my office when she'd asked me to kiss her and I'd wanted that too much to deny her. I've blotted out the sinfully good feel of her in my arms and replaced it with a patched memory of how things ended with Madeline, how it had been when she left with barely a goodbye.

"You are the key to this show." I gesture broadly to the cast and crew, encompassing them all. "We succeed or fail on how you work with each other. *Crash the Moon* is about passion and creativity and the limitless bounds of desire, both in art and in love. It's about one young woman's artistic and sexual awakening. It's about a jealous man and an intense love, and it is very physical. The thing that makes people hold off taking a piss until intermission and then race back to their seat afterward, that gets them cheering and shouting, is what you"—I pause to point to the whole cast, from the chorus members to the supporting actors to Patrick, Alexis, Jill, and Braydon—"bring to the stage."

Alexis sits in the front row, kicking one high-heeled foot back and forth, showing off bare legs even in the winter. She takes pride in dressing like a starlet, and kudos to her—she's got some Marilyn thing going on with a white, swirly dress and pinned-up hair. My eyes stray to Jill in spite of myself. I'd love to see her in a low-cut white dress and stilettos—a dress that can be bunched up for doing things behind closed doors, or in alleys, or in stairwells.

I clench my fist and release it, releasing the thoughts as well.

"And if you can't handle that," I tell the cast, "if you're afraid or you're a precious snowflake, now is the time to leave." I go to the door and pull it open, inviting anyone to go. "If you can't leave your goddamn hearts hanging out and beating, then you don't belong here. If you stay, you better be prepared to slice open a vein on stage. I will accept nothing less."

I hold the door open and wait, though I know none of them will leave. Some of them shift in their chairs, glance at each other, peek at the door. When I've made my point—this is serious to me, you are not in charge— I shut the door hard, the slam echoing in the studio. That, and their breathing, are all that punctuate the pristine quiet.

I return to the front of the room, the soles of my shoes sounding on the freshly polished hardwood floors, and face them again. "You are here because you are the best. That got you here, but it's not enough. I'm going to get you the rest of the way and, on opening night, I want the audience to feel every ounce of your pain, every molecule of your passion. Is that clear?"

"Davis?"

I don't expect a verbal response or want one. So, Alexis's raised hand is an unwelcome surprise. So is her using my first name, but there are only so many battles I want to fight with her. I save my energy for the bigger ones.

"Yes, Alexis?"

"I think I speak for all of us when I say this is going to be the greatest show Broadway has ever seen." Then she rises from her seat, turns to her castmates, encourages them to stand too, and begins a round of applause. Some stand, some stay seated. Some cheer, some don't. I glance briefly at Jill. Her hands are resting in her lap.

She's looking down at her feet now, but then she lifts her face and her blue eyes meet mine for the briefest instant. The room goes silent, and she's the only one I see.

There's something about her—her humor, her toughness, her vulnerability, her beauty—that has already hammered chunks from the fortress around my heart, threatening to undo me.

Against all my better judgment.

I wave off the clapping. "Enough." Alexis is about to open her mouth, but she's had her moment, and I hold up a hand. "Let's get to work."

And so, our first rehearsal begins.

* * *

Don is waiting in front of the rehearsal studio the next morning. As soon as I see the pinstriped suit, I groan. The billowing trench coat makes him look even more like a two-bit mobster, and the Bluetooth headset dangling from his ear just makes him look like a douchebag. His pointed glare at his watch is wasted on me. I can't be late for a meeting that doesn't exist. In fact, I'm early. The cast isn't due for another hour, but the stage manager and I need to review which songs and scenes we'll be rehearsing today.

I head for the revolving door, hoping to avoid unpleasantries, but doubting I'll be that lucky. No surprise, he flags me down, and I stop.

"Davis," he says in that grating voice.

"Don."

A cold wind whips past us and Don shivers, pulling his coat closer. "We need to talk."

"Ah, my four least favorite words. What is it, Don? Make it fast. Shannon and I have a lot of song cues to run through in the next hour."

He clucks his tongue. "It's come to my attention that you might be a little harsh with your cast."

I laugh. Oh, this is brilliant. I'd hate for him to have shown his face this fine morning over something child-ish. "Someone's run to tell teacher already? That was fast."

"No," Don lies. "But I *would* like you to tone it down a bit. You could be nicer."

"Could I? Would the actors like foot massages too? Later calls so they can sleep in? Or should I order them some nap pods?"

"Don't be ridiculous. But actors can be sensitive. And when they think you're kind of mean—"

"*Kind of mean?*" I cut him off. "Is this Broadway or the sixth-grade play? I told them to leave if they couldn't give it their all. If Alexis ran to tell you I was a jerk, then . . ."

Don affixes his best poker face. "I'm not naming names."

It doesn't take a genius to know Alexis is the narc. I saw on day one that she would be trouble. But couldn't pretend I didn't know how this business worked.

"What is it you want me to do differently?" I asked.

"Be nicer, okay?" At least he looks slightly embarrassed about it.

"Honestly? You came here to tell me to play nice?"

"Yes," he mumbles.

"And, if I don't roll over, are you going to threaten to pay my exit clause?"

"Davis," he says, trying for a softer *be reasonable* voice. "I never did that."

I step closer pointing my index finger at his lying face. "You did threaten to can me. And you won that round. But if you keep telling me how to run the show, I'll walk. Got it?"

He gulps and says nothing, which isn't good enough.

"Don't push me. Every time you pop up here because Alexis cried wolf, you're questioning my professionalism, and I won't have it. You can go find a new director."

He swallows again, then nods, looking like a scolded dog.

"Good." With that, I return to a more genial voice. "Now, if you'll excuse me, I have a show to rehearse."

I push through the revolving door into the lobby, press the elevator button, and wait, eyes fixed on the elevator doors.

Only once it's arrived and I've stepped inside do I let out the breath I've been holding. I run a hand through my hair and try to shake off my nerves. I hate it when I have to bluff.

The truth is, I'd never walk. He'll have to throw me out kicking and screaming. I am madly in love with *Crash the Moon*. I love this show so much it hurts. And that's entirely separate from the stunningly gorgeous and talented understudy who will walk into the rehearsal studio in sixty minutes.

Alone last night, I tasted her lips again, claimed her mouth with mine. I laced my fingers through hers and pressed her up against the wall so she couldn't move, and she didn't try, just gave in to the things I made her feel, and say, and scream.

Sixty minutes and counting . . .

9

JILL

This is fate.

What else could it be when the subway doors rattle open and Patrick steps inside at the first stop after mine?

He's so handsome I have to catch my breath. It's like looking at a masterpiece that somehow holds the beauty of not just one starry night but every starry night you've ever seen or will see. I grip the pole as the car jerks into motion, enjoy the rush of fluttery warmth expanding from my chest all the way to my fingertips. I am staring, which is awkward when he glances my way and we lock eyes, but then he recognizes me.

"Hey there." His smile is warm and friendly, but I already knew that.

"Hi," I manage, a little breathy, but not enough to telegraph all the years of infatuation and fantasy.

"You're in the show, aren't you?"

"Chorus. And understudy for Ms. Carbone."

"That's fantastic." His grin broadens and lights up the train. No wonder he's a star. "Is this your first show . . .?"

He waits for me to give my name, and fortunately, I remember it. "Jill. Jill McCormick."

"I'm Patrick Carlson."

I laugh, some nerves, some irony. "I know who you are."

"What did you think of yesterday's rehearsal? Of Davis's trademark first day speech?"

"It was intense." Like Davis. "But inspiring. Like the locker room pep talk in the third act of a sports movie."

Patrick chuckles, and the sound sets off firecrackers inside of me. Patrick Carlson had laughed at something I said. Only, I hadn't intended it to be at Davis's expense. It feels a bit sordid talking about him with Patrick at all. I don't want to talk about him at all except as a director. Any non-professional thoughts need to stay locked down tight.

The train shakes as it slows into the next stop, and I latch on tighter to the pole so I don't stumble into him. I'm an adult, not a heartsick teen, but I still have a sliver of fear that if we touch, a dam will burst and I'll blather about all the long, lonely self-loathing nights that dreams of him carried me through. Or I'll confess how just the possibility of him started to heal the dark places in my heart.

Patrick tilts his head, considering me. "Stop me if you've heard this before"—he flashes a rueful smile —"but I feel like we've met somewhere else, outside of *Crash the Moon.*"

The smile does me in, and I blurt out the truth. "I saw you in *Wicked* and we met outside the stage door after. You were very kind and didn't roll your eyes when I humble-bragged about being in the show at school. We even sang a few lines together."

His brows climb and he laughs in surprise. "That was you? Of course, it was you—that's why you seem familiar. That was a blast."

Praise the Lord and glory be. He remembers me. Well, he definitely remembers that moment, and fondly, because his gorgeous face brightens so genuinely I don't know how I'm not breaking out in song and dance right now.

"We did a hell of a duet, didn't we?" he says.

I nod, solemnly. "If there were any justice in the world, and anyone in the alley besides us and the rats, we'd have a recording contract by now."

He laughs, and my heart trips along in rhythm because this time I'd meant to amuse him so I feel like I've done something right.

"I dunno," he says. "I hear we got rave reviews in *Theatre Squeak*. Maybe we could parlay that into some backing."

"From who?"

He's flirting with me. Or maybe it's banter. It makes no difference because we are having a rom-com movie moment and I can't wait to tell Kat.

Patrick exaggerates a thoughtful look. "Hmm . . . Pizza Rat? It was a while ago, but ever since he went viral, he's been—"

"The big cheese?"

We say it at the same time, and maybe it *is* Fate that he stepped onto my subway car because we both laugh, looking into each other's eyes, and both glance away.

None of the perfectly scripted moments with the *possibility* of Patrick felt like this. It might be the first time I preferred *real* to the safe haven of *pretend*.

Patrick clears his throat. "What numbers should we put into our demo for the record labels? I'm thinking a retrospective of the great duets in musical theater history. 'You and I' from *Chess*. 'All I Ask Of You' from *Phantom*. 'Light my Candle' from *Rent* . . ."

"Excellent choices."

"And, of course, our signature piece from *Wicked*." As he says it, something shifts in his expression, and he frowns. "Wait a second. You're the one who sent me flowers, aren't you?"

My face flames, and as the train crawls into the theater district, I want to crawl under a seat. Forget our flirty banter. Right now, he must be rewriting our rom-com into a stalker movie.

"Yes." I look down, out the door, anywhere but at him.

"The flowers were beautiful, Jill," he says to the top of my head as we reach our stop. The doors open, and he guides me out, with a protective hand on my back, shielding me from the frenzied sardine pack of New Yorkers racing to work in the morning.

"Thank you," I mutter. We're going to the same place, so there's no getting away.

It wasn't just the awkwardness. My heart hurt like I'd had a glimpse of something I wouldn't dare wish for and then the door slammed in my face. Twice—once then and once now.

"Hey." Before we reach the turnstiles, Patrick tugs me away from the crowd, turning me toward him so I meet his gaze. "I loved the flowers. They lit up my dressing room at the Gershwin. And under different circumstances, I'd have said yes. I'd enjoyed talking to you. But I was involved with someone at the time."

I gulp to hide the hitch in my breath. A gorgeous and talented guy like him? *Of course* he'd been seeing someone. "That's good to know."

He adds with a touch of humor, "Well, I also knew you were in high school, and I didn't want to do anything inappropriate. Which, despite my youthful good looks, it would have been."

And he's a gentleman too. He didn't want to lead me on then, and he's being straight with me now. The Patrick I imagined him to be was a good guy, so I'm glad to know it hadn't been wishful thinking.

Taking my cue from him, I lighten my tone as we rejoin the flow of foot traffic. "It's okay. It was just an impulse. I was so impressed with the way you jumped into that role, and you were the first Broadway actor I'd ever met. I've admired you ever since."

He gestures for me to go through the turnstile ahead of him. "And now we're acting together. Perhaps it's fate."

My heart skips all its beats, and I manage not to blurt, "That's what *I* was just thinking!" Fate we're in the same show. Fate he took the subway.

It's impossible to talk while navigating the crowds

on the stairs and the traffic at street level. That's just as well, because what I'm thinking—that it's fate, too, that I saw him in *Wicked*—doesn't need saying.

All that went wrong with Aaron—the things he said and did when we broke up, the letters and calls and pleas—it wrecked me. Everything changed, only nobody knew it because I held myself together by my fingernails while my heart splintered invisibly inside of me.

Then I met Patrick at the stage door of the Gershwin, and he'd been gorgeous, talented, charismatic . . . and kind. Kinder than I was being to myself, if I'm honest.

Instead of admitting to anyone—my mother, any of my brothers, one of my friends—my life was in tatters, I found my way through—running when I wanted to explode, acting when I needed to escape, and when I wished for comfort, there was the daydream of Patrick Carlson and love that doesn't hurt.

I haven't been with anyone since Aaron. No one has touched me but me. Why risk the heartache when no other man can give me what the mere idea of Patrick can?

Only he's not only an idea now. Those tingles that race from the tips of my fingers and toes to my chest where they bloom into shivers . . . When had I last felt attracted to anyone?

Weeks ago. Davis's office. When he had his mouth and hands all over you.

I don't think that should count, but I can't think of a good reason why not.

* * *

I do lunges as Kat packs. She's heading to Mystic tomorrow to see her parents, and to be feted at their gift shop where her necklaces have been selling like crazy. She invited me to go with her and I want to be there, but rehearsal lasts until six and her party is at seven, so there's no way I can make it. She graduated from MBA school a few weeks ago, and her Kat Harper necklaces have become amazingly popular, carried in boutiques and in the fancy Elizabeth's department stores around the country. She's running her jewelry business full-time and planning a summer wedding in Mystic where she and Bryan first met.

I'd say it was a charmed life if I didn't know how hard she's worked for it, and the twisty road she and Bryan have taken to get to their happy-ever-after. Besides, I love her to the moon and back, and want all good things for her.

She considers a purple scarf with white stars, looping it around her neck and pouting at me like a glamour queen. "What do you think?"

"Oh, *darling*," I drawl. "Purple is *so* your color."

She tosses the scarf on top of her other clothes. "You really can't leave rehearsal early?"

I switch legs and do more lunges. I rarely sit still.

"Have you met Davis Milo? If you're late, he paddles you."

She laughs. "Really? Got a BDSM director there, do you?"

I shrug and look at the floor. Why am I even making

stupid jokes about Davis? But I can't seem to stop. "I wouldn't be surprised. I bet he ties up all his conquests."

"Maybe I should leave the scarf with you then," she says, then winks.

"His *conquests*, Kat." I roll my eyes, and specify, "Not me, in any case." Even joking around, it feels important to draw a line between Davis and me. I haven't told Kat that he kissed me at his office, or that I'd asked him to. It was a mistake, and we agreed that it won't happen again. It was a non-starter and a non-issue.

"Have you ever been? You know, tied up?" Kat asks. "Or handcuffed or anything? Like by Stefan maybe? I could see him as the type."

I focus intently on a framed vintage poster of Paris on Kat's wall. "No."

It's true, but it feels like a lie. Nearly everything she believes about Stefan is an invention. She thinks I slept with him, and that he's some sort of wizard in the sack, based on some assumptions she made that I didn't correct. That story was much more interesting than my actual love life, or lack thereof, that I rolled with it, and then broke it off with "Stefan" before I had to admit the real Stefan and I had gone out a few times and kissed exactly once.

I trust Kat more than anyone, but it's easier to let her assume I have a semi-normal dating life than to explain why I don't. I can't talk about what happened. I couldn't bear for any of my friends to know. What if it *was* my fault, like Aaron said?

Besides, I've kept the story a secret for so long that I wouldn't know where to begin to excavate it. Why conduct a full-scale archaeological dig for a relic I don't want uncovered? What happened with Aaron can stay buried, and I'm fine with that.

Am I fine, though?

I'm a twenty-three-year-old single gal in the city who's gone six years without sex. At least, sex that's a duet, not a solo. I have a good imagination, an e-library of racy books, and a healthy libido, at least according to the articles in Cosmo. I dream of passionate kisses, of lips and hands that can't get enough, of bodies entangled and heated encounters and promises of more.

But if I'm going to be with someone again, I need to know it's not a tainted kind of love. That it's not twisted. That it can't be used against me, or against someone else.

"What about you?" I layer a salacious tone in my voice, so I can shift the attention back to her and off of my fictionalized love life. "Does Bryan have ropes for you?"

She laughs and shakes her head, then places her hand on her chest. "Jill, let me introduce you to your vanilla friend Kat. But even so, it's better than anything I've ever read in a romance novel. Speaking of, I downloaded this hot new rock star romance. It's scorching. I'll gift it to you. Maybe you can use it tomorrow when I'm out of town."

I hold up my hand and waggle my fingers. "If only my e-reader could vibrate."

Kat laughs, and I say goodnight and get ready for bed, taking the time to put together an outfit for tomorrow, settling on a jean skirt, black tights, and a teal sweater. I don't link the care I put into my clothes to my earlier thoughts until I'm picking out accessories and realize—I want to look *dateable*. I want to go on a date and just see where things go. I'm ready.

Davis Milo appears center stage in my mind. Oh, no. My director is ineligible. However, talking to Patrick on the train was fun, and I think if I ask him out *now*, I'd have much better luck than six years ago. So, that's what I'm going to do.

I have a charm necklace Kat made for me last fall, with a beret on it to commemorate when I'd gotten the part in *Les Mis*. When I go to get it from my nightstand, my gaze falls on the top drawer, slightly ajar. I reach to close the drawer, but instead I pull it open.

The small wooden box inside has been beside my bed for six years. It calls to me now in a haunting voice, as if I need a reminder of what's inside. As if I could forget.

I remove the box, place it in the middle of my bed, and take a deep, calming breath. I'm about to open a bomb. It's tried to destroy me before, but I keep thinking, *This is the time I'll defuse it.*

From the same drawer, I pull out a tiny key dangling from a chain, and I unlock the wooden box. I don't need the pictures to see Aaron's perfectly–dark, close-cropped hair, light brown eyes, and that dimple on the right side of his mouth that made me fall for him. His sense of humor, the jokes he made about our school mascot, the dozens of red roses he brought me when I played in our production of *Mamma Mia*. Those are the good things.

Fingers shaky, I take out a picture. He and I at prom. I'm wearing a red dress that falls to my knees, and my hair is in a French twist with a few loose tendrils. He's unbearably handsome in his tux, and that smile gives nothing away. I open the note next, the creases in the paper as permanent as tattoos, and read the first few lines.

"God, I love you so fucking much, Jill."

That's what gets me every time. Those words. Those awful, painful words.

I close the box, lock it, and return it to the drawer.

* * *

The next morning, I take the train to the rehearsal studio, a cute knit cap pulled over my blow-dried hair, a red scarf wrapped around my neck, and a skirt—tights too, which I'm glad of as I hurry from the Fiftieth Street station to the building.

Inside, I head right to the elevator panel to press the button.

"Hold the elevator."

I turn, and it's Davis.

"*Please*," he adds when he sees me. His tone is—unless I'm imagining things—playful, and he flashes a smile just for—I check around—yes, just for me. His inky blue eyes twinkle, and I have a strange, fleeting sense of him appraising me from stem to stern and drinking me in—my cap and the blonde hair peeking from under it, to the black tights and the short gray boots that Kat brought me from Paris. It might have lasted a flick of an eyelash, or I might have imagined it entirely.

Besides, thoughts are unpredictable. I've had unprofessional thoughts pop randomly into my head, caught myself looking where I shouldn't. It didn't mean I would act on them. That is, not *again*, because I'd learned from the first *mistake*.

"Elevator's not even here yet," I say, facing the closed doors in case I'm blushing.

"I'm sure there will be another one," he replies, facing the same way.

From the corner of my eye, I notice he's not wearing a winter coat, even though he's just come in from the cold. Just jeans, shoes, and a white button-down shirt that must have been tailored for him. He's holding a coffee cup in one hand, and a sesame seed bagel in the other. It's only us in the lobby. Waiting.

I glance at Davis again, and he's not even shivering. It's like he's made of iron, impervious to the elements.

"Don't you ever get cold?"

"No."

"You're kind of badass."

His lips quirk up in a grin. "Thank you."

I clap my hand to my mouth because I don't know what's going to come out next. "Dammit," I mutter.

The grin fades to a concerned frown. He transfers

his bagel to his other hand, and reaches as if to touch my arm, but then he stops himself. Lowering his hand, he asks, "Is something wrong, Jill?"

I start to give a breezy, "Nothing," but he seems to genuinely care about my answer. So, after a moment, I say, "I forget I shouldn't say things like that to my boss." It's true, a reminder to myself, and though I didn't plan it that way, it's a bit of a rebuke. With me, he's been warm and teasing, or icily formal. He delivered, on request, the hottest kiss of my life and then went full General Patton on the cast at rehearsal the other day. . . And now whatever this is.

My finely-tuned calibrations can't get a read on him. At a glance, he's the man in the *GQ* ad, relaxing in a leather chair, a suit jacket tossed casually over the arm, a few buttons of his crisp white shirt undone, holding a sturdy glass of scotch, his midnight blue eyes hypnotizing from the page.

At work, he's the colonel keeping us in line, but he's also an artist and a gentleman. And then there's this unexpected soft side. Davis Milo is the strangest mix of sophisticated class and unbridled intensity I've ever seen. If a Merchant Ivory movie and a Quentin Tarantino flick got together and had a baby, that would be him.

"I really wish you wouldn't call me your boss," he says, in a carefully neutral tone that could mean anything. I wonder if he's having just as hard a time reading me.

"But you are, aren't you?"

The question—*aren't you?*—takes on a life of its

own. It didn't sound flirtatious when I framed it in my head. Maybe something between my brain and my vocal cords is looking out for me, because the air around us feels warmer, sharper, and I lean into it, wanting more of it.

More of the mistake.

He tilts his head and keeps his eyes on me, not letting go. That look makes me want to tell him things, to open up, to share the secrets I've never told anyone else. His dark blue eyes are pure and unflinching, and they demand total honesty, nothing less.

Of course, that's his style. He elicits the most compelling performances from actors by demanding unwavering truth on stage.

He doesn't respond to my question. The silence expands, an electric kind of quiet, and soon I can't take the tension.

"My boss," I clarify. But my feathery voice seems to belong to someone else.

"Technically, I'm not your boss," he says in that same level, could mean anything tone. "The producers are. I'm only your director."

I can't tell if he's returning the volley, or if he's just a master at handling actors. At handling me.

I look at the floor numbers above the elevator. Third floor. The elevator will be here any minute, and then I'll be alone with him in it. My mind gallops off to visit all the sexy scenes in elevators I've ever read. Part of me wants to rein in my imagination, but the other part would let it run.

I can't leave it to chance which wins.

"I'm going to take the stairs." I turn on my heel and go.

"Good idea."

His voice follows me, but I did not expect that he would follow me too.

10

DAVIS

I take a bite of my bagel as we round the first landing, chewing as I watch her walk up the stairs. I should look away, but her legs—strong, shapely, and impossibly long—have the advantage over willpower.

"How's your coaching going?" I ask as we round another flight.

She casts me a curious look over her shoulder as she keeps walking, her boots on the concrete steps resounding in the stairwell. "How did you know I was a running coach?"

"Because I looked you up before I called you in," I say. "I research all actors I seriously consider casting."

"Oh," she says. I catch a faint whiff of disappointment. Would she rather I'd looked up only her?

"Coaching is good," she continues. "I scaled back a bit when I got the part, but I'm still working with a core group of women who are training for a run to raise funds for breast cancer research."

"Takes a lot of discipline to do that, to run every day.

I imagine it takes even more discipline to have run five marathons."

"Yes. I am immensely disciplined." There's something veiled in her answer that raises intriguing questions. "In fact, I've learned all the lines already."

Oh. My mind was drifting off to far tawdrier shores.

She halts abruptly on the landing to the fourth floor and wheels on me in a startling rush of frustration and hopeless desperation. "You can't just do this." Her voice nearly breaks. "You can't keep coming in and out of my life."

I step closer to her, confused but mostly worried. "I'm sorry." But I don't know what I've done wrong. "Are you okay?"

She flashes a smug and brilliant smile. "It's from the show. Act II, Scene Five."

I can only stare for a moment then laugh at myself. "A point to you. You had me going and I didn't even recognize that it was a line." Because I know them all, of course, and I give her Paolo's line and his cocky stare. "But I'm in your life. I'm in it, Ava." I say emphatically. I'm no actor and don't wish to be one, but I shift into the scene. We're no longer in the stairwell. We're in the art gallery where this scene takes place, and Ava is angry with Paolo because he's appeared when she didn't expect him.

Ava is through with all their ups and downs. "Then be in it," she commands in clipped syllables.

I step closer to her. "I will if you'll stop pushing me out."

"I never have, and you know it." Chin lifted, she fixes me with a tough stare and doesn't back away.

I pause. Breathe. Let go of the anger. "Ava, I can't stand this fighting anymore."

She raises her eyebrows playfully. "Let's do something other than fight, then." Her eyes soften. She reaches for my face with tentative fingers. "You have something on your . . ."

That's not right. I frown, puzzled at words that don't fit. "The next line is *I have something in mind—*"

She cuts me off. "No, I was going to say you have a sesame seed right here." She taps her chin.

"Oh." I swipe once to wipe it off.

"You missed," she says softly. "Davis," she adds, so I know she's talking to me now in that inviting, seductive tone. We're done with lines. It's just us.

She sweeps her thumb across my chin. "I got it," she whispers. Still Jill or back to Ava—I don't care. She traces my jawline, and the barest touch from her makes me hard.

"Did you find any more?" I ask, low and hoarse.

She shakes her head, her hair brushing her coat. I catch a faint scent of her pineapple shampoo that already is *her* scent to me.

Now she's running her index finger across my lower lip, and that's it. That's all I can take.

"Jill," I warn.

"What?"

"If you keep doing that . . ." I trail off, leaving the possibilities open.

She keeps doing it, obliterating all my willpower. I

place my coffee and bagel on the stairs then grab her wrists, walking her two steps backward until she's up against the concrete wall. Her lips are softly parted, and her eyes are full of heat. I bend close to murmur near her ear. "Ask me again. Like you did in my office."

She tilts her head so her cheek brushes mine and whispers, "Kiss me again, like you did in your office."

I take a tighter hold on her wrists as I capture her mouth with mine.

She lets out the tiniest little whimper at the first touch of my lips, an encouraging sound. I want to kiss her hard and hungry because that's how she makes me feel. But I'm setting the tempo and tone here. Still trapping her wrists, I trace her lips with the tip of my tongue, slowly, torturously. She tries to deepen the kiss, but I take my time with her sinfully delicious mouth, tormenting her with my tongue. I want her to think only of lingering, consuming kisses any place she wants them.

I move to her jawline, kissing her there, teasing my way to her earlobe. "Is that what you wanted me to do?" I whisper.

"Yes," she pants.

"Is that why you touched me?"

"Yes."

"Have you been thinking about me since that day in my office?"

"No."

"Don't lie to me."

She inhales sharply then whispers in a ragged voice. "Yes."

I let go of her wrists, and they fall to her sides. I untie the belt of her jacket then undo each button, letting the fabric fall open. "I hate winter," I say. "Too many layers."

Then I pull back to look at her. She's wearing a V-neck sweater that makes her breasts look fantastic. Her nipples harden under my gaze. I finger the bottom of her sweater, dying to know what her skin feels like. I lift the fabric and run my fingers across the soft skin of her stomach.

She shivers, and it's as if she's been vibrating a low hum, waiting for the right person to turn her all the way up, all the way on. I want to be that person, and I slant my mouth across hers to kiss her hard and rough. I want her to feel me later when she's all alone.

She responds instantly, grabbing my hair, pulling me closer, tangling her tongue with mine. It's a hungry kiss—I explore her mouth, tasting her lipstick until I nearly lose my mind with the need to know more of her body.

Every inch of her.

Her hands drop to my waist, and she tugs me closer. I follow her cues, giving her what she wants, rolling my hips against her. Her hands are on my ass in a second, pulling me against her, thrusting her body against mine. I'm so close to hiking up her skirt, to touching her under those tights, to learning exactly how much more she wants.

Instead we kiss like that, frenzied and fast, bodies smashed together, but never quite going too far. Finally, we pull apart for air. She's breathing hard, but she's smiling too, and everything about her is lowering my defenses—the sweet curve of her lips, the glow in her blue eyes, her talent and how she was meant for this role. It's eating me alive not to ask her out, to romance her the way I want.

I let her sweetness work its way through the guarded parts of me, and I tell her something I shouldn't.

"As soon as I saw you audition, you were Ava to me."

Her eyes widen. "I was?"

"Yes." I want her to know what I see in her. I want her to know that she's my discovery. I found her, I called her in, I chose her. "You embody her. You *are* her." I leave a quick kiss on her neck, making her shudder. "I can feel her pain in you. Her secrets. Her sadness. How wounded she is. Most of all, I can feel her hope."

She bites her lip, color rising in her cheeks. Slowly, she brings her hand to her heart, as if enchanted. "Really?"

I nod. "You're going to be such a big star, Jill. A bright light of Broadway. I want the world to know I discovered you."

"Thank you," she says. "I'm so happy to have this chance so early in my career to work with you."

Her eyes hold such genuine happiness, and it's a strange thing to jolt me back in time. It's a look I recognize, along with the words. *So early in my career.* I can picture Madeline three years ago, how thrilled she was when I called her in for an audition after seeing her in a tiny little workshop production, how over the moon she was to be cast in one of my first shows, how hopelessly we fell in love as we worked together on *World Enough and Time* in San Diego.

It shatters the moment, seeing Jill look at me now the way Madeline did then. She is all my weaknesses, and I know the ending of this story. I can't go there again.

I shake my head to clear it. "Rehearsal is about to start. I can't be late. And we can't keep doing this."

"Right." Her voice is shaky.

"We just can't," I repeat, aware that I'm the one who needs convincing.

"I know," she says more forcefully. She's resigned but resolute. "The show is too important. You can't be distracted, and I don't want to do anything to mess with the cast's chemistry."

She thinks it's because of the show. But it's more than that. "Jill. I don't date actresses." It comes out more cruelly than I intended, in a firm, harsh voice that's more for me than for her.

I can see the moment when my tone and words catch up with her. "Oh." Her tone is unreadable, and she quickly and deliberately rearranges her features, erasing happiness along with the lingering glow of what we just did.

Then she adjusts her coat and smooths her hair. "Well, that's fine. There's someone else . . . I could see myself falling in love with him, and now there's nothing holding me back. So . . ." She pulls her coat closed and looks around the landing. "Thanks for the clarity."

Turning on her heel, she starts up the stairs while I'm still taking that in. In love with someone else?

"Then you really shouldn't kiss me like that," I call out to her, and this time I intend it to sound harsh.

She gives me one sharp cold stare before she pushes open the door to the fifth-floor hall. "You're right. I shouldn't."

11

JILL

As soon as rehearsal ends, I head straight for the ladies' room to lecture myself in the mirror.

What were you thinking?

Why limit it to one thing? The morning was a cascade of bad decisions. And seriously? "*There's someone else?*" That's rookie-league face-saving. I could have just said, "You don't want me, but my totally real and not at all imaginary boyfriend does."

The door opens, and I grab my lip gloss for an excuse to be there. Shelby, one of my castmates, pops in. She's in the chorus with me, a few years older, and an amazing dancer, with a sort of ballroom flare, all hips and sexy sway.

"Hey, there," she says. "The whole cast is going out to Zane's for drinks. Want to join?"

I almost decline, then I remember that, not only does our director not *date actresses*, he doesn't fraternize with the cast after rehearsal, either.

"I'm in," I say. "Let me grab my bag, and I'll meet you by the elevator."

I leave the restroom and head for the elevator. I spot Davis talking to Alexis inside the doorway of one of the rehearsal studios. Well, I can only see part of them, but he's the only one in the studio in a white button-down, and her hand rests on his arm, no mistaking those long, scarlet nails, that tighten on his sleeve. What a cliché.

Sort of seething, but mostly smarting, I angle to stay out of their line of sight. But I stop cold when I hear Davis say in a low voice, "Of course you're the best, Alexis." It sounds like he's smoothing some ruffled feathers. "These are just nerves. I knew from the first day, I had to cast you as Ava. When you're on the stage, you *are* Ava . . ."

While I'm still gasping at that sucker punch, Alexis loosens her grip and pulls him in for an embrace. I hurry by so I won't get caught listening.

What the hell? He'd said the same thing to me this morning and had seemed so incredibly sincere. Does he think actresses are interchangeable? Or is he playing us both?

Ding, ding, ding!

We have a winner. To him, we're all fragile flowers needing praise like we need the sun. So he doles it out, and that's how he coaxes out such great performances. It's insidiously clever, and totally Machiavellian.

I was easily fooled because I wanted his words to be true, to believe I was his first choice. Now all I want is to march up and demand he never toy with me or my feelings or any other part of me again. But not while he's with Alexis. Chin up, I walk right past the closed studio door on my way back, and don't give it a glance.

Shelby is waiting at the elevator and we step in and ride down. "That dance number was brutal." She stretches her neck from side to side, as I force Davis and his puppeteering ways from my brain. I don't have any extra mental real estate to devote to him. "I thought I was going to die."

"Yeah, totally," I agree. Actually, the dance number was all cardio, and I'm a wizard at cardio. But I also really like fitting in. "I think I might collapse later because of that number."

Shelby gives me a playfully stern look. "Drinks first, collapse after."

"But of course."

We head into Zane's and find our crowd. Alexis has turned up, though she's off in the back of the bar with her publicist, so I hang where a bunch of chorus members have pulled together some tables. I order a beer, and we talk about this show and other shows we've done. When Kelly Clarkson's "Catch My Breath" starts on the bar's sound system, a group of us grab our imaginary microphones and sing along—loud and boisterous and actually on pitch. When the number ends, we get a rousing ovation from the rest of the bar.

I head to the bar to order another beer. As I wait, I take out my phone and text my brother Chris in California. We talk—okay, we text—every day, and I like to keep him up to date on my life. We were close growing up, and he always looked out for me—until the business with Aaron. Somehow, I could never find the words to tell him what was going on. I guess by sharing the details of my life in New York City now, I feel like I'm making up for my silence years ago.

Rehearsal is great. But director is strange.

I send off the note, then wonder why I mentioned Davis now that I have his number. He's a master craftsman who knows how to use his tools perfectly. "Used" is how I feel after hearing him tell Alexis the same thing he'd told me. *You are Ava.*

Chris writes back quickly. *Define strange.*

You know, like Broadway director strange.

He replies *I know this may shock you, but I know nothing of Broadway directors. BTW, I'm probably coming to NYC next month for a work trip. Can you make some time for your big bro?*

I nearly squeal. I haven't seen Chris in a year.

Yes!!!!

As Shelby joins me at the bar, I put my phone away. She pushes a hand through her dark, wavy hair and asks, "On a scale of one to ten, how hot is Patrick Carlson?"

I nearly spit out my beer. Then I realize it was just a question—not a dig at the single-minded, single-sided passion of my late teens. Because no one knows about that. And everyone with eyes knows Patrick is gorgeous.

"Oh, he's all right," I downplay, and Shelby laughs and bumps my shoulder with hers as I glance back the way she came. "Is he here?"

"On his way, someone just said." She looks at me impishly. "Is there a reason you're asking? If you like him, you should go for it. I worked in *South Pacific* with him, and he's super nice."

Earlier, I'd thought I might ask him out. I didn't want it to be because of what I'd said to Davis, or in a reaction to Davis's door-slam. I didn't want Davis to factor into it at all.

I did the safe thing and turned the conversation toward her. "What about you, Shelby? Anyone special in your life?"

"Since you asked . . ." She laughs and waggles her hand, showing me a gumball-sized sparkly rhinestone ring. "I *am* involved with someone. It's not a real diamond, obviously. More a promise of a ring to come. He's an actor too."

"Oh cool. What's he in?"

She sighs, and her brown eyes look sad. "Nothing right now. He just moved to Los Angeles since pilot season is starting. He's hoping to land something soon. He's working as a personal trainer between auditions."

"What about you. Are you acting full-time?"

"I used to moonlight as a hairstylist. I worked at one of the blowout salons for a while and did a ton of updos for weddings. I loved it. I've been doing hair for fun my whole life. But now I mostly do voice-overs to support myself—and then this kind of gig, of course, when I land one."

"Can you teach me how to French braid? I grew up with two brothers and my mom worked all the time, so my French braids are disasters."

"Oh, you'd look gorgeous with a French braid, with that perfect long blonde hair. I'll do yours next rehearsal and then teach you. Mine are epic. I was a nun in *The Sound of Music* back in high school and I did Maria's hair, just messing around one day. The director saw and had me styling Maria and half the Von Trapp kids for the week-long production."

I laugh since she grins while telling the story, and I take a sip of my beer. "Maybe Davis will enlist you then for your mad hair skills."

She pulls back and eyes me with such disbelief that I'm sure I've offended her. "I'm sorry. I didn't mean to imply you would have to work double."

"No. That's not it," she says with a laugh. "Do you really call him Davis? No one calls him Davis, except for Alexis. He's Milo to everyone."

Heat rushes to my cheeks. "I didn't mean . . . I just . . ." I can't finish because I don't know what to say. I call him Davis because he asked me to. Now that's just who he is to me.

"I'd say to go for it with him, because he's got that

whole tall, dark, and broody thing going on, but he doesn't date actresses."

"Oh yeah?" I try to sound as disinterested as I want to be. But am I the only one who didn't know this about him?

"Yeah, ever since Madeline Blaine—" Shelby cuts off when she catches someone's eye and waves. "Hey, beautiful!"

I turn to look, and oh, hey, it's Patrick, walking over to us and wrapping Shelby in a big hug. When he lets go of her, it's my turn. It's nice, with potential. He feels good and strong, and as he releases me, he says, "Hey, Jill! How are you?"

"Great!"

The bartender scurries over, fast enough that I guess he recognizes Patrick. "What can I get for you, sir?"

"I'll have what they're having," he says, placing one hand on my shoulder and one on Shelby. She was right —he is super nice, the kind of nice that makes you feel like you've been friends way longer than you have.

As he waits for his beer, the three of us chat about today's rehearsal, then Shelby excuses herself for the restroom.

It's just Patrick and me at the wooden bar, with One Republic's "Feel Again" playing. "I love this song," I say, making conversation.

He grins and sings a bit with the chorus. "What else do you listen to when you get tired of show tunes?"

We talk bands for a bit, and considering he'd been my unattainable ideal for so long, it's surprisingly comfortable. And you know what? It doesn't matter what Davis would make of it. This isn't about him. It might have been, but *he doesn't date actresses.*

In the next lull in conversation, when Shelby should be coming back any minute, I ask, "So, remember that super awkward thing where I sent you flowers and asked you out?"

He looks wary but takes his cue from my tone. "Er, yes."

"Ignore that." I blew out a nervous breath. "This is just me, enjoying talking to you, and wondering if you'd like to get together for coffee sometime."

"A date?" he asks cautiously, but there's a twinkle in his eyes like he doesn't think it's the worst idea ever.

"Um . . . if you'd like it to be? It doesn't have to be anything but, you know, hot water and ground beans."

He turns and faces me, taking my hands as if he's a gentleman come to court me. Then, very seriously, he says, "I would love to go out for water and ground beans with you, Jill."

"Hot water," I correct.

"Hot water," he agrees, and breaks his straight face with a smile. My day has moved from cold and confusing to warm and wonderful.

At least until I'm drenched by a cold beer I never see coming. "What the . . .?"

I spin to see Alexis has crashed into me, and the beer from her empty glass is now soaking my clothes.

"Oh dear, I'm so sorry . . . um . . . whatever your name is." She hardly bothers to feign contrition.

"It's Jill, and you just spilled your beer all over me," I snap.

She narrows her eyes and looks down her nose at me. "I said I was sorry. You don't have to be snotty."

I hold up my hands. "I wasn't snotty. I'm just covered in hops now."

Patrick hands me a napkin. I try to blot up the mess, but it's hopeless.

"Excuse me," I say, and head for the bathroom. The cloth napkin is little help, so I grab a handful of paper towels and blot at the wettest part, but I'm fighting a losing battle. Even my tights are wet.

Someone opens the door. I look up to see Alexis stumble into the bathroom. Despite the beer on her breath, her crystal blue eyes are steely and cold. "You." She points a finger at me, and I want to slap it away. I want to smack Davis too, for telling her she was the one. "Whatever your name is. This isn't going to be some *All About Eve* situation here."

I roll my eyes. I mean really, see-it-from-the-back-row rolled them. "I'm not plotting against you, Alexis."

She snorts. "Oh right. Oh sure. I know your type. You want my part. I'll be watching you, and I won't be the only one. If I think for one second that you're trying to pull something on me, your career will be over like that."

She snaps a finger. The gesture is over-the-top and stagey, and I'm done. I have had it.

"Can we cut?"

"What?"

"The hidden cameras." I make a show of searching.

"If we're on a reality show, there must be hidden cameras somewhere."

"We're not on a reality show." Then she drops her voice and looks around a little wild-eyed. "Are we?"

"We must be. The conspiracy theories, the overacting—"

"Overacting!"

"Yes. Because that's the only place where people say annoying things like this." I gesture to her and my skirt and all of it. Gloves off, I face her and lean a bit closer, so she knows I'm serious. "So, unless we're living in a Telenovela or with the Kardashians, why don't you stop focusing on me, and save the drama for the stage?"

I turn on my heel and leave her with her mouth hanging open. It's a small victory in this roller coaster day. A victory that feels entirely Pyrrhic when I have to say goodbye to Patrick and Shelby because I'm soggy and smell like a brewery.

12

DAVIS

My sister takes a sip of the white wine she's ordered. She nods approvingly at the waiter holding the bottle. He pours more into her glass and then tips the bottle toward me. I decline with a curt wave. I'm not in the mood tonight.

He bows and walks off.

Michelle stares hard then imitates me, adopting a frown and a standoffish little shrug that mirrors mine.

"Are we going there again?" I sigh.

"Well, you've barely said a word."

"We just got here five minutes ago."

"That's five minutes of talking we could have done."

"You talk all day long for your job. Don't you ever want to *not* talk?"

"Surprising, I know, but I actually like talking. And I thought you talked too. Oh wait, you tell people what to do." She flashes me a *just kidding* smile that makes it impossible to stay annoyed with her.

"But isn't that what you do too?" I ask, arching a brow.

"Touché."

This is what my little sister and I do—needle each other, get under the skin, and don't let each other get too much in our own heads.

I take a drink of my water as Michelle savors another swallow of her wine. She rolls her eyes as she savors it, like TV chefs appreciate deliciousness with their faces. "This is divine," she says as she holds up the glass. Then she looks again at me. "So what's with the whole enigmatic, broody thing you have going on today? I'm aware that's your usual, but you're operating at double the daily dosage today. Crap day at rehearsal?"

I shrug. I can't get the details of what happened in the stairwell this morning out of my mind, but neither do I want to discuss them. "It was fine."

We're at a too-cool-for-words restaurant on Canal Street, not far from my loft. This place is called The Cutlery Drawer and there's not a matching utensil in the place. The tables are all black lacquer, the floor is charcoal gray tile and the utensils are a strange hodge-podge. My sister picked it. I think it's more fitting for a nightclub, but this is her hobby. She spends her days advising on the challenges of love and relationships as a psychologist and her nights researching the newest eateries in Manhattan for us to check out.

She narrows her dark brown eyes and leans across the table. "I don't believe you, Davis."

"You don't believe that I had a fine day at rehearsal?"

"I believe that when you say *fine* it means shitty. Something's bothering you."

"I swear, some days I wish you weren't a genius shrink at such a young age."

She raises an eyebrow. "I was right then."

I say nothing.

She softens her tone. "C'mon, Davis. What is it? I hate to see you all wound up."

"It's nothing," I huff, but I can't put that cat back in the bag.

"Are you being careful with your new show?"

I pick up a fork and twirl it between my thumb and forefinger, looking away. "Yes," I mutter, because now she sees right through me.

She presses her palms together, almost as if she's praying. "Please tell me you're not falling for some captivating young actress who'll break your heart again?"

I drop the fork.

"Oh, Davis." No teasing now. That's worry etched in her features.

"Michelle, I'm fine." It's up to me to look out for her, not the other way around. I look at the menu.

"I don't believe you. I don't want to see you get hurt again. I hate what Madeline did to you."

"She just left, that's all. Okay? Please, let's stop investing the whole affair with so much monumentality. Besides, it was a few years ago." I don't want to dwell on Madeline Blaine. I don't want to revisit all the promises we made, all the things we said to each other. Most of all, I don't want to remember how much it hurt when she walked away, too soon after the play we worked on together ended for it to be happenstance. *You gave me my first big break, and for that, I will be forever grateful, but I don't have time in my life for love. I need to focus on my career.* Then she went to L.A. and did just that.

It's not like I expected a fucking plaque for having plucked her out of the pile of young hopefuls. That's what I do. I would never expect her to owe me anything as her director.

As the man she fell in love with, though, I had hoped for a lot more than a cold goodbye after the curtains fell. But that's how it goes with actors. They fall in love with their roles, they fall in love with the show, they fall in love with you. Then it ends and they move on because they know how to turn emotions on and off.

"I read she was in talks to do that new Steve Martin play and is coming to New York. I'm totally not going to see it, even though I love his work," she says, boycotting the show preemptively.

"Let's talk about something else. Health care reform or troubles in Congress," I say sharply. My sister is the only person who really knows me. Sometimes I hate being known. Sometimes I prefer the appearance I've carefully crafted with my work.

Michelle is insistent, though. She reaches across the table to wrap her hand around mine. "I know you worry about me, but I worry about you too. Just let me, okay? You're all I have."

The waiter appears with a plate of bread.

"Thank you," I say to him.

"But of course, sir."

He leaves.

I grab a piece of bread and bite into it. When I finish, I point to the bread. "You should have some." She forgets to eat when she's sad, and I don't want her to be sad for me. I'm fine, I'll always be fine. But even though I like to think I'm the one who looks out for her, as I have since that snowy day our parents died in a car crash when I was only seventeen, the truth is we look out for each other. "I promise I won't do something as abysmally stupid as fall for an actress again."

"Good," she says and takes some bread. "There are plenty of wonderful women in the world who won't use you to get ahead."

I want to believe that Jill wouldn't do that. I want to believe she's different from Madeline.

As soon as I realize that, I know, too, that I don't really care if Madeline will be in town. What I *do* care about—maybe too much for my own good—is the sweet, sexy, vulnerable woman I kissed this morning. But that's a far bigger problem, and that's precisely why I'm going to have to resist her with everything I have.

Later that night, I'm too wired, too wound up, and I can't stay inside. I attack a late-night run with ferocity, joined by Ryder. He's recently left a relationship that I can only describe as horrid. Now he's able to take off for an after-ten run along the Hudson River Greenway. No one expects him home anymore.

"How's the new musical coming along?" he asks as our sneakers slap the pavement.

"Great. I kissed the understudy in the stairwell."

He snaps his gaze at me. "What the . . .?"

I shoot him an evil grin. "I've shocked the Consummate Wingman," I say, using his moniker. Ryder Lockhart is Manhattan's very own *Hitch*. The love doctor—he could smooth any path for any man pursuing a woman.

"You know that's hardly the role I'm playing these days," he says.

"I know. But I have faith in your wingman talent," I say as my breath comes in sharp spurts. My thighs burn as we run, and I welcome it.

"By the way, don't think you can distract me from the *kissed your understudy* comment."

I manage a mirthless laugh. "There's really not much more to tell."

"How about the story of how it happened?"

But what's the point? It won't happen again.

13

JILL

Now that my beer-soaked skirt and tights are in the hamper, I wash my face, brush my teeth, and pick a long T-shirt to sleep in. I slide under the covers and grab my e-reader. Between the messed-up morning in the stairwell and the buzzkill of Alexis in the bar, I need some reliable company, people who act in predictable ways.

I click on the title Kat gifted me. She hooked me on romance novels, and now I'm a junkie. I lose myself in the story, imagining I'm living the heroine's life, from the sweet dates to the sultry nights, to the swoony and dirty words the hero whispers in her ear.

Everything is better here.

Safer here.

I let myself linger in that world for a while, escaping into the story, but when someone from the past appears in the heroine's life, my shoulders tighten.

A memory snags.

Something tugs at the edge of my mind like I left an iron on.

I sit up straight in bed.

Look around, as if someone's here.

But no one's here, the apartment is quiet, and the only noise is in my head. It sounds like a radio tuned slightly wrong, static mixing with a song I used to know well.

I throw off the covers, pace down the hall and check my phone that I left on the coffee table.

But there are no new messages, and I'm not waiting to hear from anyone.

When I finally fall asleep, I dream of the letters in the locked box by my bed. Letters living, breathing, creepily alive. Letters making demands.

Letters that I open in the street, that the wind snatches away from me. I try to grab them and stuff them back inside, but they're rippling away in the wind, and I can't reach them anymore to hide them.

* * *

The next morning, I skip my run. I shower quickly, get dressed, and when I'm done, I take one of the letters from the wooden box. Then I catch a train to Brooklyn and head for Prospect Park.

I clutch the piece of notebook paper in my right hand. The words are faded, smudged from all the times I've read this one. It's the first of the handful of letters Aaron sent me after we split. I walk deeper into the park, following the path by memory. I spent so many days here with my brothers, riding bikes, climbing trees, playing hide and seek. When I was a teenager, I relearned all the corners of this oasis in Brooklyn that were perfect for stolen kisses, for first tastes of beers, for moonlit make-out sessions far away from parental eyes. But I haven't set foot in Prospect Park since Aaron. Not since the last time I saw him under Terrace Bridge.

Now, I have to because I can't keep holding on to the pieces of the past. I can't keep carrying all this blame with me. My life is unfurling before me, and if I don't free myself from the past it'll keep haunting me.

I weave down the path that leads under the bridge, remembering how green and lush the trees were the last time I was here—thick emerald branches hanging low and bushes bursting with life as the sun cast warm, golden rays.

Today, my heart pounds, drowning out the lone squawk of a hardy crow circling overhead, scanning for crumbs on the barren ground.

The cobblestones curve under the rusted green bridge, and I nearly stop when I see the bench with its wooden slats. He waited for me at the bench, looking so sad but determined too.

Memories flood me like a dam breaking.

"Please, don't do this to me."

"It's the only way."

"No, we can try again. We can start over. I promise to be everything you want me to be."

"I have to go. Please, let me go."

But he didn't—he never really let me go—so I went from seventeen and carefree to completely fucked in the head. I realized I could break someone, and someone could break me. But then, I clawed my way out. I threw myself into my acting, letting go of myself and all the emotions that had crushed me.

All that is left are cruel memories. It's time to let them go so I can be free.

I start with this one note.

My fingers grip the paper so tightly I think I'll have to pry them off. But instead, I open my fist, one finger at a time, and it's as if a piece of me is moving on. Then, I stand in front of the garbage can and I tear up his words.

They flutter into the metal can, unreadable, unknowable.

I don't know what I have to do for you to love me again .
. .

I wipe my hand against my cheek and then inhale deeply. "I'm just getting started."

And I walk away.

14

DAVIS

One week.

Seven days.

One hundred sixty-eight hours.

That's how long my detox from Jill has lasted. No more stairwell encounters. No more meetings alone in my office. Nothing but the necessary interaction at rehearsals, and for the last week, the assistant director has been working with the chorus on some of their numbers, so I've rarely seen her.

Now, we're blocking one of the dance numbers with Patrick, Alexis, and some of the featured actors. I lean against the wall and watch the choreographer guide the actors through the bare-bones motions of what's shaping up to be a sensuous number as Paolo and Ava dance on stage.

Then Alexis stops in the middle of a step. She raises a hand and waggles her fingers at me. Damn, that woman can act. I almost believe she's not about to waste everybody's time.

"Excuse me, Davis? What if . . .?" She sashays over to stage right in her flouncy red dress, and I brace myself for another Alexis suggestion. "Wouldn't it be better if, say, we started this number right here"—she stops and gestures dramatically to the spot downstage right that she's claimed, then tips her forehead to the back of the room—"instead of back there?"

Right. Now she's the choreographer too.

"No. We'll start the number where we always start the number."

"Of course, Davis," she continues, still syrupy. "But have you considered it might be better if we started it here?"

"No. I haven't, nor do I plan to. Let's go through the song."

I walk to the back and take a seat as the actors resume the choreography. No more than a few steps in, a phone rings, loudly beating the overture from *Fate Can Wait*.

"Oops." Alexis clasps her hand over her mouth and bats her eyes. The chorus from that wretched show plays again. "My bad," is her offhand, non-apology. "I must have forgotten to turn off my cell."

She grabs her purse from the floor, roots around in it, and snags her phone. "Oh, dear." She taps a nail against the screen. "I should probably take this call. I may be a little while."

She scampers out of the rehearsal studio, letting the door fall hard behind her. The room is silent for an awkward moment, then I turn to Shannon, the stage manager.

"Can you get Jill, please?"

She leaves to find Jill in one of the other studios, and they return shortly. Her dance leggings hide none of her shape—the curves of her body, her tiny waist, the strong legs that I want to wrap around my hips as I pin her against the wall. "We're working on 'Paint It Red,'" I tell her. "Start with the lines leading up to the song."

At the chance to do the scene, even in rehearsal, her face lights with the same bright-eyed excitement that worked its way into my head from the day I met her. Within seconds, she's at the front of the room with Patrick, who flashes her a grin that instantly twists my stomach. It's a movie-star grin that makes friends and entices lovers. I look away briefly because I don't want to see Jill's reaction.

As they run through the scene, I knit my fingers tight and focus on the performance. Jill has the lines memorized, and she's hitting the right emotional notes too. She's so at home playing this character—I'm impressed, but not surprised. Patrick is a good match on stage, pulling off the nuance, the narcissism, but also that random bit of playfulness in Paolo. They segue into the song, one that calls for them to tango briefly before they begin crooning to each other, confessing their burgeoning feelings with music. As they link hands, the worm slithers around my heart and lungs, tightening, threatening to strangle me from the inside out.

I drop my head in my hands. I can't stand watching

her with him, and it's only one scene. One fucking, make-believe scene.

"All done!" Alexis calls out cheerfully, not caring that she's interrupting the work. But for one bizarre moment, I'm grateful for her center-of-the-universe ways. My internal organs thank her because envy starts to subside.

"Alexis, take it from here." I gesture carelessly toward the front of the room. "Jill, you can just watch the rest of the number."

Alexis resumes her place, and Jill surprises me by taking a seat next to me. She's been avoiding me as much as I've been avoiding her. But now she's inches away and lit up like a sparkler from that brief moment in front of a tiny audience. She glances my way as I'm studying her, and we lock eyes.

"Thank you," she says with the same bright happiness. It dawns on me that this is why she sat by me—to tell me that. "It was thrilling. I loved it, even if it was only for a few minutes."

I stay impassive. Every new thing I learn about her ensnares me tighter, especially this hopefulness, the sheer joy she has in her work. "Like I said before, you'll likely be needed for this show," I say.

"I saw the call sheet for the next few weeks. The stage manager has me scheduled with Braydon, the understudy for Patrick." When she breathes his name, she glances at the front of the studio where Patrick is running through the song with Alexis. No—not glances. Gazes. Jill all but inhales him with her eyes. And since he's on stage, she can watch his every movement without it being obvious. But her expressive face is never quite still—avid, wistful, and affectionate.

A hot streak of jealousy pierces my chest and nearly knocks the wind out of me. It hurts more than I imagined it could or would. I'd felt the angry ache of this all-too-familiar emotion, but there's a whole new level of envy rising up in me now.

He's the one she's in love with.

Patrick *fucking* Carlson.

My lead actor.

I get up and leave the studio without a word and head to the bathroom. I turn on the cold water and wash my face. I do it again and again and again, jealousy still burning through me. I grip the edge of the sink, wanting to rip it out from the wall with my hands.

What the fuck is wrong with me? I hardly know her, and I have no justification to feel this way. Less than none—I'd rejected her. Told her I wouldn't get involved with her. She's the sensible one.

I don't want to risk another relationship with an actress, but the prospect of her with another man feels far worse. It's unreasonable, but I don't want her to be with Patrick what-so-fucking-ever. Certainly not right under my nose. Even if she's on my banned list, I can't witness the woman I want so badly fall deeper in love on my stage, in my show, in front of my eyes.

I study my reflection in the mirror. The glass is smudged and there's a crack in the corner. These old rehearsal studios in New York show their age. But I still see who I am. A man who gets what he wants. A man who knows how to do one thing incredibly well, who devotes endless hours to work. One who can move actors around like chess pieces, bring out the best in them. One who's earned awards for exactly that.

For knowing exactly how to handle actors.

I let go of the sink, turn off the water, and dry my hands, each move a step in my new strategy. Because I'm not the director for nothing.

I make the fucking rules.

I can change the rules to work for me.

She's not mine, but she can't be his.

I return to the rehearsal room, sit down next to her, and take some small bit of victory when she looks away from him and at me.

"You're not going to rehearse with Braydon," I tell her.

She looks crestfallen. "Why? I don't understand."

"Because I'm going to rehearse you as Ava. You'll rehearse with me."

15

JILL

During a break in rehearsal the next day, Shelby pulls me into the group dressing room that all the chorus gals share.

"What is it?"

She pats the chair in front of the mirror. "Sit. Time for your hairstylist to work her magic."

"Braid me, baby," I say, following her over.

"No. I changed my mind. You need a French twist. Something ridiculously alluring."

"I didn't realize a French braid was so innocent."

"French braids are for the gym and the beach." She bumps me with her hip then pushes my shoulders so I'll sit. "Twists are for the sophisticated socialite and the sexy secretary." Running her fingers through my loose waves, she adds, "Plus, I'm in the mood to get my fingers into a twist."

I wave to give her carte blanche. "Do your thing then, Miss Broadway Stylist."

Grabbing a water bottle from the dressing room table, she sprays a bit to smooth out my hair, humming the number we worked on earlier today. I watch in the mirror as she deftly coils and twists, pins and smooths, then says, "Ta da!"

She hands me a mirror and swivels me around so I can check out the style from the back—a classy, sophisticated twist, worthy of a movie star on the red carpet. I hop off the chair, and kneel down in front of her, bowing. "I'm not worthy. I'm not worthy," I tease.

"Oh, shut up. It was fun. And besides, I got my styling fix for the day."

"You can use me anytime," I tell her. We return for another round of dancing and singing and working with the music director, while our director spends the afternoon with the stars.

Then, everyone leaves, and it's only Davis and me.

* * *

We are alone in the rehearsal studio.

"Your hair is up."

"Yeah."

"You didn't have it up earlier today." It's a matter-of-fact observation, like a costuming note. But it's not a costume, it's my hair, and I bring my hand to my neck, self-consciously brushing away a few loose tendrils. "I can take it down."

He shakes his head. "Leave it up. It works for Ava."

"For Ava?"

"Of course." His message is clear—this was all about Ava, the songs, and the show. Nothing outside those lines.

While I try to think of a clever way to say "fine by me," Davis sits at the piano, something I've never seen him do before. "You play?"

He nods. "I'm not a virtuoso. But I get by."

His fingers wander through a bit of *Für Elise*. Perfectly.

"*Get by*. Please." I scoff. I do far better with Davis when I tease him, keeping things light, like that first night at Sardi's. If we're going to get past our awkwardness, I'll need to treat him like a buddy, like Reeve. I have plenty of guy friends, and there's no reason he can't move into the friend zone. Because when he's all serious and intense, I feel as if I'm walking on unsteady ground. "I bet you speak French too. And you're probably a pilot as well."

He laughs once. "No. I don't speak French. I'm not a pilot, either. Nor, if you're wondering, am I a gourmet cook," he adds. "In fact, I can't cook at all. I prefer take-out. I also don't own a yacht, a polo pony, or any vintage cars."

He's playing me now. His midnight-blue eyes have a teasing glint. This is the way I'd rather work with him, so I return the conversational volley with an arch look. "But do you like opera?"

He shoots me the barest of grins, then coaxes out a quick few notes from the piano. I recognize the music. It's from *Carmen* by Bizet.

"*Habanera*. Love is a rebellious bird." I name the famous aria he's playing. "Though, I'm not an opera fan."

"I don't care for it, either. I like Carmen though, and the way she moves. I'd like this song better if it were played like this."

I lean on the piano and watch his hands move over the keys. He has a scar across his right hand, a long, jagged worm from the wrist all the way to his ring finger. I wonder if he ever tells anyone how it happened. If he'd tell me if I asked.

His fingers move quickly on the keys—he's turned Carmen's aria into a rock tune, changing the speed, mixing it up, so it has a low, sexy beat that sounds like the song he was playing in his office a month ago.

The song I told him I loved. The song he turned off. Now he's shifting from *Carmen* to Muse, and it's as if he's playing "Madness" just for me, telling me something, using music instead of words. His eyes stay on me the whole time, and my cheeks grow hot as he plays.

Music fills the room and spreads through my body, and I have the strangest sensation that I'm his instrument. That the keys beneath his fingers hammer strings inside me, sounding notes from within me. Neither of us speaks. There is only music between us, but I know the lyrics, and when he reaches *come on and rescue me*, it all becomes too much.

"You lied," I say, speaking to break the spell. "You said you didn't play well."

He shakes his head. "I said I'm not a virtuoso. But I don't want to talk about me anymore, Jill." His voice has changed to commanding. From playful to powerful. I straighten from leaning on the piano, standing taller. He's all business, so I need to resist my instinct to lighten the mood when it gets heavy.

"I want to talk about Ava," he says. "And I want to talk about you and how you become her. How to find the truth of her and hold on to it so tightly that no one watching doubts for even a second that you're her. You won't doubt it, I won't doubt it, and the audience won't doubt it. And so, I want you to think of Carmen and *Habanera* when you work on your part."

He's shifted, leaving Muse behind us. I follow his lead, shifting my tone too. "Tell me why."

"Ava is a rebellious bird. She resists Paolo. She resists his teaching, his way of making art. She resists his love too." His eyes never stray from mine, and his gaze is so intense it could burn. Then he lowers his voice, softens it to a lover's whisper. "But then she transforms. Love changes her. Love without bounds. Love without reason. She becomes his, and that changes her."

Those last few words make me feel light-headed and woozy. I reach for the edge of the piano, holding on.

She becomes his, and that changes her.

"I love that," I manage to say. My own breathy voice surprises me, and I quickly catalogue my reaction—goosebumps dot my arms, there's a tingling in my belly, and my lips are parted.

I know what's happening.

He's doing it again.

He's enticing me with his words, and I am turned on beyond belief.

My body responds faster than my brain can apply the brakes—heat flares inside and my skin is hot all over. I know this feeling—but only through the pages of a hot scene in a novel. This is real—in my body and not in my imagination. Not a book, but Davis. I'm weak from craving something I haven't let myself have in years.

Contact.

My vision blurs for a moment, and I clutch the side of the piano so I don't fall.

"Which sentiment, Jill?"

He says my name like it's dessert. Like it's something he wants to eat. It's a simple question, but I'm unhinged by the feeling that my body is responding to someone else's cues.

His cues.

There was no reason for my head to be so cloudy and my body so hazy, or for my pulse to race like a runaway train. It would be unbearably foolish to allow the line to blur between acting and feeling. He's good with words, he's good with people, he's good with ideas. He does what Paolo does—takes nascent, unformed clay and transforms it into something alive and wondrous. That's why there's an aching between my legs, why I'm vibrating like a tuning fork. It's because Davis is making me feel like Ava, and Ava is turned on by Paolo.

I finally answer his question. "All of them."

"All of them?" He raises an eyebrow.

"The one you just said, where she becomes his," I say quickly. My skin is feverish. The heat is cranked too high in this room. I look around. "Can we turn the heat down?"

He stands and goes to the thermostat, adjusts the lever, and turns back. On his return path, he passes so near to me that I sense him, mere inches from me. For a brief moment, I expect him to trail a hand across my lower back so that I shiver.

He sits again at the bench and plays the opening notes to Ava's signature song, "Show Me the Rebel." "Show me the rebellious bird in you, Jill."

"But . . ." Hesitation is so unlike me. I know the music. I know the song. I have never been afraid of performing. Something's different here. "It comes in the middle of the show. It's not her first song."

He says nothing, just plays the intro again.

"Can't we start with something else? I haven't practiced it before."

There's a hint of a smile on his lips. "That's why *I'm* rehearsing you," he says, and his voice is like whiskey and honey. Rough and smooth at the same time. "So you can practice. I want you to be able to blow the audience away. I want them to melt for you. I want them to fall for you. You can start by making me feel that way."

My legs are wobbly, and I don't know if it's because I'm rehearsing with an award-winning director in my first Broadway show, or if it's because his words are laced with subtext and innuendo. *You can start by making me feel that way.* But this off-kilter is how Ava feels when she begins this song. She doesn't know what to make of Paolo, and I don't know what to make of Davis.

I pick a point on the opposite wall, a random nick in the plaster, and I sing to it. I serenade the dent on the wall with a rote, emotionally flat melody. I make it through only six lines of the song when he stops his accompaniment.

I turn to him, waiting.

"Is there a reason why you're staring at a spot on the wall?"

"Um . . ." This is one of those questions without a correct answer.

"Is there?" he asks again.

I shake my head.

"Do you sing any song to a spot on the wall?"

"No." My face flames red.

"Do you sing it to the audience?"

"No."

"Do you sing it to the floor?"

"No."

"Do you sing it to a random, distant point in the balcony?"

"No," I say through gritted teeth, and now I want to smack him for the way he's making me feel stupid.

"Are you mad at me, now?" he asks in the exact same tone, a professor quizzing a student, dressing her down. He doesn't rage but simply peppers her with questions until she's thoroughly unnerved.

Screw being turned on. Now I'm pissed off.

And he asks if I'm mad at him?

"No," I lie, looking down.

He rises from the piano, stalks over to me, and stands mere inches away. He doesn't lift my chin or grip my shoulders. I still respond, raising my face to meet his eyes, because I can't not. His midnight blue eyes give away nothing now except power, confidence, and absolute control. There's an electrical current between us, and it's one that he alone controls.

I bite my lip briefly, and he makes an almost imperceptible sound that borders on a growl, then asks again. "Are you mad at me?"

"Are you asking me or are you asking Ava?"

He nods approvingly, as if he likes the question.

"Jill," he answers slowly, my name becomes sound in the charged air between us. "I'm asking you as Jill."

"I'm saying no, as Jill."

He shakes his head, not fooled. "Don't lie to me. There is no right or wrong answer. There is only the truth, and I want yours right now. Are you mad at me?"

I breathe out hard and admit it. "Yes."

"Good."

"Why is that good?"

"Use it. Use it for the song. Ava is headstrong. Ava is passionate. Paolo makes her crazy. He manipulates her. Or so she thinks." He balls his fingers as if he's grabbing something. "But he does it to reach deep down inside her. To help her find her true self, her true art, her true creativity. Everything he does, he does because he believes in her."

"But why? Why does he believe in her?"

"Because he knows in his heart"—he taps his chest —"in his head"—now his forehead—"and his gut." He hits his fist against his flat stomach. "He knows. Start from the beginning. Now, take your anger and use it. Sing it to Paolo. Look in his eyes. Let your anger carry the song. Let your frustration take you through. Then let go of it and let it fade away."

I nod. I don't think I can speak. I can only feel. The anger at Davis. The frustration with myself. Then what Ava feels—the spark of hope, the possibility of becoming the person, the artist, the woman he believes she can be. I take a deep, quiet breath, imagining all those feelings living inside of me.

He returns to the bench and resumes the music, the notes falling on me like rain. Then I'm Ava, and I turn and meet my director's gaze. Only he's not Davis anymore. He's Paolo. He's the man I'm mad at, and mad with, and mad about. I sing to him—not the wall, not the floor, not the audience. Just him, the man who drives me crazy with his perfectionism, with his inscrutable side. But I need him, not only to succeed as a painter, but to break free of all the loneliness I've felt my whole life as Ava. And I sing every word, every line, every note to him.

He watches me the entire time. Lets my words, my story, my tale become a part of him. He takes what I have to give. He absorbs all my music, all my passion, all my pain. He is the reason I'm singing, and I give it all to him because he knows what to do with all I have.

Because he accepts me for who I am, and because he makes me feel again.

And as I sing, something deep inside of me loosens. A brittle piece of the make-believe heart that I've been gripping so hard for so long rattles free and tumbles away. I let it go because I'm ready. I feel buoyant, unencumbered by my past, and it's an unfamiliar feeling, but such a welcome one. It's a reprieve, and my voice hitches, hitting a note all wrong and raw, but his eyes light up at that.

With the end of the song, I take one step closer to him. "I need you, Paolo," I say, shifting from sung words to the spoken ones in the script that cap off this song. Shifting, too, from calling him Professor to calling him by his name. "I need you to make me whole again."

"I will, Ava," he says in the softest whisper, but one that carries through the whole rehearsal studio as he delivers lines that start to bring this hard-edged, mercurial man closer to falling for this woman. "I promise."

* * *

After several more rounds, I'm sweating. I've shed my sweater, and I'm wearing only a tank top with my jeans. It's a workout singing for Davis, and I'm not even dancing. I'm merely standing and singing. But the way he directs, demanding everything I have, feels like a workout. I pull at my tank so it doesn't stick to my chest.

"Ready to go again?" he asks.

"Any time you want."

He laughs once, shakes his head. "I was only teasing. I think we can call it a night."

"Oh, I can keep going," I say. "But if *you* need to stop . . ."

Davis rises from the piano, closes it, and grabs his jacket. "I don't really think there's any question about whether I can keep going. And I don't need to stop. Ever." Then his eyes rake over me, as if he's memorizing me for later. "I'm *choosing* to call it a night."

Now my chest is hot again, and I'm ready to take the sheet music and fan myself. How is it that half the things that come out of his mouth are double entendres? Is it on purpose? Sometimes, I think I have him figured out, but then he looks at me with those bedroom eyes, or he says something ridiculously sexy, and I'm reassembling puzzle pieces again.

I skirt the innuendo because I'm not quite sure what to do with it, especially when he made it clear I'm not his type. Instead, I point to his coat.

"So you do own a jacket."

"I'm not entirely impervious to the elements."

"Aha! He is human, after all." I feel a little giddy, maybe even punch drunk from singing my freaking heart out. I'm spent in the way that a good, hard run can wring you dry but leave you surging with adrenaline too.

"Don't tell anyone," he says. "I have a reputation as a badass to maintain."

He doesn't seem to mind at all that I've figured out he likes the image he's created for himself—take no prisoners, hard as hell, impossible to get to know. Sure, he is tough, but there's more to him, too, and I don't think he lets many people see his other sides. Maybe that's why he seems to enjoy it when I see through him. Maybe that's why he talks to me this way.

"Oh, you're still badass in my book," I say as I pull my sweater back on. For a moment, I wrestle with the neckline, so I can't see him as I'm stuck under my clothes.

When I emerge, he's stepped closer, all serious and smoldering again. I can't take my eyes off of him when he's like that. It scares me how my whole body feels like it's waking up when he looks at me.

"Am I? Badass in your book?" he asks in a voice that's low and smoky and makes me want to say *yes* to him over and over, to anything he'd ask.

That's why I can't answer his question. Because my body has instincts, but I'm still my mixed-up, messed-up self, and I have no idea what to do with these veiled questions that feel a lot like foreplay.

So, I dodge the heat again, take a steady breath, jam my arms into my jacket, then cinch it closed. I need to shift gears and focus only on my job. "So how did I do tonight?"

Davis seems to sense and respect the shift. "You were everything I wanted you to be," he says, returning to his crisp, professional voice. He stops to lock the door, then we head down the carpeted hallway to the elevator. Once inside, he pushes the button for the ground floor. I glance at his hand, noticing his scar again. I point to it, my finger mere inches from his hand, so close I could touch him, could trace the raised line on his skin. "How'd you get that scar?"

He doesn't answer right away, and I wonder if I've

crossed some line. I hold my breath, as I wait for either an answer or an admonishment. The gears whir as the car begins its descent. This might be the tiniest elevator ever made because I might crash into him if it stops suddenly. I imagine being jolted, being caught. His arms around me. Our bodies so close. That frozen moment when you're either colliding or you're not.

Maybe I do want more of his innuendo. Maybe I do want the elevator to topple me into him, so I can see where this goes.

But the ride is smooth, and we both stay in our places.

Then, he holds up his hand, regards it as if he hasn't seen it in ages. "This? Punched the glass window of my front door when I was seventeen."

"You did?"

"Couple of days after I found out my parents died."

He says it in the most offhand way, but my heart leaps to my throat and I want to comfort him. To wrap my arms around him, tell him how unfair it is when people you love die too soon. I lay a hand on his arm. His eyes jerk to mine, but then he quickly looks away, and I remove my hand. "I'm so sorry."

"Yeah, me too," he says in a low voice, sounding wounded. Letting down his guard.

I want to ask what happened to them, but that feels too personal, too much, too soon.

The car stops at the lobby, and the doors crank open. We step out into the cold, biting night, and the sounds of New York traffic. It's the familiar soundtrack to my days and nights in this city.

We walk down the steps to the sidewalk. A cold wind whooshes by, and I pull my jacket tighter. He moves closer, and for a second I think he may drape an arm over my shoulder, pull me near and keep me warm. But he doesn't. Instead, he points to a town car waiting at the curb.

"For you," he says.

"Me? You got me a car service?" I shouldn't be excited over a car, but I am. I've only acted in a few off-Broadway shows and a couple of commercials, and I didn't even rate a cab in my contracts for those. It was subway, all the way.

"If I'm making you work late, it's the least I can do," he says as he opens the door for me, and I slide inside.

He leans into the car, reaches for the seat belt, and pulls it across my chest, buckling me in. He's inches from me, and he smells cold like the night air. But he also smells the way a man should at the end of the day: a little bit of sweat, a lot of work, and all raw power. He brings one hand behind my head and unclips my hair, letting it fall over his fingers. I tremble from his touch as a shiver runs down my spine. "I like your hair up and I like your hair down," he whispers to me, breaking down all my resistance in an instant.

I can see this playing out if I do nothing—I'll spend the night rewinding this moment and rewatching it until dawn. But I don't want to go home with only a memory to feed my body, and I can't stand the thought of this night ending too soon.

There's only one choice. "Do you want to share?" I ask, praying he lives in the same direction.

"You're downtown, right?"

I nod.

"Me too."

Then he closes my door, and I swivel around, watching through the tinted window as he circles to the other side quickly and opens the door. His dark eyes pin me and send a rush of heat down my chest and straight to my very core. He never takes his eyes from me as he closes the door and hits a button on the console that raises the tinted privacy partition, telling the driver "Just drive."

Like it's a command.

For a long beat we are still, the air crackling in anticipation of what's next. Unquestionably next. I'm done holding back, and so is he. As the engine starts, I unbuckle myself as his hands frame my face. He sucks in a breath at the first touch, then a low growl escapes his throat as his lips find mine with a hungry kiss that ignites me.

I grab his shirt, loving the feel of his strong, firm chest. My fingers fist the fabric as I pull him closer, but he doesn't need any direction from me. His hands are in my hair, and his lips are consuming me, his tongue tangling with mine. I'm about to burst from all this sensation—from the masculine way he smells, to the delicious scratch of his stubble, to the fingers that tug on my hair.

He tastes so good that I don't want to stop. I want to be devoured by him. I want him—no, I *need* him, desperately need him—to do something about this onslaught of desire that's become a delicious ache between my legs.

"I want to be under you," I say, not sure how I formed a coherent thought. All I know is what my body demands. I need the weight of him on me. I need to feel him pressed hard against me. I take off my jacket quickly, tossing it to the floor of the car, and he does the same. Then I slide down on the leather so I'm lying flat, and he moves with me, hovering over me, braced on his strong arms.

"Who needs jackets anyway?" he asks with a wry smile, then returns his lips to my neck, trailing kisses across my skin that make me hot and wet and hungry. "Jill," he says, and he's no longer playful. He's intense and demanding, as he puts a hand on my chin and makes me look at him. "Tell me you think about me."

I don't answer. I just breathe out hard.

"Tell me I get you off when you're all alone."

I bite my lip, and my nipples harden at the way he's speaking to me. I want his hands all over me. I want his hands between my legs. I wriggle under him, arching my hips against him. He moves away, so I can't feel his erection against me, even though I'm dying to.

"Tell me you picture me doing all sorts of things to you." His hands roam down my chest, and he cups my breasts through my sweater. I nearly cry out, it feels so good, sparks of sheer pleasure rippling through my entire being. "You do, don't you?"

"Why are you asking me?" I ask in a tortured voice, because he's tormenting me with his fantastic hands, pinching my nipple between his thumb and index finger, and it's rough, but it makes me feel alive. It makes this moment feel real. I want to feel every single thing right now. Every real feeling.

"Because I don't want you thinking of someone else when I make you come tonight."

"Oh God," I gasp, and with a quickness that surprises him, I grab his ass and pull him down to me so I can feel what I've done to him, so I know I'm not tumbling toward the edge alone.

He gives me a daring look, as if he's impressed that I snagged the upper hand. But I don't care about this battle of wills because he's so hard and it's all because of me, and I can't get enough of the friction. I tug him closer, so I can feel the steel length of him against my thigh.

Before I know it, his hands are up my shirt, and he's unhooking my bra. He squeezes my breasts, and I swear it's like wildfire racing through me, and I buck my hips against him. "Please," I say.

"Please what?"

"Do something," I beg.

"Tell me I'm the only one you're going to think of when you come undone in a few minutes," he says, his voice rough against my ear.

"Isn't it obvious?" I ask through gritted teeth. My frustration provokes the most wicked grin from Davis. I have no idea what he's going to do to me, but I don't care. I can't stand how long it's been since someone's hands have been on me. I want to be touched so badly I can feel it deep in my bones, this need.

I need him.

"Say it."

"I think of you. I think of you making me come. There. Are you happy?"

"Yes. As happy as I plan to make you before I'm done."

16

DAVIS

I tug off her sweater as she shrugs out of her tank and bra, then I stop for one brief moment to savor the view. She's topless, her arms over her head, all beautiful curves and gorgeous flesh, and I want to spend hours on her body, touching and tasting her neck, and her breasts, and her absolutely enticing belly. But she's already panting, and I can feel the heat between her legs through the denim of her jeans.

I press hard against her with my hand, and she draws in a breath.

"Oh God," she says, and her voice is rising. She pushes against me, rubbing against my hand in a desperate frenzy. It strikes me that she's already close. That I could slide my hand inside her jeans, feel her wetness, and bring her to release within a few seconds.

Her face is strained, and her skin is fevered, but her eyes are closed. "Please. Please make me come. Please," she says and that last word borders on a cry. She's arching her hips, and she's fumbling at the button of her jeans. But I need to know she's with me before I go further. I press both my hands gently, but firmly, on top of hers, quieting her moves.

"Jill. Look at me."

She opens her eyes. They are wild with desire.

"I've got this. I'll get you there."

She nods and drops her hands to the leather, letting me take care of her. Her breath is coming fast, but she stays still. I unbutton her jeans, unzip them, and slide my hand between her legs. There is nothing that feels better than this, than *her* being so ready for me, so turned on that her underwear is damp with her heat. My cock strains against the fly in my jeans, and I want so badly to be inside her, but this isn't about me right now, or even about me tonight. This is about whatever desperate need is winding up her body.

"You are so wet and hot. This is all for me, isn't it?"

She gasps as I play with the waistband on her underwear. She starts to thrust her hips up, and I shake my head. "No. I told you. I'll take care of this."

My fingers inch their way between her legs, and I slide them once across her.

"Fuck, Jill," I hiss out. Then I bring my fingers to my lips and lick off her taste.

"Please," she says, wracked with the need to come right now, and there's nothing I'd rather do than be the one to satisfy her. She kicks off her boots as I pull her jeans down past her hips then tug them off. My hand is back in the promised land, and she's deliriously wet. She's the hottest woman I've ever touched and the neediest, and that's fine with me because this is what I want. Her. This woman. Screw the past. Screw my rules. I don't care about anything but making her come. I want to send her into never-ending bliss, so I slide two fingers across her, and she moans greedily, as if this is the thing she craves most in the entire world.

"God, it feels so good," she says in a ragged whisper.

I've barely given her anything, but she's already near the edge. I rub the pad of my thumb where she wants me most, and soon she's thrusting her hips, and she's no longer whispering, she's screaming out, "Oh, God, oh God, oh God."

That's it. That's all it takes. She comes, her entire body rocking against my hand, hips bucking hard and wild. She grabs at me, pulling me to her and kissing me, but she's so far gone from the orgasm that it's a supremely sloppy, intensely sexy kiss—because I made her come in seconds flat, and she's still crying out.

Her voice can really carry, and the sound of her coming echoes around the car, but the driver doesn't care. Her whole body is trembling as she starts to float down, and soon she opens her eyes and looks at me. Her eyes are dreamy now, and she has a glow that makes her even more beautiful. I want to see that look again and again. I want to be the only one who makes her feel this way.

"That was . . ." she trails off.

"That was what?" I'm pretty certain she enjoyed herself immensely, but I still like hearing it from the source.

"That was the fir—" Then she stops. "That was amazing." And she pulls me in for another kiss that makes my brain go fuzzy from the heady taste of her lips, and the way she smells even sexier after she's just come. I can barely process what she was going to say, and I'm not sure it matters right now. I nip at her bottom lip, and then break the kiss.

She reaches for me, trying to touch my cock. But I stop her hand.

"What? Why can't I touch you?"

"Because this was about you."

"But I want to."

"Trust me, there's nothing I want more than for you to feel what you do to me. But I already know you're the only one I'm thinking of. And I'm not going to let you touch me until I'm certain I'm the only one you want to be touching."

She gives me a questioning look, but there's no bending here. I've already chucked my one hard-and-fast rule, and now I'm not only caught up with an actress, I'm caught up with an actress who's told me she's in love with someone else. Double the obstacles. So I answer her by pulling her close and kissing her forehead softly. "You know it's true. But you also know that he's not the one who made you come tonight. I am. So the next time you're alone, I want you to picture what I did to you. And then I want you to imagine all the things I'm going to do with my tongue when I taste you for the first time. And then you're going to tell me if it's as good as you imagined when I go down on you sometime soon. Sometime very, very soon. Because you taste fantastic."

She shudders, bites her lip once then breathes out, hard. "Yes."

Then I push her hair away from her ear. "Do you want to come again now?"

She nods against my chest, then whispers, "I don't know if I can though."

"You can," I tell her, and this time I pull off her underwear and she's completely naked and beautiful as I slide two fingers inside her and she rocks against me, coming apart once more.

17

DAVIS

Clay holds the punching bag, and I slam a cross into it. Then I administer my best hook. Jab, cross, hook—I repeat this combination, grunting hard, putting everything I have into each punch. I feel the exertion in my stomach and shoulders. I end with a final flurry of hits and cap it off with a punishing uppercut, feeling simultaneously sated and charged.

I finish, and Clay pats the bag once then claps me on the back. I breathe out hard, panting.

"Nice," he says. "Picture anyone in particular this time?"

"Me? No. Never."

I don't think of anyone when I hit. I don't need to. There's a store of coiled-up tension already inside me from working so much, so hard, so long. This is simply the release.

"C'mon. Not your least favorite executive producer in the world? Don was a prick to deal with. Tried to pull all sorts of shit with your contract."

"I know. He's still a fucking prick. Showed up the other day at rehearsals and told me to go easy on Alexis."

"I bet you wanted to hit him then," Clay says, half joking, half knowing me.

I pretend to consider that, as I unwrap my hands. "Hmm. You know, maybe I did. You got me there, Clay."

We walk over to the water fountain at the boxing gym where we work out. It's a Tribeca gym, so it's full of men like us: guys who spend their days working in the shade, who wear white collars and ties, who make deals for a living. But still, it's more my speed than one of those 24-hour gyms with the cardio machines. I'd rather lift weights and punch the life out of a bag to burn off the day. It's a habit I picked up when I was younger, and one that helped me deal after I lost my parents.

Everyone grieves differently. My way through the pain was to punch it out. It worked, kept me sane through caring for my sister and sending her off to college. There wasn't anyone else to look after us —just me.

I take a long cold, swallow of water then grab my gym bag and pull on a sweatshirt as Clay grabs his bag from the other corner. Ryder's here, crossing the floor to one of the weight benches.

"Any more stairwell encounters?" he asks with a smirk.

"Fuck off."

He pretends to be mortified. "*Behave*. Or I'll call you out on my radio show."

"I'll consider myself duly warned."

He settles in on his bench, and I head out with Clay, the cold January air the perfect end to a workout.

"So is *Crash the Moon* coming together?"

Clay isn't just my closest friend from college. He's my lawyer now too, the best damn entertainment lawyer in the business. He handled all the negotiations with Don Kraftig, once Stillman chose him to produce.

"Going to be the best production to hit New York in years."

"That's what I love most about you. Your humble nature."

"Damn straight. And you?"

"Squeezing money out of all sorts of producers for all sorts of clients like there's no tomorrow. I'm wrapping up a deal for one of my showrunners for a new network sitcom this week. His fucking agent was a loser. He had to can the agent, so I did it all."

"Yeah. You're a modest one too. I'm sure you're hating doing all that work when you see your hours add up."

"One of the producers even sent me extra tickets to the Broadway Cares auction in a few weeks because he was so damn happy the contract was finally done. They want you to say a few words about the fundraising efforts *Crash the Moon* will be doing. You want some extra tickets too? To take Michelle?"

"Sure. She loves going to all those galas."

"Listen," he begins, drawing in a breath. "I heard from Madeline's agent."

My shoulders tense, habit when her name comes up. "Yeah?"

"Sounds like she's coming to New York soon," he says as a cab squeals to a stop at a nearby light.

"That so?" I ask. I think I know what this is about, after Michelle spilled the beans the other night.

"Hasn't been announced, but her agent just signed her for the lead in the new Steve Martin play that starts rehearsals in a few weeks," he continues as we walk past early morning runners, focused looks on their faces. "Anyway, I thought you might want to know since the play will be at the Belasco."

The Belasco Theater. One block away. Michelle hadn't mentioned that. I am more annoyed than upset. Madeline is the past. I won't go there again. "I'm a big boy. I can handle it."

"Hey, Davis? Have you met my friend Davis? He was the guy who was wrecked by this gal in San Diego three years ago."

But I'm not wrecked anymore. Not by her, at least. She's in the rearview mirror, and maybe that's why I've been loosening my rules.

"Would it make you feel better if you got her rehearsal schedule so I could plan my day around it?" I joke. "I'm sure you could even get my sister involved, and the two of you can devise new routes to work for me."

"Just looking out for you, man. Someone has to."

"I'll catch you later," I say, as we reach my loft.

* * *

Ava chases Paolo and grabs him before he leaves the classroom.

"I see you've changed your mind," Paolo says with a daring look in his eye, challenging Ava to make the next move.

"I need you, Professor Paolo."

"Don't call me professor."

"What should I call you?"

"Don't call me. Kiss me."

Then she cups his cheeks in her hands and kisses him, a long, slow, wet kiss.

It's a fantastic kiss, full of believable smolder and so much longing. But something's missing.

Alexis and Patrick pull apart, break character, and look at me expectantly, awaiting notes. This is the tenth time they've worked on this scene today.

"It's still not coming together," I say.

Alexis sighs audibly. "Well, I flossed and brushed beforehand, so it can't possibly be my fault."

"I would never think it your fault that a kiss isn't working," I say, to placate her.

"So what's the problem, then?"

"I'm trying to figure it out."

"I've never had to work this hard on a kissing scene. The audiences all love my kissing scenes," she continues in a haughty voice.

"Of course they do." I hate that she's right, but she's beloved by the fans. They have no clue what she's like to work with. All they know is she's a force of nature on stage and she possesses far too much of that most precious resource—charisma.

"Are we supposed to kiss all day?"

"Alexis, you make that sound like such a chore," Patrick huffs. He rarely has a sharp word for anyone, but I'm glad he's rising to the occasion here.

I wave them off. "It's not the two of you," I say as I pace around the studio, trying to work out what's missing. I rewind briefly to Jill's audition when she performed this scene perfectly. What was so different about it? I let myself picture her grabbing Patrick, kissing him like her life depended on it—even though the memory is even more grating now that I know she's in love with him. But the kiss isn't the problem.

Alexis and Patrick kiss like lovers who've been burning for each other.

Jill and Patrick did as well.

So why doesn't the kiss feel as authentic as it should?

With a flash of insight, I realize the problem doesn't lie in this scene. The trouble is what precedes it, the moment before she sings "Changed Your Mind."

"Here's the issue. There's no transition. I don't believe for a second they'd go from all cooped-up anger about her painting style and his teaching, and then go to a kiss. There needs to be a transition. A moment of intimacy, touching but not quite touching before they finally kiss." I stop pacing. "Thirty-minute break. I need to get out of here."

I leave the studio, take the elevator downstairs and head outside. I need fresh air. I need to think. I need to find what's missing. I push a hand roughly through my hair and lose myself in the midday crowds of tourists and locals thronging down Broadway, some in brand new *I Love New York* jackets as they snap photos, some suited up and racing to make their Midtown meetings.

I turn the corner and head toward the St. James. We're finishing with the rehearsal studio stretch and moving into the theater itself for the next several weeks. It's rare to have access to the actual stage itself at this point, but since the St. James is empty, Clay worked it into my contract for us to rehearse sooner on the stage itself.

I head toward the alley that leads to the stage door, figuring some time in the theater itself will be the inspiration I need. Then I hear a familiar laugh.

There she is, and it slays me every time I see her—how fucking beautiful she is. How effortless. How much I want her again. I see her and I want her. I talk to her and I want her. I spend time in the same five-foot radius, and I want her.

I watch her as she walks toward me with Shelby. They don't see me yet. They're chatting with each other, laughing as if they have some insider secret. A grin tugs at my lips because her smile is so radiant, so pure. Some days she seems like the most easygoing person in the world. Other times, she seems like she's hiding something. The mixture is intoxicating, and I want to be the one who unlocks her mysteries.

They near me, and Shelby sees me first. She waves. "Hello, Mr. Milo. You checking out our new rehearsal digs?"

"Of course. Can't get enough of the St. James. About to take a quick walk-through."

"Hi," Jill says, and though she's cool and casual, the slightest blush spreads across her cheeks and I know she's remembering the other night in the car.

I want to whisper "hi" back, just to her, then kiss her right below her ear in the way that drives her crazy. But I behave. The three of us stop in front of one of the glass cases on the stone and stucco wall that will soon hold a poster enticing pedestrians to come check out *Crash the Moon*.

"We were on our way to the rehearsal studio for our afternoon call," Jill says. "But does this mean we're working here today?"

She turns to point to the theater, and I notice her hair. She's wearing it in a braid today. She's only worn it up once before—the other night at our private rehearsal. Her neck is so inviting, beckoning me to touch her, to run a finger across the exposed skin. I stuff my hands in my pockets, but my prized self-control doesn't stop me from saying, before I can stop myself, "Your hair is up again."

Then Shelby pipes in. "That's my handiwork! And let me tell you, it's the best French braid the world has ever seen." She grabs Jill by the shoulders and spins her around, so I'm looking at the back of her head. "Have you ever seen a better braid?"

But I'm no longer seeing a braid. I'm seeing the answer. I'm seeing what I went looking for. Now I know exactly what the scene needs before that kiss.

I say goodbye to Jill and Shelby, duck into the St. James, and call Stillman, telling him my idea. He says yes.

18

JILL

"And now for the pièce de résistance."

Kat shows me one of her newest prototype necklaces, with a miniature padlock modeled after the ones hung on the Lover's Bridge in Paris. "A spin-off from the holiday line," she adds, referring to the Paris-themed necklaces that were sold in tandem with cufflinks made from the old locks from the bridge. Her fiancé's company made the cufflinks and then manufactured the necklaces she designed. They were a massive hit at stores, and now she's doing the *hers* version of the padlocks as a necklace.

I turn around and sweep up my hair with one hand. She loops the jewelry around my neck, letting the charm fall against my skin, then spins me around so I can face the mirror behind her door. "See? You look mah-velous, dahling! Simply mah-velous."

She's so genuinely happy, in general, but also for me, because I'm going *out* this afternoon. On a *date*.

Six years ago, I never could have imagined even a coffee date would be so far down the list of things on my mind.

At the top is the pit in my stomach—not a hollow pit—it's filled with all my guilt over what I did with my director the other night. I let him touch me. I *begged* him to touch me. I practically threw myself at him in the car, grabbing his shirt, and then pleaded with him to make me come.

I was a different person, a woman crazed with need. I wanted Davis unconditionally—no hearts, no flowers, not even dinner first. Because that would be a date.

I honestly don't know if I would feel this out of sorts if there was some kind of relationship building. One where two people get to know each other with their clothes on before—or maybe concurrently with—getting to know each other naked. Was that naïve?

Then, ironically, I have a date—a coffee date—with the man of those exact youthful fantasies, and I'm not sure I'll even be able to enjoy it.

I turn back to the mirror, eyeing my jeans, red cowboy boots and a scoop neck top. My hair is down because it doesn't remind me of Davis. Of how he can't keep his hands out of my hair. How he likes my hair up, how he likes my hair down, how he can't stop touching me. Here with my hair tucked primly behind my ears, I feel less like my own emotions and desires are going to ambush me.

"Um, no. What are you? A schoolgirl? Let it free!" Kat threads her fingers in my hair and makes it wild again. "Never tuck your hair behind your ears on a date."

"It's not a date. It's a meet up of two friends," I say, as if that makes what I'm doing okay.

She rolls her eyes. "Yeah. Go have fun with your *friend*. I'm going to go call my *friend* Bryan," she says, sketching air quotes, "to see if he wants to come over and be friends."

"I mean it, Kat. It's Sunday afternoon. It's *coffee*. It's not that way with Patrick."

She fixes me a serious look. "Make it that way then, Jill. Or if not him, then someone you want *that way*. Now's your time."

I grab my coat, my purse, and my phone and catch the subway, those last few words still echoing. *Now's my time.* Because I've done my time, right? I've beaten myself up over Aaron. I've read his letters thousands of times. They're branded on my brain. They're tattooed on my heart.

I close my eyes as the train rattles under the city, and Aaron's written words ring in his voice in my ears.

I fucking love you so much.

Do you have any idea what it feels like to love a person this much?

It's killing me to be without you.

I press my fingers against my temple, as if I can squeeze out the reminders of him. I still don't understand it. He was so good to me the whole time we were together. Captain of the swim team, president of student council, the model, upstanding guy. He was unimpeachable, and he was crazy about me. If I'd loved him as much as he loved me, would things have been different? Would I be different? But it's so hard to know anymore. All I know is that love should be free from the kind of weight that trapped me and finally crushed Aaron.

* * *

Patrick and I drink lattes and chat for an hour about our favorite shows, movies, songs . . . Standard getting-to-know-you stuff. It's fun. Really, it's fun.

It's still early as we leave the cafe, so we head to the indie bookstore on Seventy-Third. Inside, he stops at the first table and taps a celebrity tell-all tale from the reality star du jour. "God, I love these books." He opens one to a random page and speaks for the starlet subject in a high, breathy voice. *"But spending the summers in Lake Como with my movie star boyfriend isn't as glamorous as everyone thinks it would be. My iPhone has spotty reception there, so it's hard for me to keep up with Twitter."*

He chuckles deeply. "I have to get this. They're my secret addiction." He looks around like he's checking for eavesdroppers. "Junk reading, but I don't care. They make me happy."

I bring a finger to my lips. "Lips sealed."

"What do you like to read?"

Do I tell him that I read red-hot racy romance novels? That I love stories with sexy alpha males who border on bossy?

Yeah, maybe not.

"Oh, you know, this and that," I say evasively.

"C'mon, now." He cajoles me and nudges me with an elbow. "You can tell me."

I don't know how it would feel to speak the truth. To let the person I am now speak up, even about a little thing like what I read. But it's actually a big thing. I read these books because it's all I've allowed myself. Because I'm terrified of getting close to another person again. Because I'm petrified of what happens when love gets twisted into a weapon.

I pick something—my brother's favorite author.

"Elmore Leonard. *Get Shorty* is not only a terrific movie, but a fantastic book too." I'm even quoting what Chris told me about the book, and I hate that I'm lying to someone about something so minor. I shift gears and try to tell the truth, but out comes another lie. "And Carl Hiaasen too. He tells the craziest stories and they suck me into his world."

More lines from Chris. More lies to Patrick.

"Do you have his newest?"

I shake my head.

"Let me get it for you then. As a gift."

"Oh . . . thanks," I say in a strangled voice.

I hope Chris enjoys the book he'll be getting for his birthday.

* * *

My heart pounds and my legs burn, and my breath is visible in the frozen morning air. It's Monday, still early in the dawn, and the sun is barely peeking over the wintry New York horizon.

I turn around and run backward. "Almost there!" I call out to my crew of mommy warriors as we run behind the Metropolitan Museum of Art. They are a resilient group, decked out in nylon running pants and fleece jackets. This group is my most advanced set, training for the upcoming 10K to raise money for breast cancer research. It's their third year, and if they improve their times, they'll land more matching money from corporate sponsors. "Keep up your pace. Keep your elbows at your side, and don't forget to breathe."

I flash them a smile and turn back around as we run toward the reservoir in Central Park. The women are quiet in the home stretch, and so am I as I let the running do what it does: wash away yesterday's regrets. I run them off and leave it all behind me.

When we reach the end of the reservoir, I raise a fist, encouraging all of my ladies as they slow down and finish a hard morning run.

"You're amazing. You're going to do great on Saturday."

I hug them all, and soon we go our separate ways. As I walk across Eighty-Sixth Street toward the subway, I fast forward to tonight, and the next private rehearsal. Should I wear my hair up or down? Should I wear that black V-neck sweater that hugs my breasts just so? Or maybe the navy blue one since it matches my eyes?

Wait. I know what to wear.

My red sweater with the little buttons up the front.

I bet money Davis likes red.

Then I realize I'm about to walk into traffic because I've been daydreaming about a guy with a list of reasons I shouldn't be daydreaming about him. I stop at the curb, and press the crosswalk button, and tell myself to stop thinking about a man who seems to like me a lot in private, but not enough to date.

19

DAVIS

I unlock the stage door to let myself in. I'm the first to arrive, and I'll be the last to leave.

I use these moments before the stage manager, choreographer, music director, and cast arrive to walk through the theater. The St. James is a more intimate setting than many others on Broadway—not as small as some playhouses, but not a cold, heartless theater like some of the newer ones. It's the perfect size for a show like this, since *Crash the Moon* isn't about extravaganza and spectacle. It's about the relationships between the characters, about lives changing, hearts breaking, and most of all, passion. This theater is the *only* one that can handle the intensity and the sexuality of this production.

I head down the center aisle, trailing my hand over the creaky upholstered chairs that theatergoers will pay top dollar to park themselves in soon. Tickets went on sale last week, and Don emailed to tell me the show is already sold out for the first two weeks and counting.

That's 1,600 seats filled every night with people expecting to be blown away by this show. I tap the stage for good luck then turn to the empty house, picturing it full of faces, chatting, eager for the show, brushing up on actors' credits in the Playbill then tucking away phones, closing purses, and focusing as the overture to the newest Frederick Stillman show begins.

Just a handful of weeks to get it ready.

My thoughts are interrupted when Shannon marches across the floorboards, clipboard in hand. "Alexis called. She has a cold and can't make it in today."

"Color me surprised," I say dryly.

My stage manager rolls her eyes. "Shocking. I know."

"Does that make it two missed rehearsals already, Shannon?" I ask, though I already know the answer.

"Indeed it does."

"Remind me not to tell Don that I told him so when this keeps up during the show."

She laughs once. "Of course. Should I let Ms. McCormick know she'll be playing Ava today?"

"Yes. You can give her the new pages when she arrives. Same for Patrick. Give them an hour to read them over first, and we'll have them on at ten."

She nods. "Absolutely."

Minutes later, the actors trickle in, and I work on a scene with two of the supporting cast members first. Then the stage manager calls Patrick and Jill to the stage.

I'm instantly aroused when I see what she's wearing. Tight jeans and a red sweater. She looks edible in red. Then I notice it has tiny little pearl-shaped buttons on it. I can hear the sound they'd make, clattering across the floor, if I were to rip it off her.

It's going to be a long fucking day, watching her rehearse this scene with Patrick.

* * *

Shannon has one hand pressed against the stage door later that evening. "Alexis called. She'll be back tomorrow. She said she—her words—*simply cannot wait* to rehearse the new scene."

"I'm so glad she'll grace us with her presence."

"If we're lucky, she might even try to reconfigure the blocking," Shannon says in a deadpan voice as she zips up her coat. The weather forecast earlier today called for snow after midnight. Shannon taps the doorframe, as if an idea just took shape. "Maybe you could nail down some of the blocking tonight when you work with Jill. So there's no wiggle room."

I tamp down the mischievous grin that's forming. I'd certainly thought of that myself, but hearing the suggestion from my stage manager makes my task tonight feel more necessary than self-indulgent.

"Good idea, Shan. Now go get home so you can curl up by the fire and watch the snow fall."

She raises an eyebrow. "Maybe we'll even have a snow day tomorrow," she muses. "Oh wait. Davis Milo never allows snow days." She swats me playfully on the arm.

"You don't allow them, either."

"You got me there. But I learned my merciless ways from you." She tosses her scarf around her neck with a final flourish. "I'm off into the tundra."

She opens the door, letting in a cold blast of air. I'm about to close it, when a voice I long to hear calls out, "Hold the door! My hands are full."

I push back on the door and see Jill practically sprinting down the alley, holding a cup of coffee in each hand. She says a quick hello and goodbye to Shannon as she passes her.

"Good luck with the hair scene, Jill," Shannon says. "Make sure you guys finalize the blocking."

"Hair scene. I'm on it," she answers like a good soldier.

Jill reaches the door and holds up the blue paper cups. "Coffee."

"I can see that."

"I got you one," she says, and there's the slightest flutter to her voice, as if she's nervous.

She thrusts a cup at me, and I take it. I'm dying to break into a grin because it's not just coffee—it's coffee from her. It's coffee for us. It's a little something she did for our private rehearsal.

"I'm impressed you can run and not spill the coffee."

"It's all part of my marathon training. In fact, I teach that skill to the more advanced runners in my coaching group."

"But of course. Some of them probably even want to

learn how not to spill a latte, or perhaps an espresso," I say with a smirk.

"We're actually well past the how-not-to-spill espresso training. By the way, do you think you can let me in now?"

I laugh, realizing I'm standing in the doorway and she's outside, shivering, even with her coat on. I open the door wider, letting her in. I look briefly at the dark sky, brighter than usual, a sure sign the clouds are swelling with snow.

"Looks like snow." I let the door close behind us.

"You better watch out, then. I toss a mean snowball. My brothers taught me how to throw."

"I'll consider myself duly warned for a vicious snow-ball attack." We head down the backstage hallway toward the wings of the stage. As I watch her walk, her coat hitting just below her waist, I imagine her naked again. I love that I know what she looks like without anything on.

I take a drink. The coffee is perfect. Just black. Nothing added to it. Exactly how I like it.

"How did you know?"

"How did I know what?"

"How I take my coffee."

"I took a wild guess. My roommate has this theory about guys and their coffee drinks," she says as we reach the stage. She stops at the edge of the curtains.

"A theory about men and coffee?" I raise an eyebrow. "Enlighten me."

She briefly looks at her shoes, then back at me. "Well, it's just, she has this theory that the man who orders just coffee is, you know . . ." Her voice trails off, and crimson starts to flood her cheeks.

"Is just what?"

"Just . . ." She can't seem to finish the thought.

"You want me to guess?"

She shakes her head, her hair falling in a curtain around her face in the most distracting way. But she seems embarrassed, and the last thing I want to do is push her past her point of comfort.

"Well, whatever the theory is, I will choose to take it as a compliment."

She raises her face and meets my eyes. "Thank you."

"Do you want a tour of all the secret doors and backstage passages before we start? Or did you check everything out already?" I hope she'll say yes. I want to be able to do something for her that no one else can do. To show her more of the things she loves—like theater.

Her eyes sparkle. "Secret backstage stuff? Like ghosts?"

"This theater has many, many ghosts. They say the ghost of Hammerstein sometimes watches from over there."

I point past the stage to the balcony on the right-hand side.

"Do you think he's there right now?" she whispers.

"Oh no. He's far too busy. He only shows up on opening night."

She laughs and places her coffee on the floor and unbuttons her coat. She walks to the edge of the stage, leans slightly, then tosses the coat perfectly so it lands on a chair in the second row—right next to my coat. Then she retrieves her cup.

I tip my head toward the wings and crook my finger for her to follow me. I take another sip of the coffee then show her the trapdoor in the stage, the steps down to the orchestra pit that also do double duty for quick costume changes in some shows, and the catwalk above with the spotlights.

"But here's the best part. Did you know there's a dressing room above the stage?"

She grins widely, as if I've just revealed the location to buried treasure. "How did I not notice it today?"

"It's kind of hidden behind some of the crates with the set pieces we haven't unpacked yet. The star usually claims it; it's actually in Alexis's contract. But it's still worth a look." I show her back to the wings and open a black door that's painted to match the walls. "Right there. Stairs lead up to it. Like a fire escape."

"Can we go up?"

"We can't go inside. But you can go up."

She walks up the steps to the top where a small metal balcony looks out over the quiet stage, with the door to the dressing room behind.

"It's quite a view," she says drinking in the majesty of the St. James from this hideout spot that few people ever see. I love watching her reaction because I feel the same. She turns to me, and we're so close in this tiniest of balconies that I could easily grab her and kiss her and do so many other things to her, with her, for her up above the floorboards, with only the stage below to know our secrets. "Davis," she says in a low and sexy voice that nearly obliterates my self-control. "Would you go down to the stage? I want to see what it looks like from up here with a person on the stage."

"Okay," I say warily. "But I'm not going to perform."

"I won't ask you to tap dance or twirl in circles."

"Good." I oblige by heading down the metal stairs to the middle of the stage. I'm still holding my coffee, so I look up at her, and hell if she doesn't look like the most romantic woman ever written leaning on the railing in the balcony, her long hair framing her face and a wistful sigh fluttering from her lips.

It's a moment that shouldn't be ruined by words. Besides, she wanted to see how the stage looks, not how it sounds, so I say nothing. I take a drink of my coffee. I wait for her to go next.

Even from this distance, I can see her swallow and exhale as if she's about to say something that's hard for her. "Your coffee?"

"Yeah?"

"All the hot guys take their coffee black. So that's how I knew."

For the first time I can recall, I am speechless. I am reduced to nothing but this buzzing in my bones, as if every cell inside me has been dialed all the way up. My skin is hot all over, and I might be shaking as she turns down the stairs, crosses the stage, and stands in front of me.

I want to crush her against me. I want to smother her in kisses. I want to taste her, touch her, feel her.

Her lips are slightly parted, and if I stare at them any longer, I will be claiming her mouth with mine, pushing her up against a wall and owning her body. So I glance down, and that's a worse decision.

The red sweater taunts me. Those pearl buttons are beacons calling out to me, and my fingers twitch with the desire to twist one hard and let it rattle to the floor, then another, then another, exposing her breasts to me, so full and creamy.

I scrub a hand across my jaw, then find the will to turn away. If I start something now, we'll never rehearse. I force myself to focus on my job.

"We should probably get to work on that scene," I say hoarsely.

She raises an eyebrow. "The show must go on." She walks to stage left then tosses me a look over her shoulder. "As they say."

I love that she can shift back to playful so naturally, and it's one more thing that is going to ruin me.

* * *

There is only an easel on the stage. It's a temporary one, a fill-in prop from an art supply store. When the show begins, the real easel will be bigger, larger than life in many ways, befitting a Broadway show. But for now, this does the trick. It gives Ava a focal point for her work. She has been painting all day, working and reworking her newest piece under Paolo's direction. The young painter, barely into her twenties, and the world-renowned artist who's taken her under his iron-fisted wing at art school.

Paolo returns to the studio to check on her progress and finds her a painted mess.

I enter from stage left. Ava doesn't notice me at first; she's so engrossed in the work. I am quiet, walking on cat's feet to her side.

She startles. "Oh."

"You are . . ." I don't finish the sentence. Instead, I make a circular motion around her face.

"I'm what?"

"You're covered in paint."

She shrugs. "What else should I be covered in but paint?"

"Your hair is full of paint. It's getting in the way."

With one sweep of her hand, she brushes her hair off her face, leaving behind an imaginary streak from the paintbrush.

"Oops," I say, because Paolo feels playful right now.

"It's on my forehead now, right?"

I nod, then trace a quick line across her forehead. "A bright yellow streak. And your hair is the color of the sun too."

"I'm a mess," she says in a sweet, self-deprecating tone.

"Here." I hold out my hand. "Give me the brush."

She hands it to me, and I lay it on the easel. "Come with me."

She follows and we move to the middle of the stage. "Sit," I tell her.

She bites her lip then sits cross-legged. I kneel behind her, so the audience will be able to see both of us. "Let's get your hair out of the way."

"Okay," she says, in the softest, sweetest voice.

She leans her head back, closes her eyes, and lets me run my fingers through her hair. I gather it at the top of her head, the thick strands sliding across my palms like silk waterfalls. I weave one strand into another, then gather another layer, recreating the French braid I saw her wearing the other day. The one that made me think of a moment of intimacy, when Paolo and Ava come closer together through touch before they kiss in the next scene. A tender moment, where he wants to take care of her, get her painted hair out of her face.

I reach the point in the braid where I'm at her neck, and now I'm simply looping one strand over the other. There are no more lines in this scene until hers at the end, and as I finish, I stare at her neck, at the vein that seems to be beating harder, and then I listen, and her breaths sound like tiny little sighs.

I stop moving for a second, trying to collect myself. Fighting everything in me that's dying to touch her, I return to character, pulling a rubber band from my pocket and fastening her braid. She twists around and looks at me.

That's not in the blocking. That's not how she did it this afternoon with Patrick. She didn't look at him. She uttered the last lines while gazing out at the audience, her body language saying how she felt as she leaned into him, showing that she trusted him.

But now, she's leaning back against my chest, and turning to look up at me. A tiny whimper escapes her throat, before she says, "It feels so good."

I have no idea if she's acting. If she's Ava, or Jill, or both. If she's acting, she's so fucking convincing because her face says she's never been more aroused in her life.

My hands are still on her back, my thumbs tracing the tiny strands at the end of her braid. She doesn't break our gaze, nor do I. I don't know what's happening, but for the first time, I don't feel like I'm in control anymore.

She is.

I stay completely still.

She counters me by shifting closer. "What is happening here?" Her voice is unsteady as she says a line that's not in the script.

"You tell me," I say, and I'm not even sure where my own voice is coming from.

She turns around, uncrosses her legs, and mirrors me, kneeling. "You wrote that scene for me, didn't you?"

I nod. My throat is too dry to speak.

"That day you saw me with Shelby outside the theater, right?"

"Yes." I swallow. I'm an open book now.

"Did you write it because it makes the show better? Or did you write it for me?"

I close my eyes briefly. I've never had an actress question me like this. Then, I look at her. "I put the scene in the show because the show needed it," I answer with as much confidence as I can muster, grabbing the reins from her.

"But you're also kind of into my hair, aren't you?"

Now she's in control again looking at me with such

a challenging stare and so much want in her blue eyes. Her breath is staccato, like mine. She raises her hands behind her head, pulling out the rubber band, shaking out her hair, and letting it fall around her face.

I am undone by her.

My hands are twitching to touch her. I am aching to taste her lips.

"Do it," she breathes out in a voice so low it's barely audible, but it's all I need.

I place my hands on her face and cup her cheeks, and she closes her eyes and sighs. Then, I pull her to me, pressing my lips to hers again. I am unable to stay away from her.

Her lips are soft and full and greedy. But I like to lead, so I kiss her deeply, possessively, twining my hands through her glorious hair as I trace the soft underside of her lips with the tip of my tongue, eliciting the sexiest moan from her that I kiss away. I nibble on her bottom lip, and she gasps. "Davis."

My name alone sends me into another realm, and before I know it I am tugging on her hair and roaming my mouth down the gorgeous column of her neck, and right before I reach her shoulder blade, I press my teeth to her skin, lightly, but heavy enough to make the smallest of marks.

"Ouch," she says, but the word tapers off, and the next thing she says is *more*, in a breathy whisper that turns into a groan of pleasure as I give her what she wants. "Do you know why I want to have my hands in your hair?" I ask in a hoarse voice.

"Why?"

"Because I want to pull on your hair as I fuck you. I want to bend you over and take you against the wall, and I want to gather all your hair in my hands and hear you cry out."

"Oh God," she moans, her mouth in a gorgeous, perfect O that sends me spiraling further into such dark longing for her. "Do you think I'd like it?" she asks, playing along.

"You'd love it. Because I'd always make sure it was good for you. And I think you'd want me to tell you what to do. To direct you."

"Yes," she says, panting, as I bring a hand down to the little pearl buttons on her sweater. "I want to bite these off," I whisper in her ear, my breath hot on her skin and making her shiver. "But I think you like this sweater. I think you wore it for me. Did you wear it for me?"

I nibble my way down her neck to the hollow of her throat. She gasps out a yes, as I tug on the bottom of her sweater, making room for my hand to slide across her belly. Her skin is so soft.

"Were you thinking I'd like the way your breasts look in it? That I'd like you in red?"

"Yes."

She grabs my shoulders and slams me on top of her, her beautiful body against the floorboards.

"This works too, though," I tease.

She laughs, but then turns serious again. "What else do you want to do to me?"

"I want to go down on you on the piano. I want to lift you up and put you on the baby grand, and push your skirt to your hips and tell you to spread your legs for me," I tell her, and she responds by opening her legs and grabbing my ass so we are in perfect missionary except for that little problem of clothes.

"Do you think I'd do what you say?" she asks breathily, as she thrusts her hips against me.

"Yes," I say confidently. "I think you'd spread your legs for me and let me taste you."

"Do you think I'll taste good?"

"I bet you taste like sin and heaven at the same time. I bet you taste fucking delicious coming on my tongue." I look straight into her eyes, and they are full of fire and lust. "And I'm going to find out right now, Jill."

I offer her a hand and pull her up, bringing her to the piano at stage right. Then I take off her boots, unzip her jeans, and leave them in a pile on the floor. I lift her up and gently lower her on top of the piano.

Her eyes widen with the realization that I wasn't joking.

"Are you really going to?"

"Do you want me to stop?"

"No. The last thing I want is for you to stop."

"Good. Now, let me admire you."

I step back as if I'm appraising her. All she wears are red lace panties, the red sweater, and the look in her eyes.

"Take off your sweater," I tell her.

"Don't you want to take it off of me?"

"Yes. But I want to watch you undress more."

She nods, and reaches down to the waistband,

crossing her hands, and tugging her sweater over her head. She wears a white strappy tank.

"Now the tank."

She inhales sharply and does as I ask, tossing it into the growing pile of her clothes on the stage. She's wearing only her matching bra and underwear, and she's a sight to behold in all that red. My eyes roam her body, memorizing her skin, her curves, the way she's so sexy in anything and nothing. Then I stalk over to her and place my hands on her thighs. She quivers as I touch her, and arches her back instantly. I run my thumbs along her inner thighs, and she gasps. Then I reach her panties and trace a finger over the thin fabric between her legs that can't hide how turned on she is. She grabs my hair and tries to pull me closer.

I meet her gaze, and her eyes are fiery.

"Please stop teasing me."

"I'm not teasing you."

"You are."

"I would only be teasing if I planned to stop."

She presses her hand against her mouth. "I can't take it anymore. Just touch me. Please."

"Take off your bra."

She reaches behind her back, and unclasps it instantly, handing it to me. I drop it on the floor then cup her breasts. "So beautiful," I murmur. I lavish attention first on one breast, tugging on her nipple as she moans, then the other, and the noises she makes drive me on. Then I pull back. "But that's not what I promised you tonight."

"I know, and I want what you promised," she says,

and her voice is full of reckless desire. There's something so wild in her, so untamed, as if she's been waiting to be unleashed like this and wants me to do it.

I stare at her, then give her the next bit of direction. "Let me see what you look like on my stage with nothing on."

20

JILL

I shimmy out of my panties and hitch in a breath. My whole body is vibrating, and I am lit up from the inside out. Every part of me is screaming for him. I'm completely naked on top of the piano and he rakes me over with his eyes, making me feel like I'm the only one he's ever wanted like this. I don't know how he does this to me, how he makes me feel charged all over, but I've never been this turned on. I didn't know I *could* be this turned on, but this man makes me feel like my body belongs to him, like he can bring me places I never thought I could be. Like he can take me way past this reckless longing into some sort of altered state of bliss.

"Jill. Fucking Jill," he says in a rough voice. He steps closer, curves a hand around my neck, and kisses me gently on the lips, then pulls back to drink me in with his eyes. "You are the most beautiful woman I've ever met. You have to know that. You have to know how beautiful and intoxicating you are to me. Now, spread your legs for me."

I am aching for him, throbbing past the point of no return. I want him so badly it's like my desire has become its own life force here in the theater with him. I scoot back on the top of the piano and part my legs, my knees falling open for him.

Then his hands are on my thighs and I cry out. He hasn't even tasted me yet, and I'm already in heaven with him so near me. He bends down and traces his tongue across all the wetness between my legs. Sparks of sheer pleasure shoot through me, from the center of my body all the way to my fingertips. I loop my hands in his hair, holding on to him and pulling him closer. I want him so badly, I want his mouth, and his tongue, and his lips, and I even want the bristly scratch of his stubble against me. I want every single sensation all over me. But mostly, I want him to quench this burning need in my body, because it feels like I might die if I don't come. I know that's not true, yet nothing has ever felt more true, because I've been reduced to nothing but feelings, to the constant bursts of pleasure that he brings as he licks me, his moans the sexiest sounds I've ever heard in my life as he tastes me, savoring me.

I didn't know it was possible to be wanted this much, but Davis makes me feel as if no woman in the world has ever felt like this before, as if all the pleasure cascading through my body is happening for the first time. He flicks his tongue against my clit, and I grab his hair harder and buck against him. Then his lips are on me, kissing me between my legs, and it's beyond amazing the things he can do with his mouth.

Until I learn what he can do with his fingers at the

same time. He thrusts two inside me, and my head falls back from the dizzying feel—the softness of his mouth, the roughness of his fingers. He swirls delirious lines with the tip of his tongue, all while fucking me hard and deep with his fingers, and all I can picture is him inside me, filling me up, stretching me. Soon, my world spins off its axis, sending me into a place of pure and absolute bliss, like every molecule and atom inside of me is vibrating, and I've never felt more alive.

Somewhere, somehow, I'm vaguely aware of all these sounds I'm making, these wild moans, and pants, as I cry out, and beg for more and more because I'm racing, rocking against him, reaching for his hair, his shoulders, as I move harder and faster, my breaths erratic as I climb my way to the far edge of desire.

I am devastated by the feelings that wrack my body.

I am undone. Completely and utterly undone for him.

I call out his name, and it echoes around the theater, reverberating across the walls and crashing all over the empty auditorium as I come on his mouth, his tongue, his lips. He holds tight to my hips, slowing his moves, but still kissing me until I can't take it anymore, and he pulls away.

My shoulders heave, and I pant hard, as if I've just finished a race, and maybe I have. Soon, I open my eyes, but I still feel woozy, as if I'm barely grasping at reality, as if I'm still on the edge of a dream. But he's here, looking at me with the same wildness in his eyes that I felt moments before.

"Did you picture that before I did it to you?"

I press my teeth into my lips once, then nod, still dazed on the aftereffects. "Yes."

"Was it how you imagined it? Coming for me?"

I shake my head. "It was so much better."

He inhales sharply, and his expression says he wishes he could take me now—yank me off the piano, and slam me down hard on his cock, and take me right here, like this.

"Do you want to have me now?" I ask in a voice that's comprised solely of lust.

"Yes. But I'm not going to."

21

JILL

I wash my hands then dry them, checking out my reflection one last time. My cheeks are still rosy, and I have that just-been-fucked look still. I don't think that's going to disappear any time soon, and I'm okay with that. I toss the paper towel in the trash can, smooth my hands over my red sweater and return to the backstage hallway, then to the stage. I still feel like I'm floating, but there's another feeling surrounding me, and it's harder to get a handle on.

Nervousness maybe? Chased with a touch of hope? I'm not sure of anything that's happening inside me. I hardly understand who I become around him, how I can spin out of my carefully constructed world of happy-go-lucky, everything-is-fine, and transform into this ravenous woman grasping at pleasure as if I need it for my very survival. When did the release I feel with Davis become as necessary as breath and air?

I move the curtains aside and walk to the piano,

trying to compose myself. But into who, I don't know. The actress here for rehearsal? The woman unfazed by her boss? Or the person who doesn't have a handle on herself?

He's on the bench, straddling it rather than sitting at it, and he's swiping his index finger across his phone.

"Texting someone?" There's something unsettling about him doing something so ordinary as texting while I'm having some kind of identity crisis that he caused.

He shakes his head. "No. I'm reading the news."

"Oh." That's better, I suppose. I sit down next to him. "Anything interesting going on in the world?"

"It's snowing, and the government still has a deficit," he says with that wry smile. I want to reach out and touch his face, trace the outline of his lips. So I do, and he leans into me, like a cat who likes being petted. Then I stop because I want to know more about him. I want to understand him.

"Are you a news junkie or a weather junkie?"

"Both. But in this case, news. I read the *New York Times* religiously."

"What else? Do you read books?"

"I have nothing against books. But I would have to say nearly all my reading is the newspaper. Well, the paper online."

"Cover to cover?"

He nods, and it seems fitting that he's a newshound. It suits him. He seems like a man who wants to understand the world, and so that's what he does. But I also think there's more to it. "Do you think you lean toward news so much because you spend your day with make-believe?"

His lips quirk up as if he's intrigued by the question, considering it. "I hadn't thought of it that way. But you're right. I spend all my hours constructing the most believable artifice I can, so when I'm not playing pretend, I want to know what's real."

Real. There it is again. The word makes me wince because I'm struggling so much with holding on to real and make-believe, and they seem to be seeping into each other.

He fingers a strand of my hair absently, and it's such a sweet gesture because that's all it is. It's not the start of something. It is what it is. "What about you, Jill? What do you read?"

I take a long but quiet inhale and stare off at the faraway balcony of the theater. The balcony that will be full of people soon. I flash back to Sunday with Patrick, to how I was paralyzed with fear about answering truthfully. Maybe that's why I've been asking Davis these questions—so he would ask me back. So I can test myself. See if I can speak a simple truth.

I look at him, and it doesn't hurt. I don't feel like all my words are stuck. It's remarkably easy to answer.

"Romance," I say, and it's as if a piece of my regret floats away. It feels good, so I keep going. "Racy romance, to be precise."

A grin tugs at his lips. "Of course you read racy romance." His voice is flirty, sexy. No judgment. No teasing. Just knowing.

"Why do you say *of course*?"

"Because you couldn't play this part if you weren't a romantic. Because I see it in you. Because I see all this passion, all this pain, all this hope. All this sexiness."

I can feel it again. The same thing I felt when I sang in our first private rehearsal. As if a fragment of my frozen heart is breaking away, as if the ice I've encased myself in is calving off, freeing up a tiny part of me that wants to be known. I give up more words, like a confessional. "I read dirty stuff. And racy stuff. And erotic romance. And I love books with heroes who talk dirty," I say as I move closer, and run my fingers along the smooth buttons on his shirt.

"I had a feeling you did," he says, grinning like he can't stop.

"It doesn't bother you?"

"Why would it bother me?"

"I don't know," I say with a shrug.

"Do you masturbate when you read your erotic novels?"

"Yes."

"I would love to watch you sometime."

My eyes widen with shock. "You would?"

"Of course," he says, as if it's the most normal thing in the world, when the idea never occurred to me. "I want to know how you touch yourself."

My skin is burning again, and if we keep talking like this, I'll be doing a striptease for him in the middle of the stage. But I can't seem to resist. I reach for him, trailing my hand through his hair. I love how soft it is under my fingers. He sighs deeply and leans close to me, resting his forehead against mine. "Jill," he says in a low voice.

"Davis," I say, and that's all. We're silent like that for a few moments, and there's something very comforting about being with him while the snow falls outside and we're warm and safe inside.

But soon I break the silence. "Can I ask you a question?"

"Yes."

"Did I taste like sin and heaven?"

He nods, then presses his lips lightly to my forehead. "You are my sin." He brushes them gently against my earlobe. "And my heaven." Next, the barest of kisses on my lips. "And everything between."

Then he pulls back, and his expression has changed from soft to steely. "And I hate that you're in love with Patrick. I hate it. Because it makes me crazy to want you this much and to know how you feel for him. It makes me utterly insane."

I open my mouth to ask why he thinks—then remember him shutting me out that morning in the stairwell, and my pride-saving response. I don't know what keeps me from correcting the mistake. From saying, "No, I'm not in love with Patrick. Not at all. Not the way you think." I don't say that though. Maybe my pride still wants protecting.

The words—whatever they might be—take longer than he's willing to wait. He stands up and turns away from me, coolly reminding me why I'm here. "We need to get back to work."

"Do you want to do that scene again?" I ask tentatively, the words coming out all choppy.

He shakes his head and waves a dismissive hand. "The blocking is fine. We'll work on your solos."

So we spend the next two hours working and nothing more. When we're done, he holds open the door for the car, but doesn't join me. Of course, I'm an actress, and maybe riding in a car together is too much like a date.

* * *

Reeve grunts as he bench-presses a heavy set of barbells. He's working out even more as he preps for his leading role in *Escorted Lives*.

We're at his gym in the East Village early the next morning after a run. I do bicep curls with ten-pound weights to the sounds of dumbbells hitting the floor and machines slamming down.

"How did you know it was real?"

He gives me a curious look. "What do you mean?"

"With Sutton," I say, as if he should be able to follow the random thoughts that have percolated in my head since my last private rehearsal with Davis.

"Ah," he says with a twinkle in his eye. "With the complicated, vexing, inscrutable Ms. Brenner."

"Yeah. How did you know that you were feeling something for real?" I switch to triceps. "Or that she was?"

He pushes the barbell up for one more rep then

places it in the rack, sitting up on the bench, elbows on his knees.

"It wasn't easy, let me tell you. She was a tough one. Hard to read. Lots of layers of self-protection there. Took a while before I could really figure out if it was real."

"And even then, she tried to deny it," I say, remembering when Reeve came to my apartment a few days before my *Crash the Moon* audition, completely flummoxed over what to do to win her over. Before he laid it all on the line for her.

"That's my woman. She could put up walls like no one I've ever seen."

"Hmm," I say, as I push my arm back for another curl. If Reeve only knew about my walls. My secrets.

"Is this about Patrick?" he asks, tilting his head to the side and pushing a hand through his brown hair.

"Um, sure," I say.

He gives me a look that says I haven't fooled him. "Should I ask?"

"Please, God, no."

Nearby, a burly man with a worn blue T-shirt that shows off arms as big as tires brings a set of weights to the floor. They clang loud enough to make me wince.

"So, how is it going with Patrick? Still going on these *friends* dates?" Reeve helpfully sketches air quotes.

"I hope so." It would not be the worst thing to end up with a friend in Patrick. Until Davis brought it up— a mild way of putting it—I hadn't thought beyond the friend zone. "I could use an idea for a non-date activity."

"Oh, I know what you should do. Bowling. There's that bowling alley in Port Authority. It's awesome. It's two blocks from the St. James so you can go there some evening after rehearsal."

"That does sound fun." It sounds like a way to get away from confusing, unsettling things that I don't know how to fit into my life. And Patrick is even-tempered, low-key, and comfortable after an afternoon with Hurricane Davis.

My phone buzzes. I reach into the pocket of my workout shorts, and for the briefest of seconds, I find myself hoping it's a text about another private rehearsal. But it's from Kat, and it's a picture of a wedding gown she wants to try on this weekend.

I smile and write back. *Can't wait.*

She's going to look beautiful when she walks down the aisle to marry the only man she's ever loved.

* * *

Patrick holds the green bowling ball in front of his chest, pausing on the polished wood floor. He bends, his arm swinging gracefully behind him, then in front of him as he shoots the ball down the lane.

Lifehouse plays loudly in the Port Authority bowling alley, a strange choice. I'd expected a bouncy Katy Perry tune, or even some hair metal from the 80s, like Poison. But the guy who runs this place loves his alt-pop music, so we're treated to one of my favorite songs—"Broken"—mixed with the sound of arcade games and gutter balls.

Patrick's ball rolls in a perfectly straight line. Ten pins spill with a loud crash, rattling under the lane, and he raises his arms, does a victory spin, and smiles widely.

"Strike!"

"You are a rock star," I say as I high-five him. This guy is a unicorn. Good at everything and literally the nicest guy I've ever met.

He waves off my compliment, as if it's nothing. "Nah. I'm just having fun."

At the St. James, they're working with other chorus members, so we had two hours free at lunch and slipped out to the nearby lanes at the Port Authority. It's been a welcomed break from the building, rehearsal, and Davis's broody mood.

Patrick is easy company. He doesn't blow hot and cold. He doesn't make my brain hurt. He doesn't confuse me with all his mixed messages.

No drama. No angst. No worrying.

I can't imagine it would be different if we were more than friends.

The scores come up as 188 for Patrick and 102 for me. We congratulate ourselves on a good game and head the few blocks back to the theater.

"This was a good idea," Patrick says as we reach the alley behind the St. James. "We have to remember this place."

"For when the cast needs a break before their brains leak out onto the stage floor?"

"Or for less dire situations. What are your feelings on mini-golf, and where can we find that in Manhattan?" Patrick asks as we reach the stage door.

"Randall's Island," I tell him, as he holds open the door for me. "There's mini-golf on Randall's Island."

"Then, Jill, that's exactly what we're going to do the next time we get together," he declares as he bounds up the steps and into the hallway. I'm right behind him as we round the corner, but I freeze when I see Davis at the end of the hall, head down and wrapped up in a conversation with Shannon who's holding her clipboard and taking notes.

He doesn't even see me, but an icy dread spreads through my bones, as if I've been caught. I'm ready to turn around, run, hide. Then I remind myself I did nothing wrong. There's no reason I can't hang out with my castmate. No reason at all. So I tell myself to pick up my boots and put one foot in front of the other and walk on.

I keep pace next to Patrick, who's musing about whether the mini-golf range at Randall's Island has one of those crazy, macabre clowns for the final hole, and I force a smile on my face, and then I even manage a laugh, because I'm sure I'll feel as lighthearted as I possibly can while whacking a small white ball into a clown's face.

The sound of Patrick's voice chatting about mini-golf and bowling carries in these cramped hallways, and it's enough for Davis to look away from Shannon.

He appraises the scene instantly—Patrick and I coming from outside, Patrick and I gone for two hours, Patrick and I chatting. His blue eyes turn dark and steely, and I can almost feel the anger radiating from him as we pass by. He's like a high-tension line, and his jaw is set hard, his eyes narrowed.

"Hey, Milo," Patrick says amiably, giving him a quick salute. "I'm ready to start on whatever you've got for me this afternoon."

"Great," Davis says through gritted teeth.

I tell Patrick I'll see him out on stage and then duck into the bathroom where I lean against the wall, taking deep and shaky breaths. I press my thumb and fore-finger against the bridge of my nose, wishing I could erase that encounter. Wishing I knew what I would do differently. But I can't go out and face Davis right now, so I lean forward, my hands on my thighs, as if I'm winded and need air.

Then I stand up straight, open the door, and head back into the hall. It's empty—everyone must be gath-ered on the stage now. I hold my head up high, my spine straight, and remind myself that everything is fine.

There's a hand on my waist, gripping me. I spin around, and Davis is staring hard at me. He pulls me into a dressing room and shuts the door behind us. It's empty, but the exposed bulbs are bright and glaring around one of the mirrors, and makeup and brushes litter the counter.

He backs me up against the closed door, caging me

in his arms as he presses his hands against the door on either side of me. My pulse speeds up.

"You were out with him, weren't you?"

I narrow my eyes. "We were out of the theater in each other's company."

"Were you on a date?"

"Why should I tell you?"

"Did he take you out? Did he romance you? Did he kiss you?" He looks tortured as he asks the last question, and my breath catches. I never wanted to torment him.

I never wanted to torment Aaron, either. Comparing him to Davis is laughable, but the intensity around us is setting my nerves on end.

When Davis breathes out it's hard, almost feral. His eyes blaze at me, and his hands shake. He's so mad he's shaking. His voice is low and measured as he bites out the next words. "Did. He. Kiss. You?"

Angst and anger mix and rise up in me like a thick plume. I don't like being talked to this way. I don't like *feeling* this way. "Why should I tell you? You don't take me out. You don't call me. You don't even text me," I say as if that proves all my points.

He scoffs. "I should send you texts with smiley faces? That would change things?"

"No," I spit back. "But you're acting like you own me. And you don't. You don't own me just because you want to fuck me."

He heaves a rough sigh and looks away, his lips pressed tight together as if he's trying to collect himself. He looks back at me, almost forcing himself to calm down. "I can't stand the thought of him kissing you. I can't stand the thought of his hands on you. I can't stand the thought of anyone's hands on you." He brings a hand to my shoulder blade, traces my collarbone with his knuckles. "Except mine," he says in a rough voice, as he trails his fingers down to my waist then wraps them around my hip. He bends his head to my ear and whispers harshly. "I can still taste you."

His words make me lightheaded, and my knees nearly buckle. I feel like my world has been twisted inside out, and I've lost all sense of direction. I can't find my way through anymore. "Why are you doing this to me?" I ask him in a strained voice.

"What am I doing to you, Jill? Tell me. Tell me what I'm doing to you."

"Acting like this."

"How am I acting?" His question is half-curious, half-demanding. As if he can't go on until he knows the answer.

He's still inches away from me. His eyes are so dark they're nearly black now, but they don't let me go. He's so near to me that I can smell his anger, his heat. I can smell how much he wants me too. His shirt collar is open, unbuttoned once, exposing a patch of skin below his throat. I could press my lips to him, taste him, run the tip of my tongue over him. See how he reacts to me.

"Like a jealous lover," I answer, and I don't bother to mask my anger either.

He pushes a hand through his hair then lets go, his fingers now touching my face gently. He traces the outline of my cheek. Then my jaw. Then across my lips. I wish it didn't feel so good.

"Maybe I am," he whispers. "Maybe that's how I feel about you."

I clench my teeth, place a hand on his chest, ready to push him away. "But don't you get it? You don't have the right to be. All we do is find each other in the dark. In hallways. In dressing rooms. In stairwells. Why? Because you. Don't. Date. Actresses." Then I pause for effect and add bitterly, "You've told me that. Hell, even Shelby knows that." I hold out my hands wide as if to say *so there.*

He grabs my hands, laces his fingers through mine, and brings our clasped hands to his chest. I look down at our linked fingers, surprised he would make such an intimate gesture in such an angry moment. This isn't what I thought would come next. Then he squeezes my fingers, as if he's pleading for me to understand him. "Do you want to know why?"

"Yes," I say, letting go of all my anger. Because beneath my frustration, I desperately want him to tell me. I think I know the answer. But I want to hear it from him, not from gossip. I want him to trust me.

"Because the last time I did, it wrecked me." His face softens as he admits that, and I can tell how hard it is for him to say. Instinct takes over, and I tighten my hold on his hands, letting him know I'm listening. "And I don't want to feel like a fucking mess again. Not if I can help it. Not if I can stop it. But I can't get you out of my mind, Jill, and I haven't been able to for a long, long time. I don't want anyone else touching you, and I don't want anyone else going out with you either, whether it's to bowling or even to mini-golf," he says with sneer.

"Hey, what's wrong with mini-golf?" I risk teasing him gently, knowing it might be too soon, but also knowing it would break the intense mood.

"Nothing. If you go with me," he says, and the anger is gone now. "And I don't want you having dinner with anyone else either. So you're going to make me break all my rules, right now." Then his expression changes, and he looks vulnerable in a way I haven't seen. "Have dinner with me, please." His voice rises just a bit as he lets down his guard for me.

For me.

It guts me, his honesty. The risk he's taking. How it changes everything if I go out with him.

"So you want to date an actress after all?" I ask, smiling a little, so he knows where I'm going. I already know my answer, but I can't resist flirting with him.

"Yes. You," he says, and now the nerves have gone, and he's all confidence and control again. "I want to send a car for you, and I want you to wear a dress, and count the seconds until you walk into the restaurant. Because I'll be there at the bar, waiting for you. Every head will turn to watch you walk over to me, and they'll all want to know what that guy has that the most beautiful, breathtaking woman is there for him. To be with him." He stops for a beat, and I'm melting for him as he lays his heart on the line. "Say yes, Jill. Say yes to me."

Every inch of me is goosebumps. The soft little hairs on my arms stand on end, and I am breathless. I can't say anything to him but yes. I want the same thing he wants.

More.

"You know my answer, Davis," I say.

"Say yes," he implores me one more time.

"Yes."

He relaxes into me, as if that one word has let out all the tension from his body.

"But now I want you to say yes to something," I say, and I finger his crisp, white collar.

He raises an eyebrow, inviting me to say more.

"I want to unbutton your shirt. I want to feel your chest against my hands."

"We have to get back out there, though," he says, but I'm already making quick work of the first button. He breathes out, and I can tell that he's giving in to me, that he can't *not* give in to me right now. "But Shannon can handle it," he says, answering for himself. Then the words trail off like vapor as I undo each button, spreading the fabric, and revealing his chest for the first time.

I've felt him through his shirt plenty of times. I've outlined his muscles with my hands. But there's always been a barrier. Now there's none as I reach his waist, and he helps me by untucking his shirt from the waistband of his dark gray pants. There. Now he's mine to look at, and he's so gorgeous it makes my heart hurt.

Then it stops hurting as a warm flush spreads through me because I'm going to that place I go only with him, where the heat between us takes over, and cocoons us. He closes his eyes, letting himself savor my touch as I run my index finger down the line of his chest, through the slightest bit of hair, down to his flat abs, stopping at that delicious V. His skin is smooth, and he's so toned, and he clearly takes care of his body because he's carved and cut and I want to bend down and trail my tongue across his flat belly and all the way up his chest. I want to kiss him everywhere. I want to touch him everywhere. I want to know his body.

He lets out a low growl as I explore his chest, then my hands have a mind of their own and I push his shirt down to his elbows, feeling his strong, toned arms. Every inch of him I've seen is beautiful, and I want so deeply to know what all of him looks like.

But I respect his boundaries. I understand that this is all he'll allow, so I pull his shirt back up, then button my way down. He tucks it into his pants, and I adjust the collar, smoothing it out.

Then I cup his cheeks in my hands. He inhales sharply, but doesn't close his eyes, doesn't look away.

"Davis," I say softly, "you have to know you're beautiful too."

"Thank you," he says, leaning into my palm.

"I want you to kiss me now. Kiss me like I'm the woman you're breaking all your rules for." I tilt my chin and bring my lips to his, and he kisses me, a soft, tender kiss that I never want to end.

But soon it does.

Only, instead of leaving the dressing room, he leans over to lock the door.

I raise an eyebrow.

"This will only take a few minutes," he says with a

glint in his eye. "Besides, I need to make up to you properly."

"You do?"

"I need to show you how contrite I am for behaving like a jealous ass," he says, then places his hand on my shoulders and gently turns me around so I'm facing the door. He runs his hand down my back, sending shivers through my whole body, as a delicious pull begins in my belly. He pushes up my sweater, unhooks my bra, and loops his hands around to cup my breasts.

I gasp and close my eyes as he palms my breasts, teasing my nipples with his fingers until they harden into peaks.

"Is this how you say you're sorry?" I ask, as my breathing grows shallow.

"No." He brings his mouth to my upper back, and trails hot kisses down my spine. I whimper as he licks his way down my back, then as his quick hands undo my jeans. He pushes them down to my knees and does the same with my pink panties. I move with him, letting him touch me, kiss me, taste my body like I'm his canvas and he's painting me with his tongue. I press my palms into the door, and he hooks his strong fingers around my hips and tugs me so I bend, my back almost flat, my behind in the air. I want to turn around and watch, but I also love this feeling of letting go, of surrendering to his touch as he kneels and presses his thumbs against my cheeks, spreading me open. He moves closer, blowing warm breath between my legs, making me ache for his tongue.

"This is how I say I'm sorry."

I gasp as he kisses my throbbing center, tasting how wet I am for him, enjoying how my body responds instantly to his touch. My breathing quickens as he flicks his tongue against my clit, swirling and licking and sucking me, until soon I'm panting and moaning as quietly as I possibly can so no one can hear, though I am desperate, absolutely desperate, for the release he's about to bring me. He grips me firmly with his strong hands on my hips, and strokes me with his tongue, working relentlessly until I shatter. Even then he pulls me closer, his lips needing me, his tongue still savoring me, drinking me in as if he can't get enough of me as I come again.

I don't move for a few minutes as the sensations wash over me, the aftereffects of two powerful orgasms lingering in my body.

Soon, he pulls up my lacy pink underwear, then my jeans, and I turn around. I'm sure I'm a lightheaded, woozy mess as I snap my bra and adjust my sweater.

"I suppose you're forgiven," I say, and he grins wickedly.

"Good. And I suppose I'd better head out first, seeing as you look like you've just come hard." Then he pauses, raking his eyes over every inch of me. "And twice."

He brushes his lips against my forehead and leaves.

Five minutes later, after a quick bathroom visit, I join the cast and crew on stage. I can't help but wonder if anyone can know from looking at us that our hands have been on each other, that our lips have meshed together, that we've done so much more.

Or if we're both fantastic at make-believe, because even as I practice the numbers on the call sheet, I'm thinking of my closet and the dresses I have, and the one I want to wear to dinner with my director, because I know he'll find a way to have his hands underneath my clothes.

And that's more than fine with me.

22

JILL

There is no question that this is *the* dress. With its sleeveless scoop neck, plunging V back, and a hand-beaded bodice with intricate crystals woven throughout, it is sheer perfection.

"Oh, Kat." Tears well up in my eyes. "This is the one. This is the dress you're going to get married in."

She smooths her hands over the organza that extends into a cathedral train behind her. A short, dark-haired woman who owns this bridal shop in the West Village watches patiently from her post a few feet away. Kat appraises herself in the three-way mirror, the soft light of the shop making her look even more stunning. "You think so?"

"I know that's a rhetorical question." I stand up from the cushiony white chair I've been parked in as she's tried on a strapless lace dress, a satin sheath, and many more. Soft, classical music plays through an unseen sound system. High-class bridal magazines lie elegantly on top of an oval glass coffee table next to the chair. A vase of jasmine flowers fills the boutique with a sweet floral scent. All these touches are enough to make anyone in here forget that beyond the shop doors lies grimy, noisy, crowded Manhattan. "Look at yourself. It's perfect and you know it. It's you."

I stand behind her, so she can see me in the mirror now, smiling at her. She glances at her reflection one more time, considering the dress from every angle. I can practically see the cogs whirring in her head, inching closer to the moment when she reaches 100 percent certainty. Her brow is furrowed then a grin starts to form, slowly at first, until it quickly becomes a full-blown smile.

She turns around, and she's simply glowing with happiness. "I'll take it," she declares.

"Wonderful," says the shop owner. "It is perfect for you, Ms. Harper."

"I'm so glad I found your store. I'm so glad I found this dress," Kat says, the words spilling out in a happy rush. Then she turns to me. "And thank you for coming with me. I couldn't do this without you. You're the best maid of honor and the best friend I could ever hope to have."

"Oh please. I did nothing except gaze upon your beauty," I say playfully, but my voice breaks, and I swipe at a tear that rolls down my cheeks. I'm so happy for her.

"Oh, you're so cute when you're all emotional and teary," she says, and crushes me in a hug.

"I'm going to miss you when you move in with him.

I can't believe you're only my roommate for a few more months."

"I know. But I'll still see you. We'll still hang out."

"Always. We'll always hang out."

We pull apart, and the shop owner helps Kat take off the dress, and they make arrangements for it as I wander through the tiny store with its cream walls and gold-framed vintage pictures of garden weddings and sunset vows. When they're done, the shop owner asks Kat about her bridesmaids' dresses.

"Something classy. Something she could wear again," Kat says, nodding to me.

"I need a dress for tonight is what I need," I say under my breath.

Kat turns to me, gives me a curious look. I wave my hand as if to wipe away the comment I should have kept to myself.

"I have a black and white dress in mind," the shop owner says. "Sleeveless and above the knee. Straight lines. Very sophisticated. I'll have it in the store next week if you'd like your maid of honor to try it on when you come back for a fitting?"

"That sounds fantastic," Kat says, then we exit the store. "Are you holding out on me? You have a Saturday night date with Patrick, and this is the first I'm hearing about it?"

My stomach twists, and I feel like I can't get air for a moment. As if my lungs are crushing me from the inside out. I flash back to all the lies I've told over the years. To all the fables I've carefully constructed to seem as if I really am this person. This *what-you-see-is-*

what-you-get person. But I'm too many people. I'm Eponine. I'm Ava. I'm the woman who claims her brother's favorite books for her own. I'm the running coach. I'm the jokey, happy friend. I am the girl who stopped feeling things for real after Aaron.

And I am tired of that girl. I'm ready to start saying goodbye to her. I take another small step and speak a simple truth to my best friend. "Actually, I'm going out with Davis Milo tonight."

Her eyes widen with shock, and her purse slides down her shoulder, the bag dangling dangerously close to the cobblestone sidewalk. She yanks it back up. "Oh. My. God."

"Why do you say it like that?"

"You're going out with your director?" she asks, as if it's not computing.

This is what I get for telling the truth? She's berating me? "I was just joking," I say, regressing in an instant. Who wants progress if it comes with that kind of hassle?

"You were not," she says, waggling a finger at me, but her tone shifts from shocked to eager, and she's not going to let me slip out of this unscathed by honesty. "Is there something going on between you two? Do you like him?"

I shrug and hold my hands out as if to say *I don't know*. Because I *don't* know what's between us. I barely understand what's happening. "Do you think it's terrible that he's my director?"

"Hello? Pot. Kettle. I fell for my mentor last semester. No, I don't think it's terrible at all. I think it might be incredibly hot, and I want to know everything. Spill," she says authoritatively.

I don't know that I can tell her everything. I'm still reeling from having told her anything at all. But I tell her we've kissed more than once, and I tell her that I want to find a new dress for tonight.

A new dress for a new date with a new man.

"What kind of dress?"

"Something that's unbearably sexy but that leaves a lot to the imagination."

"I know just the shop." She grabs my hand and takes me to one of her favorite boutiques and then finds a dress that's equally perfect—perfect for me.

23

DAVIS

As I leave my apartment, I see Ryder at the end of the block, heading out of the gym. He gives a nod, then a once-over. When I catch up, he tips his chin at me.

"Date night for the director?"

I scoff.

"You can just admit it. I can tell."

I huff. "Maybe."

"Ah, I see my suggestion to behave fell on deaf ears."

"Maybe I am behaving."

"Is it the understudy?" He arches a brow as we chat on the street corner.

"That obvious?"

He claps a hand on my shoulder. "I'm not going to say be careful because I know you know what you're doing. And I'm not going to say don't do it, because life is short. Just watch out for the ticker. I know you pretend yours is made of steel, but I think it might be softer."

"Just like yours?"

He shrugs. "Unfortunately." Then he fixes on a smile. "But hey, that's why I'm never going to fall in love again."

I laugh hard. "Yeah. Right. And on that note, I have a lovely woman to take to dinner."

I turn to go, and Ryder calls out. "Davis."

I turn around and wait.

"Have some fucking fun. You deserve it, man."

"So do you."

A rush of cold air invades the restaurant. The guy in the untucked shirt perched on the stool next to me whips his head around, but I doubt it's because of the chill. I grin privately, take a drink of my scotch, then place the sturdy glass on the smooth chrome bar at Vertigo, a new fish restaurant in Soho that Michelle raved about. Anticipation winds through me, as a picture of Jill forms in my mind. I lick my lips then turn around.

She's handing the hostess her coat as she scans the restaurant. Then she finds me, and her eyes lock on mine. My blood heats as I take her in. She's more stunning than I imagined, wearing a black knit dress that hugs her body and hits right above the knees, exposing inches of her bare legs before they're covered up in the sexiest black boots I've ever seen. I toss a twenty on the bar without turning around and walk up to her.

Placing a hand on her lower back, I plant a chaste

kiss on her cheek. "You're playing dirty, dressed like that. But I'm behaving myself and it's killing me," I say.

"I'm so impressed with your self-control," she teases.

"You should be. It's excellent, in case you haven't noticed."

"Oh, I've noticed."

I turn to the hostess. "Is our table ready?"

"Yes, Mr. Milo. Right this way." She leads us through the restaurant with its white-tiled floors, sleek silver tables, and gray leather booths. "The one you reserved," she says, and lays the menus on the table in the back. I gesture for Jill to slide in first to the curved booth.

"Thank you very much," I say to the hostess, who gives a quick nod, then leaves.

I sit down as Jill smooths out her skirt, then fingers the crisp white tablecloth. "Nice tablecloth," she says in a knowing voice.

"Isn't it, though?"

Then she looks me over, her eyes flicking from my green-and-white checkered shirt to my dark pants. She leans closer, her soft breath on my neck, her pineapple scent taunting me as her long hair brushes my shoulder.

"You look very handsome," she says in a soft voice, almost as if she's nervous and unused to giving compliments.

"You're beautiful," I tell her. "I hope you're not tired of hearing it from me."

She shakes her head, a small smile tugging at her

lips, and all these little gestures remind me that this really is a first date. But the moment is shattered when the waiter appears.

"Can I start you off with something to drink?"

I turn to Jill. "Belvedere and soda?"

She smiles instantly. "You remember."

"Of course."

"And are you going to have Glenlivet on the rocks?"

"You remember too," I say, and I tell myself not to read anything into it, but it's too late. It already makes me want her even more. All of her. I turn to the waiter and give him our drink order, and he leaves.

"I remember everything about having drinks with you at Sardi's," she says in a sweet voice that damn near melts me.

"You do?"

She nods, and I wait a beat, thinking she'll tell me next that it was because I cast her, because I gave her her first big break. But instead, she says, "Because I was with you." Then her hand is on my shirt, and she traces lazy circles around one of the buttons, whispering in my ear, "I want to kiss you, but I'm afraid to do it in public."

"Why?"

"Because I worry if someone might see us."

"And so what if someone does?"

"Davis," she chides.

"What? I don't know why it's a big thing."

"Maybe not to you. But to me it would be," she says, and there's the slightest note of hurt.

"Why?"

She pulls back to give me a curious look. "Really? You can't figure it out?"

"No. Maybe you could just say it," I say, a bit irritated.

"I don't want anyone to think I got the part in the show because I'm sleeping with you."

It dawns on me that she'd want to protect her reputation as a rising star. I get it. I do. Still, it's a reminder that actresses put their careers first. I don't know why I'm doing this. I don't know why I'm chasing a woman who has erected so many barriers for me—from her job to her love of another man.

But the answer dawns on me too.

I'm doing it because she's worth it. Everything about her, from her talent to her beauty to her gorgeous heart, is worth any trouble. All the obstacles.

"You've already made it," she continues. "You have three Tonys, an Oscar, you have producers probably falling at your feet to have you direct. I'm just starting out, and I want to have a long career in this business."

"I guess I don't worry that much about what people think about my private life. And I don't think you should either." And then, because I can't resist pointing out the flaw in her logic, I add, "But I'm not sleeping with you."

"Not yet," she says, and her hands are still on my shirt. I glance down at the way she's tracing the buttons, as if she's dying to take my shirt off.

"But if you don't want anyone to think that, why are you touching me like this?"

"Because it's hard for me to keep my hands off you."

But she says it in a brusque voice as she turns away to pick up the menu. This woman is hot and cold, and almost impossible to read.

"Let's figure out what to order," I say.

After the waiter brings our drinks, Jill orders the wild salmon with green beans and I opt for the sautéed filet of sturgeon. Then, I hold up my glass. "To the long and ridiculously successful career I know you're going to have."

She smiles, softening once more, then clinks her glass to mine. "And to dinner."

Her eyes stray, and she looks at my hand. She takes a drink, puts her glass down, and reaches for it, tracing a soft finger across the scar. Her tone shifts to a more serious one, as if she's let go of the sexy Jill and now she's a more emotional one.

"You said this happened when your parents died. You punched the glass window of the door. Can I ask what happened to them?"

I like that she's direct. That she's asking me without hesitation. Because I don't want her or anyone to feel sorry for me. "They died in a car crash one February night. They were in the city. They were huge theater fans—that's where I got it from—and had actually been seeing a play the night they died. It had started snowing, and my dad was driving them home to where we lived in Westchester. A car coming the other way lost control on an ice patch, and they died instantly on impact. Police came later that night. Told me what happened." As I recount that awful night, my chest tightens, remembering how I opened the door to be greeted, not by my parents, but by the solemn-faced officer come to bear bad news. It's been more than a decade since that night, and I've managed. I've moved past it the only way you can—by going through it. Still, the memory is like a knife reopening an old wound, letting it bleed out yet another time. "I didn't believe it at first."

"You were in shock," she says softly, and there's something in her voice that says she knows the feeling all too well. She runs her finger across the scar.

"Yeah, exactly. I was that way for a few days. Then pretty soon, I was angry. That's when I slammed my fist through the glass pane on the door. Not my brightest decision, especially if I had ever wanted to have a professional boxing career," I say, managing a slight laugh to lighten the mood.

"Did you? Want that?"

I shake my head. "No. Theater is in my blood. My dad was a theater history professor. Mom was a choreographer, and there was never any question about what I wanted to do." Then I shift back to the story. "The worst part, though, was having to tell my younger sister. It was only us then. It's only us now."

"You took care of your sister?"

I nod. "I delayed college for a year to stay home with her, get her through the rest of high school."

"You're a good brother," she says in a kind voice, and squeezes my hand tight.

"Thank you for saying that. What about you? You said you have two brothers?"

"My brother Jay is working in Europe for a

company there. And my oldest brother, Chris, lives in San Francisco and is this huge video game guy. Hosts his own Webflix show about geek culture, and just started getting serious with this gal who's a fashion blogger. He's actually coming here soon for work, so I get to see him and to meet her. I can't wait."

"You're close to him?"

She nods, but then holds up her hand and moves it back and forth like a seesaw.

"Close, but maybe not so close?" I ask, raising an eyebrow as I try to understand her.

She chews the inside of her lip as if she's considering the question, and it's fascinating to see a new side of her. How she seems to genuinely connect with people and care about them, but can be so guarded too.

"No. I mean . . . we're close," she offers, but that's all. Then in a small, fragile voice, she adds, "Maybe you can meet him."

All my frustration from earlier, all my fear vanishes with those words. I don't know that I will ever meet her brother, but the fact that she makes the offer at all is huge for Jill.

"That would be nice," I say, and now her eyes have gone glassy as if she's sad and drifting off someplace. But before I can ask what's wrong, I follow her gaze back to my hand.

"I'm sorry you have this scar," she says as she strokes a finger across the top of my hand. "I'm sorry for what happened to you. But since you do have this scar, and you can't change the past, is it okay if I tell you I think it's kinda sexy that you just told me all that?

Maybe because it's so real. And the scar is a visible reminder of who you are, and what you went through, and you don't hide from it. You own it."

"I don't know any other way to be," I tell her, because it's the truth. I might traffic in illusions, but they all first come from truths. From who we all are deep down, from what makes us tick. That's my stock-in-trade. I take another swallow of my scotch, the ice cubes clinking against the glass. A waiter passes by bearing small salads for another couple at a nearby table, but I barely notice them. I put the glass down, touch her cheek, then thread my fingers through her hair. "Now it's my turn to ask you a question."

Her eyes widen with worry then she takes a breath as if she's steeling herself. "Okay," she says tentatively.

"Do you remember the night in the car, the first time I made you come?"

She nearly spits out her drink. "You cut to the chase."

"I do. It seemed as if you were saying it was the first . . ." I let my voice trail off, tilting my head to the side to see if she'll let me get to know her. Get to see inside her.

She doesn't answer right away. Just takes a drink, fiddles with her napkin.

"I want to get to know you," I say and run a finger along her arm. "That's all."

She looks afraid. She looks lost. But she parts her lips and sighs. "I'm not a virgin, but I haven't been with anyone in a long time," she says quietly, as if it's the first time she's said that out loud.

I want to reassure her that whatever her history is,

it's all fine with me. "That's okay. There's nothing wrong with that."

"I haven't been with anyone since my high school boyfriend. I mean, I kissed a few guys in college. And please don't go all protective caveman and get upset that I've kissed people. Because I'm not the Virgin Mary and don't want to be treated as such." She holds up a hand, dropping her vulnerable self to return to her tough-as-nails one.

"Duly noted."

"It's just that . . ."

"It's just what? There's nothing wrong with that. Unless it's for a particular reason?" I ask carefully, because we're treading on sensitive terrain.

She simply shrugs.

"Jill," I say, keeping my voice low but steady. I don't want to scare her. I don't want to let on exactly what I'd do to someone who hurt her. But I need to know. "Did this guy hurt you?"

"No," she says quickly, and she looks away from me. She swallows then looks back at me. "The opposite. I hurt him."

Her eyes are wet, and she looks like she's about to cry, and all my instincts in reading people's emotions are turned upside down right now because she's so hard to figure out. But I also know she'll only let me in so far at a time. "Do you want to talk about it?"

"I think that's all I can manage for now."

"Well, whatever it was, I think you have to forgive yourself for hurting him. I'm sure even if you did break his heart, or whatever happened, he's managed to move on. I did after Madeline. She's the reason I didn't want to go out with an actress again. We were very serious about each other, and then she left me in the lurch when her career took off."

"Would you think it's terrible that I'm glad she left you?" Then she moves in and silences any more conversation with a kiss. I can taste the Belvedere on her lips, and I can taste her, and it's the most delirious sensation in the world to have her here with me. She pulls away for a moment. "I know I said I didn't want anyone to see us kissing, but I hope there's no one here who knows us, because I've been wanting to do that since I walked in the door." It's one of the first times she's talked to me like this. As if she's shedding all the ways she protects herself. "I've been wanting to do that since my roommate helped me pick out this dress this afternoon. I've been wanting to do that since I thought about you on the way over in the car, like you wanted me to."

For a moment I feel as if the ground is swaying, as if we're being rocked by unexpected waves. I thought I could protect myself. I once stupidly thought I could stay away from her. I even toyed with the idea that I could keep this strictly physical. But the more I get to know her, the deeper I fall. She is the most complicated and sexy and beautiful and vulnerable woman I've ever met. Maybe she's hurt someone in the past, and maybe I'm next in line, but there's a part of me that is willing to sign up for it because it's impossible to stay away from her.

Especially when she gives me a very sexy grin. "Do you want to know what I'm wearing under this dress?"

"Now that you mention it, I think I'd like to find out." I slide my hand below the hem of the dress, feeling the soft naked skin of her legs under my calloused fingers. Then I move my hand to the underside of her thigh, taking my time as I explore, enjoying her invitation to find out what she has in store for me. I watch the expression on her face change as she hitches in her breath and parts her legs the slightest bit. She gives an audible gasp when I reach that delicious part on a woman's body when her leg meets her ass. Then I cup her between her legs, and she's naked against my hand, her body already hot and wet.

"Now you'll really see why I picked this table," I tell her.

24

JILL

I wonder if he knows I've shared more with him than with anyone else. That I give him more glimpses than I have anyone before. Maybe it's because sometimes I feel as if he can see inside me, as if he senses things about me and knows there's more than I've let on. I've kept my past with Aaron hidden—literally hidden, under lock and key—but he alone seems to be able to see through all my defenses, all the ways I've built up this persona, and he can gently pull back the curtain, bit by bit, in a way that doesn't rip me apart. Because he's so patently open with me.

No faking, no pretending. Only truth.

Which makes me wonder if that's why my body responds like it belongs to him. If there's more to this thing between us than just his amazing hands, or the way he kisses me both rough and tender, or how he talks dirty in one moment and then romantic the next.

I wonder if I'm feeling things for him that go

beyond these sensations that send me to another world with him.

But right now, I let go of all those questions because he's learning that I wore nothing for him, so he could do exactly this, so he could touch me under the table.

Then he removes his hand from under my dress and shoots me a mischievous grin.

"Um, hello," I say playfully. "Maybe you could put your hand back there. Not sure if you got the memo, but I kinda want you."

"I know," he says, leaning back against the gray leather and reaching for his scotch. "And I want something too. I want to know what you look like when you make yourself come."

A shiver runs through me. Is there anything this man can say that won't make my body high on him? "You're going to torture me."

"And you're going to torture me. But I know you like to touch yourself. And I bet you can do it quietly too."

"Why do you say that?"

He leans into me, twines his fingers into my hair once more, and I melt into his touch. "Because you have a roommate. Because you told me you read erotic novels. Because I bet you've learned how to make yourself come quietly."

My breath stills, and heat spreads through my body. "How do you do that? How do you just know things about me?"

"Because it's my job to understand people and emotions and secrets, and the things we do in the dark and the things we tell others and don't tell others.

That's why I do what I do. And I know you're absolutely turned on right now."

"How do you know?" I ask in a challenging voice, even though I'm sure I'm an open book.

He brushes my hair away from my shoulder, trails his tongue from my collarbone to my earlobe. "Because your cheeks have this pink glow, and your eyes go all hazy, and you part your lips, and I know it means you're aching for me to touch you," he says, and I can't help myself. I breathe harder and gasp out, "Oh God." Neither one of us is touching me right now, but I can feel how hot I'm getting between my legs, how I'm aching for pressure, for touch, for release. "Touch yourself," he commands.

I nod, close my eyes, and slip my hand under my dress until my fingers reach my wetness.

"Tell me how wet you are now."

"More than I've ever been," I say as a low moan escapes my lips.

He brings my face closer to his, so he's wrapped an arm around me, as if he's shielding me from anyone who might see or hear. "And how does it feel to have your fingers on your clit while I'm right here next to you, and I can smell how turned on you are?"

"Oh God," I gasp. He's sending me to another plane of pleasure with the way he strips me bare. I am burning all over, my whole body lit up by how he talks to me. "I'm so turned on."

"And have you masturbated thinking about me fucking you?"

"Yes," I say, as sparks of pleasure careen through my body with every dirty word from his mouth.

"And how do I do it?"

"Any way. You do it any and every way."

"Do I fuck you from behind? With you bent over the bed?"

"Yes."

"And do I fuck you up against the wall, with your legs wrapped around me?"

"Yes, yes, yes," I answer in heavy pants, my breath wildly erratic as electric heat ripples through my veins.

"And do you take me in your mouth?"

"God, yes. I want to do that to you. I want you to let me," I whisper to him in a hungry, needy voice, because he's driving me absolutely insane and to the far edge of pleasure.

He traces my top lip with his finger. "You think you'd like having my cock in your mouth?"

"Yes. I want to. I want to taste you," I say, then he slips his finger into my mouth and I close my lips around it.

"You're so close now to coming, aren't you?"

I breathe out a strangled yes, as he takes his finger away.

"I don't want anyone else to hear you," he says in a firm voice. "The noises you make are only for me."

"Yes." I'm barely in this restaurant anymore. I'm someplace else with him, a dark and desperate place, as he cups the back of my head and brings my face to his neck, so my mouth is near his ear. "Now pretend you're home, and you have to be quiet, but it's so fucking hard to be quiet, because you're picturing my cock in your mouth, and your beautiful lips wrapped around me."

It's all I can see, all I can picture, and I want to touch him, to know how hard he is, if he's as turned on as I am right now, because I'm well past caring about anything except the way my body screams for him. I could hike up my dress, unzip his pants, and slide on top of him right now. I could ride him right here in the far back corner of this too-cool-for-school restaurant and I honestly wouldn't care if anyone saw me, because I am mindless with my desire for him. I am adrift in lust, and all I want is release, and I start to cry out because it feels so good. But he silences me quickly, rasping his knuckles against my lips. "Bite down when you come."

And I do, as my fingers fly and an orgasm starts deep in my belly and then spreads through my body, making me quiver and shake and want to shout and moan and thrash, but instead I bite down on him to muffle my sounds as I shudder and come for him in the restaurant where we'll be eating dinner any minute.

Finally, when I can breathe and speak and recognize reality, I look at him, and he has the most satisfied grin on his face when he shows me the bite marks I left on his knuckles.

"I'm so sorry," I say.

"Don't ever be sorry for that." Then he takes my hand, and he presses it against his pants so I can feel his cock straining against the fabric. He unzips the fly, locks my fingers into his, and brings my hand inside his pants, then down his boxer briefs, and I nearly combust when I touch him for the first time. He's so hard and big and velvety smooth. He's throbbing in my hands, and I can tell how much he wants me to touch him.

"Let me," I plead.

He gives me a smirk, then shakes his head playfully as if I've been naughty.

"God, when are you going to sleep with me?" I ask because I'm so keyed up and so frustrated. "I want you inside me."

He removes my hand from his pants, zips them up, and fastens the button.

"When I can fuck you and make love to you at the same time, Jill. Because that's what I want from you," he says, so matter-of-factly he could be giving me a note on how to do a scene better in the show. This is what he wants. This is what he expects from me. This is what I'll have to deliver. "That's how I want to have you. Now it looks like our food is here, and I'm hungry."

The waiter serves our fish. Davis says thank you, and all I can do is mumble a thanks. He is so cool and collected and yet I'm the one who got off. This man vexes me with the way he takes care of me so thoroughly and protects his own heart so fiercely.

But then, I suppose I know what that's like. I've been doing it for years.

He slices his fish and spears a forkful. "Now, I want to ask you to go out with me again."

"A second date?" I ask, as he takes a bite of his dinner.

"Yes. Come with me to the Broadway Cares event."

"It's one thing for me to be at a restaurant with you. But there will be people there we know."

He huffs out a sigh. "Fine. You'll come in a restaurant for me, but you won't attend a formal event where I have to say a few words about the fundraising," he teases, shaking his head.

"It's not the same," I try to point out, but my argument seems invalid, even to me.

"You're right, Jill," he says, playing along, as he places his fork and knife down to take a drink. "That's why it's a good thing I have access to extra tickets. Perhaps you can go with Shelby, and I can look at you across the room and pretend I don't know what you look like and sound like and feel like when you come for me."

A charge races through me, and I'm about ready to grab him, pull him into the bathroom and insist on what I want right now. Instead, I try my hand at negotiation. "I'm pretty good at acting. Maybe I'll go and act as if I'm not dying to have you. Maybe then you'll finally let me."

The gauntlet is thrown.

25

DAVIS

Clay calls as I'm leaving Times Square subway station, heading up the steps to the street.

"Are you emailing me that new route to work? Because I'm walking precariously close to the Belasco in about thirty seconds when I cross Forty-Fourth Street," I say, and the funny thing is it wouldn't bother me if I bumped into Madeline.

"Man, you are just a tough bastard, aren't you? But that's not why I'm calling."

"Ah, you miss me, even though I saw you an hour ago at the gym," I joke, as the smell of pretzels wafts past me from a nearby street vendor.

"Yeah, exactly. So, I'm calling with a heads-up."

I groan. A heads-up is never good.

"Don is at the St. James already. He's got some film producers there to check out Patrick."

My shoulders tighten. "What? Nobody told me about this."

"It's the Pinkertons," he says, mentioning the names

of a pair of British brothers who bankroll films. "For the second picture in *Escorted Lives*."

"The first hasn't even started shooting yet. They're turning it into a trilogy already?"

"Books were so damn popular, the Pinkertons are doing all three. And there's a new-guy-in-town role for the second film, so they want to consider Patrick for it. You know his *Crash the Moon* contract is for ten months, so his agent brought in the producers since they're in town for a few days."

"Do they think they're going to watch the rehearsal? Because that's not how it works," I say firmly, my muscles tensing all over. "It's not a goddamn open rehearsal. If the film producers want to see him play Paolo, they buy a ticket to the show when it opens in two weeks."

"I know," Clay says, heaving a sigh. "I said the same thing to Don. But you know Don."

"Yeah, he's an ass. What's the deal? Is he in bed with the film producers? Is he getting a cut?"

"I think he's vying for some small producer credit on the film. That's why he brought them in. It should only be a few more minutes. He's got that understudy with him."

I stop in my tracks, feeling punched in the ribs. A woman in a suit and heels bumps into me, and I mutter an apology, then step into the doorway of Sardi's to get out of the way.

"That understudy?" I ask through clenched teeth.

"McCormick? Is that her name?"

"Jill McCormick." I shut my eyes. My blood feels

like it's boiling, and I don't know what pisses me off more—Don commandeering the stage or Jill not mentioning she'd be doing a scene with Patrick for the producers of a romantic movie.

Rationally, I know she'll play many romantic roles throughout her career. Logically, I would never do anything to stop her. But seeing as she's auditioning for all intents and purposes with *him,* I would have appreciated a heads-up from her. I don't know why she wouldn't tell me she was reading with him, but the omission sends a hot rush of jealousy through my veins.

"Patrick likes working with her, so he wanted to do a scene with her for the producers. Not from *Crash the Moon* though. Don't worry about that. They're just running lines from the next book."

"Oh great," I say sarcastically. "That just makes it all fucking better."

"Yeah, sorry, man." But he doesn't know the half of why I'm angry. "And listen, I know you can't stand Don. But the show opens in two weeks, so if you could do your best to let this go that would help me a ton as I work on what's next for you. Got a few possibilities I'm working on. Maybe some *Twelfth Night* in London. Maybe a film."

"Let me know what you come up with. I'm always ready for the next challenge."

I resume my path to the theater. I turn into the alley, and Don is walking toward me with the Pinkertons. Don smiles broadly, and I seethe inside, but do my best to follow Clay's advice. "Davis," he calls out as if we're pals happy to see each other. "Have you met Nicholas and Jonathan Pinkerton?"

I extend a hand, keeping my anger tightly wrapped inside as I meet the two brothers. "Pleasure to meet you both."

Jonathan Pinkerton shakes my hand enthusiastically and beams a bright smile that takes me by surprise. "I'm a huge fan of your work," Jonathan says. "I've seen all your shows on Broadway. *South Pacific*, and *Anything for You*, and *The Saying Goes*. Loved your film too. And I also saw *World Enough and Time* at La Jolla. Thought it was utterly brilliant."

I'm taken aback. I didn't expect Pinkerton to be anything but a dick. But then, that's because he's guilty by association with Don in my book. "Thank you very much."

"I've often thought that play would make a wonderful film adaptation," he says, glancing up pensively at the gray February sky. Then he begins reciting lines from the Andrew Marvelle poem. "*Had we but world enough, and time. This coyness, Lady, were no crime. We would sit down and think which way to walk and pass our long love's day.*"

I flash back to the play. To Madeline playing the lead role. To the days and nights when those lines and many others from the play were all I lived and breathed. When I felt that way for her. Now, three years later, the lines are only lines, the memory just that. Only a memory, and it doesn't hurt anymore.

"Helluva poem," I say, because it's true, and because that's all the poem is anymore.

Nicholas gives me a serious look. "You know, Mr. Milo. We should talk about you turning that into a film quite soon. Shall we set up a meeting for later this week?"

"Absolutely," I say, and I'm honestly not sure how the morning is working itself into such a strange turn of events. I've gone from being blindsided, to being offered a possible next job. But the fact is, I need to think about what I want to do next. The work of a director is done once the show opens. The actors keep it going, and I move on to the next job.

Don and the Pinkertons walk away, and I head inside the theater as Patrick and Jill leave the stage. The guilty look in her eyes makes my heart stop, but she's desperately trying to make eye contact with me, and she's mouthing the words *I didn't know* under her breath.

Patrick calls out to me. "Milo!"

He has such a bright smile that he makes it nearly impossible to dislike him. Especially when I can't let my professional side pander to my personal one. "Hey! That was totally last minute. Agent called late last night since the Pinkertons were in town, and Don okayed it. Hope you don't mind us using the stage for it."

"Of course not, Patrick," I say, in my calmest voice because the last thing I need is for Patrick to be anything other than happy. He's a linchpin in this show, and if I want it to be the hit it can be, I have to make sure the leading man has no clue I've dreamed of all the ways I can take him out of the running with Jill. "The stage is always available for you."

"You're the best, man."

Then he bounds down the hall to his dressing room, singing a cappella to a Jack Johnson tune about beaches and sunny skies. I turn around to see Jill standing in the hallway. "I tried to call you this morning to tell you," she says quietly so no one else can hear.

"You did?"

"Yeah. About thirty minutes ago. I got a crazy call this morning from my agent to be here, so I rushed to get ready, and I called you when I was in a cab. But you didn't pick up."

"Must have been on the subway."

"I would have told you. You have to know that, Davis." There's real worry in her voice that she might have crossed some sort of line. The genuine concern in her eyes erases all my irritation from before. Then it hits me, like a blow I didn't see coming—she can do this to me. She has this power over me. She alone has a direct line to my heart. Where I was jealous and angry minutes ago, now I am reduced to an all too familiar feeling when I'm with her.

The feeling of not wanting to be without her.

I press a hand against the wall, and curse under my breath.

"Are you okay?" She lays a hand on my arm.

No. I'm totally screwed.

I momentarily flash on Ryder's words before dinner —*have some fucking fun*. He could probably already tell that it was more than fun for me. That it was fun, and much more than I expected.

"Yeah. Just need to get started. That little stunt cut

into the day." I push all my frustration onto Don, even though it's with me and with how I feel for her. I head for the stage, leaving her behind. I need to focus on getting this show ready, because that's why I'm here. Not for any other reason.

* * *

Everyone is gone now. I'm sitting on the edge of the stage, and Jill's walking down the aisle of the theater for one of our last private rehearsals.

"Are you still mad at me?" she asks in a small, nervous voice when she reaches me. It's the first time we've been alone today. The theater is quiet and her footsteps echo.

"I was never really mad at you."

She holds up her thumb and forefinger. "Just a tiny bit?"

I run a hand through my hair. "Just annoyed in general," I admit. "But I'm not anymore." I pat the edge of the stage. "Come here."

She hops up on the stage and sits next to me. She fidgets with the cuffs on her sweater. Rolling them up. Pushing them down. "I was worried all day."

"You were?" There's a part of me that's glad she felt that way, though I know that makes me seem cruel. But it gives me a flicker of hope that maybe this isn't a one-way street.

"I don't want you to be mad at me and think things with Patrick . . ." She doesn't finish the thought.

I want to ask if she's still in love with him. I want to

know if he's still on her mind all the time. But I also know I can't handle the answer if it's yes. I can't keep going there.

"Jill, if you have a chance to act in a film when your contract is up, and that's what you want, you should pursue it. Even if it's with him." I focus on the professional side of things, though it takes every ounce of my strength to get those words out without sounding like a jerk.

"Can I ask you a question? Why are you so nice to him? I know how you really feel about him. But you're always so nice to him, like this morning in the hallway."

"Because that's what he needs to perform," I say, as if the answer is obvious. But it's only obvious to me, because this is the way I work. This is the way I manage actors to get the best from them. "I know Patrick. I've worked with him. He's one of those people who was born skipping, and he's an amazing talent, and he needs to be happy all the time. That's what he needs to give the best performances. And that's what I want."

"The best performance?" She raises an eyebrow, as if she's considering this for the first time.

"Yes. Of course, I want the best performance. Nothing less."

"So why did you tell Alexis that day at the studio that she was your Ava?"

"You heard me say that?"

She nods.

"Because that's what *she* needs." I run my index finger along her face. Her skin is so soft, and it's impossible not to touch her. A soft sigh escapes her lips.

"So, you give her what she needs?"

"Look," I say firmly. "Alexis needs to feel as if she's the center of the universe. That's how she gives the best performance that her fans love. But even though I told her she was meant to play Ava, that doesn't change that you're the one I wanted *more* for the part. But that's what I had to tell her to get her to deliver for me."

"So, you play us all?"

I give her a look as if she can't be serious. "Is that what you think I'm doing to you?"

I shake my head. Because I don't want to think he'd do that. I can't even contemplate that he'd toy with me.

"Jill, you have to know I'm not playing you," he says in his cool and controlled voice. He's the consummate pro now. The man who wins awards and rains money down on the show's backers. He's not talking to me as a lover. He's talking to me as a director. "But this is how I work, and every actor needs something different."

"What do I need then, as an actress?" I want to know how he categorizes me. He's brilliant at his job, and I want to understand how he does it. How he knows what we need. How he makes us give it to him. How he drives us to work harder for him.

"You," he says, then stares out at the audience as if he'll find the answer there in the vast expanse of empty chairs. In the row after row of red upholstered seats that will creak and groan with theatergoers in two more weeks. With patrons who will never know the blood, sweat, and tears that were shed on the path to opening night, but will hopefully fall in love with the artifice that seems real. "You need someone to see you. To know you. To understand you. That's what makes you so good in this role. Ava needs so many of the same things, and that's why you connect with her character."

I am reminded of the day he told me the news. Of the time we had drinks and talked about what he saw in me when I played Eponine. Maybe it sounds vain, maybe it sounds egotistical, but it thrills me deep in my heart and soul to know that he admires my talent. That he thinks I have talent. That he thinks I'm more than good enough. This is what I've always wanted, to be able to move people with a performance.

I swivel around so I'm sitting cross-legged, and I take his hand in mine. "It means the world to me that you gave me this chance. You know that right?"

"Of course I know that," he says in a callous voice that surprises me. Maybe he'd rather not hear how much I admire his work. Maybe what he wants from me right now is something I'm not sure how to give.

"Now let's get to work because if I spend all night talking to you, we'll never get this show ready. I want to work on the scene where Paolo finally breaks down Ava. Where he gets her to open up to him and admit all her truths about being alone her whole life, and he helps her make the best art."

Breaks down Ava. Those words reverberate in my head. Paolo breaks down Ava, and there's a voice inside me, a quiet little voice that's asking if Davis is doing the same to me. If that's how he's getting what he needs from this actress.

But maybe I want to be broken down.

We are oddly silent as we pack up three hours later. I grab my coat and my purse, and he gathers his phone and his notes, and the silence between us is full of unsaid things. As if neither one of us knows what happens next. Do we go our separate ways, or do we find a way to reconnect after we leave the theater together? I want to say something, to ask a question, to make a joke. But I don't know where to start. I don't know what's happening with us.

Then my stomach growls loudly as if it's an ornery creature begging for food, and he laughs deeply. It's the first time I've heard him laugh like this, the kind of laugh that takes over your body.

"Do I need to feed you?" he asks in that playful way he has, and I can't help but smile and crack up too.

"Evidently, I could really go for a burger and fries. Would you care to take me out on another date?"

His eyes light up, and whatever sadness filled the day is wiped out in that grumbling sound. I'd like to send a thank-you note to my hungry belly for giving me a reason to spend more time with him. Time away from the play. "Yes."

At the diner, we talk more, and I ask him questions about all the shows he's done, and he tells me about his productions, sharing stories and anecdotes. I love hearing him talk about what he loves, and as he does, I realize that what he does for me is much more lasting than what a handsome actor in *Wicked* did for seven-teen-year-old me. That idealized man smoothed over my pain and gave me hope that there would still be love in my life.

But this man is changing me. The protective layer between the world and me has been cracking, but it's just now that I want to hurry it, not hold it back. I want to be my true self, and I want people to see my true self. Like Davis had said . . . I want to be seen.

And I don't know what the hell to do next.

"What are you thinking?" he asks, as he bends his head to kiss my neck. A soft kiss. A sweet kiss.

That you make me feel all sorts of things. That everything with you scares the hell out of me. That I don't know how to hide or pretend this isn't happening anymore.

"That these fries are awesome. Did you know they're my favorite food?"

"Ah. You say that as if you let me in on your darkest secret. But I suspect that's not what you were thinking."

"Chinese food is actually my favorite. Cold sesame noodles," I say. Then I look away and he pets my hair. "But, that's not what I was thinking."

"What were you thinking about?"

I can't tell him my darkest secret. I can't tell him all that I'm feeling. I'm not even sure what this is, or what it could be. But I manage one small step.

"You," I whisper, and he leans his forehead against mine, sighing deeply as I trace the ends of his hair with my fingers. "I was thinking about you. I think about you all the time," I say, and the admission terrifies me, but it also makes me feel lighter. Like I can start to have all the things I've denied myself. All the real things.

"You do?"

"Yes. So much it scares me," I say, and my throat hitches, but I keep it together.

"It's okay to be scared. It's okay to feel," he says in a soft, tender voice. It's such a contrast to how he spoke to me back at the theater.

And because he's done so much for me, I need to do something for him. Something that will be good for me too. Something necessary. "I was never dating Patrick. We only spent time as friends. But I'm not going to anymore."

He tries to fight a smile, but it's no use. The smile owns him. He glances away then back at me at last, uttering a confident "good."

"It is good," I second.

I pull back and look at him, seeing him in a newer light than before. He's always been heart-stoppingly gorgeous with his dark hair, ink blue eyes, and strong jawline. But he's beautiful in a different way now. Because I know who he is, beyond the man in the second row of the St. James Theater who called me in for the chance of a lifetime. That chance still exists though, and I need to protect it. "We still have to be careful at the event this weekend, okay? I don't want people to talk about me. We can't arrive together, and we can't leave together."

"Can I get you a dress, though?" He looks so hopeful, like he's been dying to do this for me.

"You don't have to do that. I can find something to wear."

"I know you *can*, Jill. I know you're perfectly capable of doing everything on your own. And I know I don't have to. But I *want* to do something special for you."

"Then I would love to see what you choose for me. Because everything you do for me is special. That's why I'm going to do what I need to do tomorrow. For me, and for us."

There's that smile again, and I think I might have made him the happiest I've ever seen him. Then he smothers me in a kiss that makes me forget we are in a public place. But there's a part of me that no longer cares.

I trot up the steps to the stage door, light-footed considering I'm going to friend zone possibly the nicest guy on earth. I head down the carpeted hallway to his dressing room and hear The Black Eyed Peas "I Gotta Feeling" before I get there. It's just what I'd expect him to listen to. The happy guy who needs to be in a good mood all the time.

I tap on the half-open door, and Patrick waves me in. "Jill! Come in."

"Hey!" I copy his tone, then bring it down. "I need to tell you that I won't be able to go to mini-golf with you."

"That's all right. We can reschedule."

"Actually . . ." It's hard to keep the smile completely from my face. "I've started seeing someone. So probably best if I give it a miss."

"Oh." He seems a little perturbed. Then his expression clears, and he points at me with a grin. "I thought you had a happy glow about you."

"So, we're good?" I bite my lip. "Because I have had fun with you."

He gets up from his chair to give me a hug. "I had a good time too. And I think it's great you found someone who makes you so happy. And we can still mini-golf. We'll just get a group together. Problem solved."

"Problem solved," I agree with a grin as happy as his.

And loose end knotted.

The cream-colored box from Neiman Marcus is so stunning I don't want to ruin the beautifully tied bow by opening it. But I'm the kid at Christmas, and I'm dying to know what he picked out. I tug on one end of the gold-trimmed bow, undoing the knot and tossing it on my couch. Excitement races through me as I wiggle off the top, then unfold the tissue paper carefully.

I gasp and bring my hand to my mouth.

"Oh my God," I say out loud.

I'm home alone and grateful because I need to have a moment with this dress. I lift it up, reverently, because I've never had a dress like this, and then I stand and hold it against me, running my hand along the sapphire fabric, savoring the hourglass shape. I'm about to go check it out in the mirror on my closet door, when I see a note in the box. Gingerly, I lay the dress down then reach for the note. It's on stiff cardboard, and I open it. Butterflies make a quick visit to my belly, but I shoo them away. I want to know what he's written.

I've never had so much as a text message from him, so I don't know what to expect.

For the most beautiful and captivating woman I know. And hope to know.
    Davis

My heart leaps to my throat, and all my instincts tell me to shut it down. To run. To *act*. A million malformed ideas invade my brain on how to pretend, avoid, hide. My heart knocks hard against my chest like it wants so desperately to escape, to stop the flood of feelings this note has unleashed.

But then I flash onto the show I'm doing in one more week. Onto the role I'll be ready to step into at a moment's notice. Into Ava. I picture the moments when she lets Paolo in. I see the scenes play out in my mind when she finally can move past the physical and accept all that he wants from her—for her art, for her love.

I close my eyes, take a deep breath, and remind myself that I am like her. She is strong. She is brave. She is more than the damage she's done. I open my eyes, run my fingers over his words then tuck the note safely into my purse. This note won't be locked away. This note will stay with me.

* * *

I gather a small section of the fabric on the skirt as I

walk up the red-carpeted steps of the Plaza Hotel on Friday night. I'm in shoes my size. Shoes I bought for myself—my own Louboutins. I wanted to have something I chose for me, even though I can't fault Davis's taste. It's impeccable.

A man in a black jacket with gold piping stands elegantly by the Roman columns, then quickly reaches for the door and opens it for us with a grand gesture.

Shelby and I walk inside the luxury hotel, and I'm immediately assaulted with images of *Eloise, The Great Gatsby,* and the history of this icon of New York City. I imagine all the other men and women, in evening dresses and tuxes, who've walked through this lobby as we do, across the polished tiles on the floor, the red leaf pattern on the carpet, and through the French doors of the Palm Court to the Terrace Room just beyond.

An attendant takes our coats, and Shelby gives me another once-over, shaking her head in admiration.

"If I had your body, I'd wear a Herve Leger form-fitting bandage dress too," she says.

"Oh stop. You have a perfect body. You're a Broadway baby, just like me. We have to look good," I say playfully.

Naturally, Shelby begins humming *Lullaby of Broadway*, and I join in, but then our little rendition fades out as we head into the Terrace Room. I've been in the Plaza. I've had high tea in the Palm Court. I even stayed in this hotel one night with my mom when we went on a shopping trip when I was a little girl. But I've never entered this room as a guest at a formal event, and the word *awestruck* takes on a new meaning.

Soft light from crystal chandeliers bathes the opulent room in a warm glow. The walls are lined with replicas of Italian Renaissance-style paintings, while the archways that ring the main floor bring majesty to this jewel of a room. Steps on each side lead up to another level that wraps the main area so you can stand at the railing and watch the mingling, the dancing, the champagne-drinking, and all the beautiful people below.

We walk down the steps, and I spy all sorts of Broadway star wattage, from my idol Audra McDonald to one of my favorite actors of all time, Michael Cerveris. There are producers and agents, choreographers, and music directors, and of course, the money men and women who make the shows go round. I even spy Joyelle Kristy, a rising film starlet who played a leather-clad superhero in a hit film and is said to be on the hunt for a juicy theater role so she can follow in Scarlett Johansson's footsteps.

"Fancy meeting you here."

I turn, and it's Reeve. He told me he'd be attending when we worked out yesterday morning.

"Hey gorgeous," I say, and give him a quick kiss on the cheek then introduce him to Shelby. Reeve is joined shortly by Sutton Brenner, the casting director and the woman who stole his heart.

"So good to see you again, Jill," she says in her crisp, British accent, and leans in to give me cheek kisses. "How's everything going with *Crash the Moon*? We're so excited for opening night, and I know you're going to be the best one in the whole show."

"Well, I'm only in the chorus."

She blows air through her lips as if to dismiss the thought. "That's where all the stars begin, my darling. And I have no doubt yours will be the brightest on all Broadway. I can't wait."

"Do you ladies need a beverage?" Reeve suggests and nods to the bar. We follow him, and I want to tease him that he's now flanked by three women, but then I see Davis talking to a woman with dark hair and a fabulous figure, his hand is on her elbow. I'm about to get all territorial, until I realize they have the same cheekbones.

She must be his sister.

But I don't spend much time appraising her because he's so sexy and so sophisticated in his tux, and when I see him in it, I swear that tuxes were made for men like him. My blood heats as I look him over, and even from across this spacious room, with all these people between us, and the piped-in show tunes playing overhead, and the twinkling lights, I can't help but want to be all alone with him. Can he feel the pull through the crowd? Sense that I'm here, wearing the dress he picked out for me? Goosebumps rise on my skin as I remember the last time I walked into a public place and he looked me over as if he would only ever have eyes for me. I lick my lips briefly at the memory, and it's then that he happens to look up from his sister and notice me. He raises an eyebrow ever so slightly and shoots me a quick grin, but then returns his attention to her as I make my way to the bar.

"Isn't it great that he'll be coming back to New York soon?"

"Hmm?" I ask, when I realize Shelby's been chatting with me the whole time as we weave through the sea of Broadway beautiful and benefactors alike.

"My boyfriend. From Los Angeles. Hello, earth to Jill?"

I shake my head, as if I can quiet all these thoughts of Davis. I tell myself the curtains are rising, and I am shedding myself and becoming a character. Tonight I'm playing the part of someone who has supreme focus on her friends, not on the man across the room who has slowly, carefully, wonderfully worked his way into her heart.

"That's awesome. I'm sure you're totally psyched," I say.

"He's going to concentrate on his commercial work and voiceovers for a while since pilot season didn't pan out."

"That's too bad about pilot season, but it'll be nice for you to see him," I say, and then Reeve turns around and hands me a champagne glass. The bubbles tickle my nose, but it tastes crisp and light.

Then I can feel a tingling in my neck, and a quick ribbon of desire unspools in me. For the briefest of moments, fingertips graze the skin on my back exposed by the V in the dress. But then they're phantom fingers, and they're no longer on me. I turn around, and Davis is at the far end of the bar, his back to me, as he chats with Michael Cerveris.

How does he do that? Just set me aflame with one

touch? I down the rest of my champagne, and Shelby gives me a wide-eyed look.

"I'm thirsty," I say. "I need another."

"You go, girl," she says, "Besides, I see Jane Black setting up over there for her set. I worship the ground her high-heeled boots walk on, so I need to go kowtow."

"She's pretty rocking," I say, referring to the singer who just won a Grammy for an absolutely epic breakup album she wrote. Reeve and Sutton are engrossed in each other's company, so I squeeze past a gray-haired man in a double-breasted suit and snag a spot near the end of the bar so I can people watch.

"I'd love to see your band," Davis says to Michael in his smooth and friendly voice. "Heard great things about Loose Cattle. Great name, by the way."

I smile privately as Davis talks to actors in his professional demeanor, and I feel like I have a delicious secret because I know all the other things he says. I know how sexy his voice is when he tells me how to touch myself, I know how it goes low and husky when he's taking my clothes off, I know how he can be sweet and tender when he's tucking a strand of hair behind my ear and asking to see me again.

I know how he sounds when he's not the director.

When he's not the man in the tux.

When he's not this incredibly powerful presence in the world of New York City performing arts.

I know how rough and hungry he gets when he's desperate for me to want him as much as he wants me.

"Absolutely. Next Thursday, I'll be there," he says,

then he shakes Michael's hand and turns to me. "Oh, by the way, Michael. Do you know Jill McCormick? She's the understudy for Alexis in *Crash the Moon*."

Michael takes my hand and gives me a quick peck. "Alexis?" He raises an eyebrow. "My condolences," he teases. "But it's a pleasure to meet you, and may she give you no trouble at all."

"Good to meet you as well," I say, avoiding my least favorite topic—Alexis.

"And on that note, I should go prepare for my song with Ms. Black."

"A duet with Ms. Black? How lucky can we possibly be?" Davis says to Michael, as if they know something I don't.

Then Michael says a quick goodbye, and it's just us at the bar. Well, us and five hundred other people. But he's the only one I notice.

"I knew you'd look stunning in this dress," he says casually as he surveys the room, standing side to side by me, so he's not looking at me. He's playing by my rules, acting as if we're two colleagues who happen to be checking out the human scenery at this gala. He speaks as if he's saying something as mundane as *nice weather*, but that's why it's such a turn-on, because it's our secret. "And the slit up the side could come in handy."

I bite my lip, so I don't start breathing loudly from all these excruciatingly delicious feelings racing through my bloodstream and turning me all the way up. I try to gather myself, to play it as cleverly as he is.

"Yes. You never know when you might have to run,"

I fire back, as if the quip can help me regain the equilibrium, but then I'm face to face with him and it's as if all the air has been sucked out of the room, everything has stopped, and no one is moving, and it's just us. I want to run my hand across his face, and play with the collar on his shirt, then smooth out the lapel. I want to slide my hand inside the jacket, touch his back. I want to mark him, so everyone knows this man is taken. This man is mine.

For a second I can't breathe when the realization hits me: I want him to be mine.

"Don't run on me," he says in a casual voice, but I know there's real meaning beneath it.

"I won't."

He takes a step closer. "I fucking want you so much," he whispers in a rough scrape, and heat surges through me, centering between my legs. I'm sure my cheeks are turning that rosy pink that lets him know I feel completely the same, and I'm about to inch closer to feel more of this heat, when I see another blonde approaching him. It takes me a few seconds to place her, but when I do my veins turn to ice, and I'm sure my mouth is hanging open.

She's so gorgeous, and she's so poised, with perfect cheekbones, deep brown eyes that could melt any man's cold heart, and the body of a Victoria's Secret angel. She stops at Davis and flashes a classy smile.

"What a delight to see you again, Davis." Then before he can even respond, she leans in and gives him a kiss on the cheek. I'd love to peel her off of him, but

I'm too shocked to say anything, too embarrassed to even move.

"Madeline," he says coolly, as if he's completely unsurprised to see her.

"I just arrived in town two days ago to start rehearsals for the Steve Martin play."

He nods. I seem to recall her being cast, but I didn't pay much attention. Then he introduces me, and it's as if I'm having an out-of-body experience, because everything about this moment is completely surreal. Davis, introducing me to the woman he was once in love with. The actress he fell hard for. The person who single-handedly broke his heart. I'm split between the desire to throttle her for hurting him, and the bizarre wish to thank her for leaving him so that I could have him now.

Instead, I simply go along with the pleasantries, shaking *her* hand. It's a lovely hand, a soft hand, but I still feel as if I'm touching an eel because it's *her* hand. She shoots me a gorgeous smile, and it's almost enough to seem real, but I can tell it's her red-carpet smile, her professional smile. That's all. Nothing more. She doesn't even say *Nice to meet you*. Her focus is only on Davis, yet she's not looking at him as a former lover. Instead, she seems all business.

"Have the Pinkertons gotten in touch with you about . . ." She pauses and shifts her eyes to me as if she doesn't want to say what it's about, and I get the message. She doesn't want me around for their work conversation. "Because I think it sounds like a brilliant idea."

"Yes, they have."

"Well?"

I'm so agitated right now that I need to make an exit. "Oh, look. I see my friend Reeve. I need to catch up with him about where we're running tomorrow."

And I walk away, pushing past other people. A tiny bead of sweat slides down my spine, and I doubt it's because I'm hot. It's more because I'm embarrassed. She's the woman who wrecked him. She's the reason he didn't want to date me. She's here, and she has something private to discuss with him.

I bump into Alexis.

She rolls her eyes. "You're here?"

"Honestly. Don't start, Alexis. Now is not the time."

I continue on, looking for Reeve or Shelby, but I don't see either of my friends. I figure a bit of fresh air would do me good. I eye the doorway and count down the seconds till I reach it, like I'm finishing a marathon, when Davis's sister cuts me off. It's like I'm being cornered everywhere I go.

"Hi. I'm Michelle Milo," she says and extends a hand. First Madeline. Now Michelle. Women connected to Davis everywhere I turn. It's like whiplash. I don't know why I thought it would be a good idea to attend this event.

"Hi, Michelle. I'm Jill. I'm in the show."

"I know who you are," she says, and then she rests her palm against my arm and it's a strange gesture. But she tips her forehead to the stairs, suggesting we go up to the second level. I go along with her.

"Listen, I know how my brother feels about you."

"What?" I don't have to act confused, because I am. I'm surprised he'd talk to anyone.

"You have to know he's the most important person in the world to me. The last thing I want is for him to be hurt again. If you're not serious about him, if this is some kind of career move, if you're going to use him, then please, I'm asking you, woman to woman, to leave him now."

I feel like she just dropped from the sky, like she's some sort of benevolent superhero, because there's something kind in her voice. Kind, but determined.

"I don't know what to say."

"If you care about my brother at all, please think seriously about what you're doing," she implores me. "I don't want him to go through that again. He doesn't do anything halfway, Jill. He doesn't do his job halfway, and he doesn't do relationships halfway. He's nothing or he's all in. So, unless you're there with him, unless you're all in, please get out before you hurt him."

I glance over at Davis, and he's still with Madeline. We're too far away for me to guess at what they're saying, but he's not trying to get away from her, and he's not looking for me.

"I don't want to hurt him. I care about him. But he's with her right now."

Michelle narrows her eyes. She looks like she's about to bum rush Madeline and tackle her from behind.

Then a loud voice fills the room. "What an honor to be here tonight."

Michelle and I turn to the small stage to see Jane

Black with a microphone in hand. "I'm still waiting for my chance to star in a Broadway musical, so any of you big name producers, just call me up. Nah, I'm just kidding. I'm all about the singing, and tonight we have a very special song for tonight's event. Have you all heard of this musical *Once*?"

The crowd cheers its answer, and Michelle claps half-heartedly too, as she scans the room for her brother. I don't see him or Madeline, and my heart goes cold with the possibility that they could be alone together.

"I thought you might have," Jane continues. "Would anyone want to hear Tony Award-winning Broadway star Michael Cerveris, who originated the role of Tommy, sing a bit of 'Falling Slowly' with me?"

The room erupts into a chorus of yeses.

"Well, you should all grab a girl, grab a guy, grab a friend, and dance."

Then Michael joins Jane on stage. He has a guitar slung around his chest and begins plucking the first notes from the romantic song first made famous in the movie before it became a musical. The notes pierce me, even in the midst of all this strangeness— Michelle's protective warnings, and Madeline's appearance out of nowhere—and now two gorgeous voices stamp out all the confusion and I feel the music doing what it does. Touching me, even though I don't want to be affected by anything right now. As Jane's gorgeous voice fills the room, Michael's beautiful baritone layering into hers, I see Davis walking toward me. Purposefully, deliberately, with a sly little grin on his fabulous face. He walks up the steps and finds me with Michelle.

"Michelle, I'm going to need to take Jill away from you right now."

He turns to me and offers his hand. "Dance with me." He holds my gaze with his deep blue eyes and says it with such tenderness that I simply nod a yes. He takes my hand, and pulls me away from his sister, and soon my hands are on his shoulders and his are on my waist.

"Are you enjoying yourself?"

"No."

"Why not?"

"Why do you think? Because of *her*."

"It was about work. The Pinkertons are considering doing a movie of *World Enough and Time* and they approached me about directing, and they're talking to Madeline about reprising her role."

"Do you want to do it?"

"I'm not sure. That's what Madeline was asking me about. She was trying to convince me, but I'm not entirely sure I want to go back to something I've already worked on."

"Was she convincing?" I ask and I can't hide the jealousy.

"Are you jealous?"

"Yes," I say, letting my irritation show. I want him to know that I don't like her being around. He's mine.

"Why?"

"Why do you think?"

"Say it, Jill."

I sigh heavily, then manage to get the words out. "Because I don't want anyone else to have you. Just like how you feel about me."

He lowers his voice more, his words only for me. "Nobody else has me. Nobody else will. Nobody else can."

I close my eyes for a moment. There are too many warring emotions in me, battling with each other. "Your sister told me to stay away from you," I tell him, because I know he loves his sister, but I want to know, too, that he disagrees with her directive.

"Did she?"

I nod as we sway in a small circle.

"Are you going to stay away?"

"It doesn't seem that way, does it?"

"Don't stay away," he says, his strong hand on my waist bringing me closer.

"I should ignore your sister?" I challenge. I don't like all these women who have their hooks in him in different ways.

"Ignore her."

"What about Madeline?"

"It's just work. I don't feel anything for her anymore. How could I?" he asks with such certainty, such confidence. "Everything I feel is for you."

A heady feeling swoops through me, and I don't know what it is. It feels like I'm flying and being cut open at the same time. As if I can feel all the good things and all the awful things at once. I don't know what's going on, especially since he moves his hand from my waist to the open V on my back. He doesn't say anything, and my mouth is too dry to speak. He strokes my back with his finger, sending shivers radiating across my skin.

"You're touching me," I say in a low voice, as Jane and Michael sing about falling so deeply you can't go back. The song might as well have been written for me right now. I can't go back to who I was, that carefully constructed self. But more than that, I don't *want* to return to the Jill I was before. I have to be this new person who doesn't have a mask or a costume to hide behind. If I want to have the things on the other side, I have to start anew. "Do you think everyone knows?" I ask.

"Knows what?"

"How we feel."

"How do you feel?"

"I think you know," I say, and we haven't once looked away from each other. The connection between us is so intense it's like nothing else exists but us and this tiny little patch of the Terrace Room where we barely move our feet, and dancing is just a euphemism for being able to touch each other in public, even if it's only a hand on a shoulder. But that bit of contact with him makes me tipsy.

"I think I'd rather hear it from you."

"Davis," I say, but that's all. I can't get any more words out.

"This song," he says, and now there's a touch of nerves in his voice. But he pushes through them. "This song is for you. I asked them to sing it for you."

And that's when I know. I feel it all through my

body and my heart and my mind. I feel *everything*. Like all the pieces of pretend that encased my heart shear off and splinter, leaving me with only the real thing. Because these words, this song about two people falling in love, is all too true, and all too real. There's nothing fake about it, and nothing happening from afar. It's happening right here, to me, and I can barely comprehend how I might feel when there are no more walls. But I need him. I need to be close to him. I need to touch him.

"I can't be on this dance floor with you right now." I can hardly get air. I'm overcome with all these feelings crashing through my body.

"Are you okay?"

"I need to be alone with you for a minute."

He places a hand on my lower back and guides me out of the Terrace Room, down the hall and to a nearby bathroom. He opens the door, shuts, and locks it. He looks me over like he wants to kiss me senseless from head to toe. Everything is electric between us as I wait in that sliver of a moment for him.

Then he leans into me, pushes one strap off my shoulder and kisses my bare skin. I am lightheaded and woozy. I want so much more, but even the slightest touch sends me into another world. He rains hot, shivery kisses all along my shoulder and to my neck, blazing a trail up to my ear.

"Are you finally going to put me out of my misery?" I might be begging, but I don't care. I'm beyond ready for him. The question is—is he ready for me?

His lips brush my earlobe, and I think he's about to

whisper a *yes* in my ear. Instead, he breaks the contact and pulls back to look at me, his dark eyes seeing me as I truly am. As the woman who wants only him. He finally knows it, and finally believes it. He is as stripped bare as I am right now with this consuming need for each other. I am on edge, holding my breath for an answer.

"Yes. Tonight."

Tonight.

It's finally going to happen. The possibility of being with him is terrifying and thrilling at the same time. Then we smash into each other and we kiss in a frenzy, as if we are claiming each other, marking this moment when everything is so completely clear between us. His hands are on my face instantly, and his tongue is searching my lips, my mouth, and I can't get enough of him. I want to crawl up him, and wrap my legs around him, and slam him into me. Instead, he pushes me against the wall, trapping me with his body, the way I like it.

"I like it when you do that," I whisper.

"I know."

He presses against me, and the feel of him is extraordinary. Even while standing, I love the pressure and weight of him. He runs his hands from my neck down to my breasts, then he turns me around and I'm looking at the mirror. He kneels behind me, so I can't see him. I tremble with anticipation, then I feel his breath along my calf, and he's kissing his way up my leg, stopping to trace his tongue along the back of my knee in such a delicious way that sparks of heat shoot across my body. Now, he's bunching up the fabric of my dress at my waist and he kisses my thigh. He reaches my ass, and I cry out because everything he does feels so incredible, especially as he runs the tip of his tongue along one cheek, then flicks it against my lace panties. I bow my back, giving him better access for anything and everything he wants.

"Whatever you're doing feels amazing," I say between broken breaths.

"Good. That's how it should feel." Then he stands, moves his hands to my hips, and yanks me against him. I start to circle my hips without being aware of it. I want him so badly, and he knows it. He knows what he does to me, and he enjoys it as he hooks his arm between my legs, his fingers touching me through my panties. I shudder, and desire spreads through my whole body, as if every cell is comprised solely of the dark craving to be touched by him.

"Look at yourself," he says, grabbing my wrists and pinning them above my head. I look at my reflection. My face is flushed, and my hair is wild, and my lips have that just-been-kissed look.

"I look like I've just been fucked," I say.

"No. That's how you'll look later tonight, when this damn event is over, and I can take you out of here and finally have you the way I want," he says, and an image of later, of him inside me, flashes by, making me hotter. Then he lowers his voice. "The way you want too."

"I do. I do want that," I say, breathless with my need for him.

"Now press your hands against the mirror because I

want us both to watch you as you come," he tells me, and I do. Then, I hear him unzip his pants, and soon I can feel him press his erection against my backside. God, he feels amazing, and reflexively, I push back, trying desperately to lure him in for more contact. "Please," I whimper.

"Jill," he says, tsk-tsking me. "I promise you, there will be plenty of time for that. But I'll give you an idea."

Then, maybe just to tease me, he slides his cock between my legs, and I nearly scream. It feels so good to have him against me, even for one brief moment, and I am absolutely aching to be filled up by him. But all he gives me is that—a taste, before he returns to that tantalizing way of holding me tight, his hard length against me, taunting me with what I want.

"Oh, Jill. The things I'm going to do to you," he says, as if he's simply musing on the topic.

"What are you going to do to me?"

Holding my wrists firmly in place, he dips his other hand inside my panties, and rubs his finger in dizzying circles against me. Then proceeds to tell me what he'll do.

Put you on your knees.

Grab your hair.

Spread your legs.

Taste you, touch you, tell you to fuck my face.

My mind races with images of all we will do, and when he rubs his finger against me, it's sweet agony. I am burning all over for him, my entire body a delicious ache.

He slides his finger hard inside me, crooking it, and

reaching that spot where he starts to send me over the edge.

"Oh, God. I can't wait much longer."

"It won't be much longer," he says. "Now open your eyes and watch in the mirror."

I do as he says. My hair is a wanton tumble, my shoulders rise and fall, and Davis looks like he wants to consume me.

I can't form words anymore. All I can manage is a loud moan. He strokes me harder, pushing me closer to release, and all the while, he keeps whispering, a low, dirty growl that sends new shivers pulsating through me, as I race to the edge. "The next time you come, I'm going to be inside you," he breathes, his strong arm locking me in place, his steel length pressed hard against my back.

That's all it takes—those dirty, sexy words he whispers to me, for me, about me, and I am lost in this haze of desire he's unleashed in my body. An orgasm careens through me, and I shudder violently against his hand. I'm about to scream, when he clasps his hand over my mouth to muffle my sounds.

"You feel that?" he demands as the waves of pleasure slowly start to fade away. I manage a weak nod, because I am awash in the fog.

"This is only the beginning, Jill."

Then he lets go of my wrists, and I fall into his arms. He catches me, spins me so I'm facing him, then kisses me softly on the forehead. "Do you have any idea how much I love making you come?"

"I think I have a clue," I say, with a happy, woozy smile.

"It is my favorite thing in the world. I love how fearless you are. I love how much you want it. I love the way you let go when I touch you," he says, returning to a tender voice, his lover's voice that melts me even more.

"You should know by now I love everything about the way you touch me," I say, as I loop my arms around him.

"I love the sounds you make, how you smell, the way your body responds to me, and, most of all, how you give yourself over to me. But the reason I love all that is because I'm so fucking crazy about you." Then he stops, takes a beat, and becomes more serious. "Jill, what am I going to do with you?"

"I thought you just told me what you were going to do with me," I tease as I lay my head against his strong chest and adjust my dress.

He cups my chin, so I have to look up at him.

"No. Not that. What am I going to do about the fact that I'm not just falling for you," he says, and his eyes never stray from mine. They hold me tight, and I can't look away, nor do I want to. "I am so completely in love with you that I can't imagine ever being without you."

Time stops in a second, and then it unwinds in a flash. Six years unspool behind me, and my blood goes cold. The floor seems to fall out from under me, and I tumble into the past I've struggled to break free from.

Those same words Aaron said to me. His last words.

I'm barely here anymore. I've been kicked back in time to the moment when I stopped feeling.

Davis presses a finger to my lips. "I have to go back out there and say a few words. Wait for me. I'll have the car meet us at the front in ten minutes, and you'll come home with me, okay?"

I nod, unable to speak, to move.

Because I don't want to be loved like that. I don't want to be loved madly, deeply, and, most of all, I don't want to be loved without reason.

Because I know the outcome.

I know the end, and I'm starting to shut down already.

He presses another kiss against my forehead, but I'm numb, blindsided by his words. The exact same things Aaron said before he killed himself.

Over me.

DAVIS

After I finish, I look for her. She is nowhere to be seen. She's not waiting in the hallway. She's not in the Terrace Room, and I don't see her in the Palm Court. I bump into Shelby as she's heading back inside.

"Shelby, have you seen Jill?"

"She ran out of here five minutes ago. She said she had a horrible headache and had to go. And she asked me to let you know for some reason," Shelby says, then shrugs as if she's not entirely sure why Jill would want to pass that message on to me.

"Thanks for letting me know," I say, wishing my heart weren't beating fast with worry. But I already know Jill's done it. The thing she said she wouldn't do. *Run.*

Shelby returns to the Terrace Room, and I'm alone in the hall briefly and I clench my fists then push my hand roughly through my hair.

"Fuck," I say under my breath, and turn toward the wall, wishing it were a punching bag and I could slam it

several times. I should have known better. I should
have known it would be too soon for her. That she'd
need to take it slow. But hell, I thought she was right
there with me. I could have sworn she was feeling the
same things. She nearly said as much when we danced.
I grab my phone from my pocket, but as I'm about to
call her, I spot my sister walking toward me, her head
cocked to the side in question. "What happened?"

"Nothing," I answer gruffly. I don't want to get into it
with her, given how she tried to stage an intervention
earlier.

She tilts her head to the side, her eyes demanding
an answer.

"She left, okay?" I admit because Michelle would
pry it out of me soon enough.

"She left?" Her voice wavers.

"Yes. And would you like to tell me why you told
her to stay away?"

Now she's steely again as she places a hand on my
arm. "You know why, and I don't regret it."

I shrug off her hand and stare hard into her eyes.
"What. Did. You. Tell. Her?"

Her lips are pressed together, her jaw is set. She is
the most determined person I've ever met. "I told her
not to play with your heart," she says with a fierce
protectiveness.

"And what exactly does that mean?" My entire body
tenses, bracing for words I'm sure I don't want to hear.
"You need to tell me exactly what you said."

She sighs heavily, as if this pains her as much as it
pains me. "I told her if she wasn't serious about you,

that she should leave. That if she was making some kind of career move or using you that she should get out," she tells me, and it feels as if she reached her hands into my chest, grabbed my heart, and squeezed. I can't breathe. There's a vise around me.

I drop my face into my hands, shaking my head over and over. "No. That's not what you said. Please tell me that's not what you said."

She wraps her arms around me, and whispers in a soft, caring voice, "I'm so sorry."

But she's not sorry for what she said. She's sorry for me. And she should be, because she was right. She was right when she warned me at our dinner. Because this is Madeline all over again.

I knew better. I fucking knew how this would end, and I did it anyway, against all my better judgment. I took a chance and chucked all my rules for Jill. And for what? To have her turn out to be like the last actress I fell for. Damn all the fucking actresses in the world who love playing pretend more than anything. Who put their careers first. Who move on to the next job without even looking behind at the people they discard.

I thought Jill was different, but really that was a stupid hope, because she did exactly what my sister asked her to do.

Leave if she didn't feel the same.

I hate that I'm standing in this hotel with my sister hugging me, while the woman who doesn't love me enough is gone. I hate everything about this, and I can't stand to be here another second.

"I need to go."

"I'm coming with you," Michelle says.

And that seems fitting. It's been the two of us for the longest time, and we have to look out for each other. Because no one else will.

I turn off my phone on the way to the car. She's not going to call, anyway, so there's no point in leaving it on. The driver holds open the door and Michelle slides in first. I follow, though I'd rather another woman be the one joining me as the driver pulls out into the late-night traffic by the hotel.

I groan and bang my head several times against the back of the seat as I bite off a string of curse words. "This wasn't how this evening was supposed to go," I mutter, loosening my bow tie as we drive along Fifth Avenue.

Michelle rubs her hand gently along my arm. "I know. But this is for the best. You know that, right?"

I nod. "Yeah."

"It's better that it ended now than later," she continues, and I'm reminded of why she's good at her job as a shrink, because she knows what to say. She knows what people need.

"I know," I say with a heavy sigh.

"Why don't we go somewhere and get a drink?"

"I cannot think of a better thing to do right now. I need a whole fucking bottle, in fact."

"Then a bottle it is." She leans forward and gives the driver the address of a bar a few blocks away. Then she says to me, "Good thing I know all the best places in Manhattan for drinking and eating. This is the perfect spot to forget about a girl. Want me to call Clay to join us?"

"Let's make it a party," I say dryly, and she calls Clay and tells him his presence is required. I text Ryder, and he says he's on his way.

Soon we pull up to the Last Stand on Lexington, and the name is apropos. I toss my bow tie and jacket on the seat of the car, unbutton the top two buttons on my shirt and head inside with my sister.

The Last Stand is like a railroad compartment, long, narrow, and all bar. There are no cozy booths for intimate encounters, or low-lit nooks where you'd take someone you'd want to touch under the table. This watering hole has one purpose—to get smashed.

"Glenlivet?" Michelle asks.

"Fuck Glenlivet. I'll take a Macallan tonight." I don't need anything to remind me of *her*.

Clay joins us, along with Ryder, and it's scotch all around.

"Only the strong stuff for times like these," Ryder says, handing me a shot, and the man knows what it's like to be pummeled by love.

"Times like these can fuck off," I say, then down a shot.

"I'll second that," he says, finishing his.

My sister and Clay follow suit.

It feels right to be with these three people right now. People I know, people I trust. Soon, I've downed my third glass, and my head is feeling fuzzy, and the vise around my heart is starting to loosen as we drink and talk about everything except show business.

Later, *much later*, the bartender says it's last call and far be it from me to deny the Last Stand another chance to pour another drink. We finish off a final round and stumble out into the middle of the night.

"You guys take my car uptown. I'm going to take the subway."

Michelle raises an eyebrow. "In your state?"

"The subway was made for times like this."

On the train, there's a woman in a nurse's uniform dozing off a few seats away, a hipster in a hoodie listening to music on his phone, and a skinny guy weaving down the car who's probably had more drinks than I have. I slump in my seat, the guy in the tux who spoke at the Plaza, who dedicated a song to an actress.

Who's heading home well past midnight, in a lonely subway car.

It's better this way. It's better this way. It's better this way.

I repeat that all night long as I sleep fitfully. I say it over and over in the morning as I run along the West Side Bike Path. I mutter it under my breath as I head over to Central Park.

This is who I am. I am a girl who runs, and today some of the ladies I coach are running a half-marathon so I am here to cheer them on. I blot out the fact that they didn't expect to see me at the finish line. I told them I had an event the night before but would be rooting for them from far away. But this is where I should be because there's no room in my life for anything more. There's no room in my heart for Davis, or Patrick, or anyone.

And when I'm alone, I can't hurt anyone again.

As the first of my gals cross the finish line, I raise an arm in the air and cheer wildly, as loud as I possibly can. I jump up and down to prove how goddamn happy I am. She sees me and smiles broadly.

"You did it!"

She jogs over to me and collapses into my arms, and I hug her.

"I'm so happy for you," I say, because I am. I am happy, I am happy, I am happy.

This is my life. This is safe. Running.

But after they've all crossed the finish line, and celebrated, and had their pictures taken, and high-fived each other, they disperse. Heading home to families. Heading elsewhere. And I'm alone, with this bruised and worn-out heart.

I leave the park, and though I'm tempted to walk past the Plaza, what would be the point? I can't have him, I can't have us, and I can't bear the reminder, so I walk down Broadway, thinking that I could get lost in the theater district, I could buy a ticket, catch a matinee, and let myself *believe* that the razzle-dazzle of *Chicago* or the underground lake in *Phantom* could take all my cares away. I make a go of it. I buy a nosebleed seat for the matinee of *The Lion King,* since it's as far from my life as a show can be.

For a few hours, I forget about the past. But when the curtain rises and the actors take their bows, I remember that I've been there, done that, and still have the empty space in my chest that my tricks and techniques can't fix.

I leave and wander downtown, check my phone once, but he hasn't called, and he hasn't texted. Not that I expect him to either. He's not a texter, and I don't deserve a call.

I don't deserve him.

There is nothing left to save me from what I did this time. By tomorrow I'll have to woman up and say I'm sorry, but I won't be able to explain, because I never have been able to explain it. To talk about it.

I return to my apartment. It's early evening now, and Kat is curled up on the couch watching *You've Got Mail*, one of her favorite movies. One she made me watch a year ago, and I fell in love with it too.

"Bryan's out of town for the weekend," she says, patting the couch. "Come join me."

I shake my head. "I'm tired."

She hits pause on the laptop, and eyes me up and down, taking in my fleece jacket and running pants. It occurs to me that I went to the theater dressed like this. It also occurs to me that I don't care.

"Have you been running all day long?"

"Something like that."

"Hey, you don't seem like yourself. What's going on?"

"Nothing."

"I don't believe you, Jill." She sits up straighter and asks, "Did something happen with Davis at the gala last night?"

I flinch, but then turn stoic. "No. Nothing happened. It was fine. We had a fine time. I'm beat though. I need to go nap."

I don't nap. I shower, put on pajama bottoms and a T-shirt and settle into my room. I read Aaron's last letter again and again.

30

DAVIS

The punching bag swings wildly after my final hit. I've been pummeling it for the last hour, but as I unwrap my hands, zip up my sweatshirt, and leave the gym, I feel as if I'm the one who's been pummeled.

I've somehow made it through the day though, and each one that follows will be easier. I return to my loft, strip off my gym clothes and take a long, hot shower, washing away the remains of the day.

I pull on jeans and a casual button-down, but don't tuck it in, then find my phone and dial the nearby Chinese takeout. I place an order, but when I hang up something feels eerily familiar and I can't quite place it. I furrow my brow, trying to pull the memory to the surface. Then it's there as I flash back to a few nights ago. When Jill said Chinese takeout was her favorite food. When she *also* said she thought about us so much it scared her. Then I remember last night on the dance floor when she very nearly told me how she felt.

"Do you think everyone knows?"

"*Knows what?*"

"*How we feel.*"

Those words echo loudly, clanging in my head, reverberating around my whole apartment. Like neon lights blaring on. Like a goddamn marquee in Times Square. The sign that was in front of me the whole time, but I didn't see it until now.

We.

How we feel.

I rewind the night once more to be sure, replaying every moment with her, every word, every second. Then farther back to the diner when she told me she wasn't going to spend time with Patrick anymore, then to the restaurant when she told me about the last guy she was with.

How she hurt him.

I've always sensed she's hiding something, hiding her true self. I've always believed she wants to be seen, wants to be understood, wants to be known. And now, twenty-four hours after she ran away from me, my gut is finally talking to me, and it's telling me there's something else going on.

I've always known when she's acting. She wasn't acting with me.

Jill wasn't using me, I was never a career move for her, and Michelle's advice isn't the reason she took off last night. When she bolted, it wasn't about me, or us, or what's been happening over the last several weeks. It was something that goes back much farther for her. It's about her, and it's about why she hasn't been close to anyone in a long time.

Whatever it is, I'm not walking away without understanding her.

I reach for my wallet, slip on a pair of shoes, and grab a jacket. Outside, I hail a cab, and on the ride, I call the Chinese takeout and cancel my order. I don't call Jill because I don't want to talk to her on the phone. I want to see her in person.

Soon, the taxi pulls up to her building in Chelsea, and I'm at the door in seconds, pressing the buzzer.

"Hello?"

It's not Jill's voice.

"Hi. I'm looking for Jill. This is Davis –"

But I don't even finish. The door buzzes, and a voice calls out through the speaker, "Second floor."

I realize I don't know the apartment number, but I don't need it. When I reach the second floor, there's a woman with light brown hair holding open a yellow door.

"I'm Kat," she says and extends a hand, and it's weird that we're shaking hands at a time like this. But formalities still exist even when the woman you love is running from the world.

"Davis Milo," I say. "But you knew that, evidently."

"I had a feeling you might be coming. Come in." She ushers me inside, and it's strange to get a glimpse of Jill's life and where she lives. I survey the living room with its old beat-up couch, a coffee table with a silver laptop on it, several necklaces, and a vase of flowers. On the wall are framed posters of Paris and a photograph of the first woman to run the Boston Marathon.

"She's kind of a wreck right now," Kat adds, then

gestures for me to follow her down the hall. "She didn't really feel like talking to me. But I have a feeling she probably wants to see you."

I stop walking. "Really?"

Kat nods. "She likes you. A lot. And I've never seen her like this. She's usually the happiest person in the world."

I nod but say nothing. Because she can be the happiest person, and she can also be the saddest.

Kat knocks on the door to Jill's room, and I wait, more nervous than I've ever been. Because I don't know what to expect.

"Come in." Her voice is empty, devoid of any emotion.

Kat opens the door, lets me in, and closes it behind me, leaving us alone.

Jill's sitting cross-legged on her bed, wearing pajama bottoms and a T-shirt. Her hair is pulled into a high ponytail and her face is scrubbed free of makeup. She's clutching a letter in one hand. Next to her on the red comforter is an open brown box that seems to hold mementos, photos, and letters.

"You're here," she says in a monotone.

"I'm here," I say, and I have no idea if she wants me to stay or to go.

"My brother's coming to town tomorrow," she says in the same dead voice.

"He is?"

I lean against the closed door. I haven't been invited in, technically, so I don't want to sit next to her, even though all I want is to be with her. What I really want to ask is what the fuck is wrong, and why she ran out, and when is she going to tell me what the hell is going on in her head. But the moment is a delicate one, and she's not truly present. She's someplace else, and I have to find a way to bring her back.

"I can't wait to see him. He's so happy. He met this woman. They're perfect for each other." She still doesn't look at me. "They're happy," she says in a barren voice. "He's so happy with McKenna. And Reeve is with Sutton. And then, look at Kat. She's so happy it's like she has extra servings."

She lifts her eyes to me, and I've never seen her so heartbroken. Even in all the scenes she's played where Ava is bereft, she has never looked this ruined. My heart pounds with the fear that I've lost her. That she's completely slipping away. Still, I have to ask.

"Are you happy?" I brace myself for whatever she might answer. "*Were* you happy?"

She just shrugs, jutting up her shoulders, and grips the letter tighter. "How can I be? I can't be happy. I can't be happy because of this. Don't you understand? Don't you get it? It's not possible. I can't have this," she says, gesturing from her to me, the look in her beautiful eyes so immensely sad. This isn't the woman I know. But this is the woman I fell in love with, and I want to do everything I can for her.

"Can't have what, Jill?" I take a tentative step toward her bed, and when she doesn't recoil, I take another, then sit on the corner of her bed.

"This. You. Us." She says each word like she's biting off something bitter.

"Why?"

"Because I'm damaged. Because I'm broken. Because nothing good can come from being with me," she says, her voice breaking, tears welling up in her eyes. She thrusts the note at me.

"Do you want me to read it?" I ask her, carefully.

"Yes."

I unfold the note, worn at the folds, with tattered edges and thinning paper. It's a short note, on a sheet of lined notebook paper, written in blue ink with slanted, choppy handwriting.

Dear Jill,

I guess I always knew I loved you more. Somehow, I knew I loved you more than you'd ever love me. But I learned to live with it. I was okay with it just to be with this girl I was crazy about. And then you broke my fucking heart when you left me. You just ripped me apart and for no good reason. I don't get it. I've tried everything to get you back, and all you do is tell me to leave you alone. You tell me to stop calling, stop talking to you. Well, you'll get what you want now. You'll get everything you ever wanted, and all I ever wanted was you. I can't imagine being without you, but I am, so I'll stop imagining.

I'm outta here.

Aaron

In an instant, I understand everything about her.

31

JILL

Nothing hurts anymore. Because I won't let it. I can't let it. I can't stand *feeling*.

But then he lays the letter on the bed and looks at me with such care in his eyes.

"Jill," he says, softly. "It's not your fault."

"IT. IS!" I shout and I push my hands into my hair, holding tight and hard to my scalp. "It is my fault. It's there. In writing. In black and white. Letters don't lie. I got this after the funeral. One day later in the mail. I'd sat there in the cemetery, my brothers next to me, my parents there. We all knew him. He was my high school boyfriend, and he killed himself. Because of me."

"It's terrible, and it's tragic, and I'm so sorry he made that choice, and I'm sorry for him, and for his family to have to live with that. But you didn't cause it."

"But I did! He said I did! I broke up with him three months before it happened. Because I didn't love him." I hold my hands out wide, balling my fists in my frustration. "That was the problem. If I had loved him like he loved me, this would never have happened. But I didn't feel the way he did. And I ended it, but he kept coming around, and he got crazier and needier, telling me he couldn't live without me, and he would track me down after school, and he would find me after cross-country. And I kept pushing him away. I even met him at the bridge in Prospect Park to ask him to please stop. But he wouldn't. He kept showing up. And he started freaking me out, so I went to tell his parents. I told them what he was doing, and the things he was saying, and how scared I was for him." There are potholes in my voice as I recount the story, the day I will never forget.

Aaron had left me another note, and the tone had grown more desperate, ending with, *I don't know what I have to do for you to love me again . . .*

Those words had sent a ripple of fear through me when I found the slip of paper in my locker in the morning. My hands shook as I read the note, and my heart beat wildly out of control with worry, like a deer trying to cross a congested highway, not knowing which way to go. The bell had rung for first period, but I stayed frozen in place, my mind racing with what to do next. As the halls thinned, I turned on my heel and headed straight for the guidance counselor's office. Because that's what you're taught to do. *Say something.* But she was out sick that day, so when Aaron wasn't at swim practice after school, I walked to his house, knocked with nervous fingers, then stepped inside when his parents answered the door.

I tried to explain what was going on. But I didn't

even truly know. Aaron had never threatened to take his life. He'd never hinted that he'd had enough of this world. But his behavior had grown so erratic, so confusing, that I had to let someone know about the notes, about the calls, about the desperate ways he kept trying to get my attention.

"I'm worried about him," I said in a small voice as I picked at the worn cuticles on my hand. "I don't know what's going on, but he doesn't seem like himself."

His mom gave me a sympathetic smile, as if I were overreacting.

Now, I look at Davis, and he's listening, patiently letting me tell the story. "And you know what they said when I told them that?"

He shakes his head. "No, what did they say?"

I take a deep breath, steeling myself. I've never said these words out loud. I've never told anyone that I warned Aaron's parents. That I was terrified he was depressed and would do something to hurt himself. That he needed help, someone to talk to. "They said he was just a heartbroken teen." I press my lips together, trying to stem the tears, the lump in my throat, the stinging in my eyes. "That's what they said. That he was just still wrecked over me. And that he'd be fine. And then, three days later, he took an overdose of pills."

"Oh, Jill. I'm so sorry for your friend," he says, and he reaches across the bed, but doesn't take my hand. Just rests his near mine. All he wants is to comfort me, but I don't deserve it. I swipe a hand across my cheek.

"He's gone. He's gone because I didn't love him enough."

"No," Davis says firmly. "No. That's not why he's gone. He's gone because he had an illness. He's gone because he needed help, and he didn't get it. He's gone because there were other things at play in his head, and in his heart. He's not gone because of you. You did everything you could."

"But it wasn't enough!" I shout and slam my fist into the bed. Then in a low voice, laced with pain, "It wasn't enough."

He inches closer. "And it might not ever have been enough. You might have knocked on their door and warned them every day. And it still might have happened. I'm not blaming them, no one's to blame. But you tried, and they didn't see what was happening. Even if they did, they might not have been able to stop it. That's the absolute tragedy of all of this. Far too many people feel things only inside themselves," he says, and he taps on his chest to make his point. "And they don't share it. He was going through something awful, and he didn't know what to do. And now you are. And you've been beating yourself up for years over this, haven't you?"

I sigh, a long, low keening sigh full of years of regret. "Yes," I whisper.

"But you have to let it go. You have to move on." He reaches for my hand, and I hate and I love that any contact with him is what I need. I hate it because I can't rely on anyone. And I love it because I *want* to rely on him. I let him take my hand, and when he does, I don't feel numb anymore. I scoot forward and throw my arms around him, bury my head in his chest, and let all the unshed tears fall, until his shirt is streaked with my regret.

"You have to forgive yourself," he whispers as he holds me tight, rocking me gently. "Life is tragic. I know that firsthand. But *things* happen. And this happened. And all you can do is keep on living, because you did everything you could. And sometimes everything you can do still isn't enough, but that's life. And that's death. And that's the way it is."

I squeeze my eyes shut, as if I can hold in the one thing that's still gnawing away at my heart. "But what if I can't love you like that? What if I can't love you enough? What if it happens again?"

He places his fingers under my chin and makes me look at him. "I'm not going anywhere," he says, the slightest trace of a smile on his face. "Jill, when I said I can't imagine being without you, it's a figure of speech. It's because I don't *want* to be without you. It's not because I'm going to kill myself if I can't. I like myself too much. Trust me, I won't go quietly from this lifetime. I will be kicking and screaming. I will be fighting and working and loving until my last dying day. I want you, and I want you to be mine. But you have to know I only want you if I can have you, all of you. I want your body, and I want your heart, and I want your mind, and I hope you feel the same," he says, then takes a beat to make sure I'm still here, still listening.

I hold his gaze, and he keeps going. "But if you don't, I'll go on. You don't have to love me from afar so you won't get hurt, or so you won't hurt me." He talks to me in the most tender, gentle voice, but it cuts through all my defenses and walls. "Because we *will* hurt each other, and we will fight, and we will argue. And sometimes it'll be less than perfect. But it'll be real. Every second of it will be completely real."

Real.

That word echoes in my mind and my body and all the way through to my frozen, make-believe heart that's been on standstill for six long years. That's been protecting me, and saving me from the possibility of heartbreak, the possibility of pain. But Davis is right. I did everything I could, and I can't keep punishing myself with an artificial life. I might do it on stage, but I don't want that when the curtain falls. I want a real life, and real love, and real pain.

I fidget with the collar on his shirt, then play with the top button. I am all nerves, but also determination as I let go and place my hands on his cheeks, looking at him. My throat feels dry and raspy, and no amount of acting, or singing, or running has ever prepared me for what I'm about to say. I'm improvising, going completely off-script, as I speak from the heart.

"I think I'm in love with you too," I whisper.

He plays with a strand of my hair as he raises an eyebrow. "You think?"

I nod and manage a smile. "Fine," I say in a begrudging voice. "I *know*."

Then I wrap my arms around him and everything —Every. Single. Thing—about this moment hurts and feels right at the same time.

"Will you spend the night?" I ask. "But just to sleep. That's all I can do right now."

"Of course."

I undo my ponytail as he takes off his shirt and jeans and leaves them on a chair in the corner of my room. He's wearing only snug black boxer briefs, and even though I've been so ready to get him undressed, there's a different reason tonight. I need to feel the connection between us—his warm body next to mine, skin against skin, as he joins me under the covers, holding me close all through the night.

32

JILL

"I like your casual shirt, but you looked pretty good the other night in a tux too," I say as Davis buttons his shirt the next morning. "I don't think anyone has ever looked so good in a tux before."

"Because it's tailored for me," he says with a sly smile.

I pretend to smack my forehead. "Of course," I say and roll my eyes playfully. "Of course you own a tux."

"What? You think I'd rent one?"

I shake my head and laugh. "God forbid." I watch him as he tucks his shirt into his jeans. "I'm really glad you came here last night."

He smiles softly. "Me too."

"I mean it," I say in a firm voice, as if I'm giving a speech. One that comes straight from the heart. "I don't know what I would have done without you. I was lost. I was totally lost, and I had no idea how much I needed you until you walked through my door. I'm so glad you found me."

"You weren't that hard to find. I knew your address," he says and cups my chin tenderly.

I shake my head, giving him a fierce stare, my eyes blazing. "I know, but that's not what I mean. What I mean is thank you for not giving up on me." I grab his shirt and grip it tightly for emphasis. "Thank you for knowing me better than I know myself. Thank you for not letting me slip away. Because I am so in love with you. I am so completely in love with you."

He pulls me close and wraps me in his arms. "That's why I didn't let you slip away. Because you're worth it. You're worth everything to me." Then he bends down to kiss me on the forehead. "But I need to go. I have a meeting."

"On a Sunday?"

He nods. "Yes. Amazingly, I still have to work on Sundays. My lawyer and I are meeting with some producers about doing *Twelfth Night* in London soon."

"Really?"

"They happen to like their Shakespeare across the pond."

"Does that mean you'll be leaving New York soon?" I ask, and my heart's beating faster now. I don't want him to leave when this is starting.

"I don't know. That's what the meeting is about. But if I go to London, I'll return," he says, and curves his hand around my neck. "I won't be able to stay away from you, Jill."

I loop my arms around him. "I feel the same, but I still don't want you to go."

"Would you rather I stay here and do the film?"

I sneer. "No."

"Maybe I'll just do nothing then for a few months. Take some time off. Sit in the park and feed bread-crumbs to the pigeons."

I laugh. "As if you could do nothing." He buttons the second-to-last button on his white shirt. His one-day stubble on his jawline is so sexy. I've never seen him in the morning after he's gone without shaving.

Then I remember something I read in the trades about *Twelfth Night*. "Hey, isn't that actress Joyelle Kristy supposed to be interested in doing the play? I saw her at the gala the other night."

"I'll find out in my meetings today. When will I see you tonight? I believe we have unfinished business," he says, then kisses my neck and I shiver.

"We do. Can I come over after I see my brother?"

"Yes."

I run a hand through his hair. "Can I ask you a question?"

"Of course."

"This is kind of awkward, but I figured we should just get it out of the way."

"Why yes. I do require the extra-large condoms," he says.

I swat his arm playfully. "Hey! How did you know what I was going to ask?"

"Lucky guess."

"But it's on that subject," I say tentatively at first, but then I just rip off the Band-Aid. "Here's the deal. I haven't been with anyone in years, as you know. And

I'm clean. And I'm also on the pill. So what I'm asking is—"

He answers quickly. "Yes. I'm clean. So are you saying . . .?" He lets his voice trail off.

I nod. "I don't want any barriers."

He presses me against his body. "God, how am I going to get through these meetings today?"

I fling a hand over my eyes dramatically when I walk into Wendy's Diner and see Chris.

"Don't even tell me. No. Don't even tell me you are actually playing Qbert on your phone."

My brother gives me a sheepish grin, tosses his phone onto the table, and stands up to wrap me in a huge hug. "What can I say? I like Qbert. And I have to keep up my skills so I can always stay ahead of my fiancée."

"As if anyone can ever beat you in a game, even McKenna," I say, and then hug him back harder. "I miss you, you knucklehead. Why do you have to live so freaking far away?"

We pull apart, and I sit down across from him. Chris flashes his signature smile, all gleaming white teeth and twinkling green eyes. He shrugs. "I hate the cold. Speaking of, what the hell? How do you survive in this weather? It's like thirty degrees out."

"That's nothing. Some days, it gets as cold as—gasp —five degrees."

He pretends to shiver. "Brutal. Can't believe I ever lived here."

"Want pancakes?"

"Always."

We order and spend the next thirty minutes catching up. I learn that things are going so fabulously with McKenna that he's even taught her dog to surf, and he shows me a picture of the blond lab-husky mix riding a wave on a banana yellow surfboard.

"Damn. And I thought it was impressive when you built that treehouse when we were twelve. But a surfing dog?"

"I know," he jokes. "Some days I amaze myself."

"So how's your woman?"

He blushes for a second or two, and I point a finger at him. "You still haven't gotten over that blushing thing you do?"

"You do it too!"

"Yeah, but I'm a girl."

"Don't make me put you in a chokehold."

"Ha. I learned how to get out of them like a ninja."

"Yeah, you learned from the best. Me. Anyway, she's great. I'm crazy about her."

"I'm so glad you found her."

When we finish with breakfast, I take a deep breath. I can't only tell Davis all my secrets. I have to be open with my family. With my brother. Because I want to have the kind of relationship with him where I'm not harboring lies and secrets.

"There's something I want to tell you."

Then I tell him all the things I never said to him when I was seventeen. His eyes widen with shock when he learns of the letter I received, then he drops his head into his hands when he hears that I kept it with me for years, in its own secret little chamber by my bed. He wraps an arm around me as I share how I felt about myself for all that time. He shakes his head over and over.

"I wish I'd known, Jill. I wish you'd let me help you get through all that."

"I know. Me too."

"But I'm here now. For whatever you need."

"Thank you."

"And I want to help you. I wasn't able to be there when you went through it, but I think there's one more thing you need to do. To finally put everything behind you."

"What is it?"

"Sort of like a memorial. A ceremony. A last goodbye."

"What do you mean?"

He tosses some cash on the table and hands me my coat. "You need to get rid of that letter. You need to set yourself free from the past. Set him free too," he says, softening his tone on the last words.

I balk at the idea initially. The letter is like a part of me; it's been my weight, my debt. "I don't know, Chris."

But he nods, resolute with this plan. "Look, I know it seems scary. But it sounds like it's been haunting you. You carried that letter, slept with it next to you. We need to say goodbye to Aaron and to all the guilt you carried around, okay?"

Haunting me.

He's right. It has haunted me, and I know this is how I can finally forgive myself.

Forty-five minutes later we are in our hometown, the borough of Brooklyn, and Chris is holding my hand as we walk across the cold grass in the cemetery where Aaron was buried. As the wind snaps cold air, I wrap my scarf tighter around my neck. Gravestones stretch far across the hills, row after row of markers, of memories. We find Aaron's headstone, and I kneel down and trace the numbers of the year he died. My chest tightens, and my throat hitches, remembering the good times. I'm glad to see a bouquet of lilies on the ground that must have been left here a few days ago. From someone who still thinks of him. Still cares for him. I add another bouquet, this time leaving forget-me-nots. Because I don't want to forget him, and I don't want him to be forgotten, despite everything that went wrong.

"Goodbye, Aaron," I say, my heart heavy, but this time for the right reasons. This time because I'm not hiding how I'm feeling.

Rising, I reach into my purse, find the letter, and hand it to my brother. It feels like a strange part of me that I'm giving up, but I know I need to let go of those words that I carried around for years like a chain. Just like I had to say goodbye to my ideal of Patrick.

Chris opens a matchbox we picked up at a nearby

deli. He flicks a match across the strip on the front, lighting it. Then he brings the small flame to the corner of the paper, and I watch, solemnly, as the paper curls into the orange light, turning black and becoming ash in my brother's hand. When the flame reaches the final slip of white, Chris flicks his wrist, putting out the match. Then he dusts off the tiny bit of ash in his hands.

And I say a last goodbye to all that I held on to. To all that I don't need anymore.

Later that day, we're in Bryant Park watching some young guys scooter around the library steps when Chris turns to me. "Remember when we rode our scooters to the pizza place we loved?"

"That was the best," I say, and we chat more about how much we liked to ride scooters when we were kids.

We talk about the board games we played and his obsession with vintage games that still runs strong.

We even talk about the San Francisco football team.

It's nothing special but it's wonderful, talking to him like this.

Before we part, I reach into my purse and hand him a book. "I thought you might like this."

"Yes! The new Carl Hiaasen. Awesome!"

I smile, knowing the book has found its proper home.

33

JILL

As the industrial elevator chugs upward, I watch the numbers on the dial trudge closer to his floor. With a loud groan, the elevator settles onto the fifth floor, and I am so jumpy inside that I think my internal organs are conducting an impromptu game of musical chairs. I'm a mix of nerves and excitement as the doors open and I step into a brightly lit hallway with four doors. Each loft must have its own corner view.

I knock on his door and ten seconds later he opens it, and I catch my breath. The ends of his hair are wet, as if he just stepped out of the shower, and he's wearing a gray T-shirt that shows off his strong arms, and jeans that hang so delectably on his hips. His feet are bare. I've never seen him dressed so casually before, and it's yet another look I want to add to the portfolio in my mind of my beautiful man.

"Hi."

"Hi." It's only one word, only one syllable from him, but it is charged. We are both combustible right now.

I quickly scan his loft with its hardwood floors, wide open spaces, exposed brick walls, and windows everywhere. I want to explore every nook and cranny of his home, see what's on the coffee table, and inside the fridge, but that can all wait, because he is all I want right now. "I'm dying to see where you live, but I can't get past how sexy you look right now," I say.

Like I'm operating only on instinct, my hands home in on his midsection, and I inhale sharply when I feel the outlines of his abs beneath his T-shirt. I slide my hands under the cotton fabric, luxuriating in the feel of his firm stomach. He cups my face in his hands and gives me a quick kiss. Then he pulls back. "So, the master bath has two vanities," he says, as if he's a realtor showing me around, then trails off, shutting the door behind us. "Fuck tours. I'll show you around later."

"I missed you today," I whisper.

"You did?"

I nod. "I had a great time with Chris, but I really wanted to see you."

"What am I going to do with this new you? This you who actually says what she feels?"

I freeze up for a moment. "Don't tell me it was all about the chase?"

He shakes his head. "It was all about the prize. It was all about you. I wanted you from the second you stepped onto my stage. But I should be a gentleman and offer you a drink."

"I don't want a drink," I say, and I tip my forehead to the open doorway that leads to his bedroom.

"As you wish," he says, hungrily, as he takes my hand and leads me into his bedroom.

Though I've barely taken a minute to notice any other surroundings, I sure as hell notice the king-size bed, white comforter, and chrome frame, and the huge window that runs floor to ceiling. I wish I could say I hope no one notices us, but I honestly don't care who sees.

His phone plays on the nightstand, and I grin when I hear the music. "Madness" by Muse.

"Did you time that song to be playing for the moment you got me in your bedroom?"

"Maybe I did," he says with a wink, and then stands back to rake his eyes over me, taking in my jeans and black sweater. I know they won't be on me for long. His eyes are darker as he drinks me in, and I watch him as he reacts to me, his breathing intensifying and I haven't even taken a thing off. I don't think I'll ever stop enjoying the way he looks at me, the way his eyes sear into me and he memorizes me with his heated gaze.

I want that from him. I want him to know every part of me by heart, and yet still want to discover me again and again. And I know he wants that too.

"I'm kind of nervous," I admit in a soft voice, unsure where it's coming from.

"Don't be. You're with me. I'll always take care of you." He steps forward, threading his fingers into my hair. I close my eyes and lean into his hands, as he laces them through my long hair. Then he gives a quick gentle tug. I open my eyes, and there's that mischievous expression on his face.

"You're going to have those hands in my hair all night, aren't you?"

"I'm going to have my hands everywhere on you."

"You already have. I think it's my turn to get my hands on you."

I grab the hem of his T-shirt and pull up. He raises his arms, letting me take his shirt off. Sharp, hot tingles race through me as I run my palms over his toned shoulders, cut biceps, and his fabulous forearms that are strong from the workouts he does in his boxing gym. He's such a fascinating man to me—he works in the arts, and he works out with a punching bag. I love the incongruities in him, how he can fit in seamlessly at an elegant reception and how he can hold his own in a rough and tumble world too.

He draws in a deep breath and sighs as I traverse his muscles with my hands, learning how they feel, uncovering the ridges and hard planes of his body. Then my fingertips reach the waistband of his jeans, dancing around the edge, tapping out a fast rhythm of desire.

His breath quickens, he opens his eyes, grabs my hips hard, and slams me against him. "That's enough playing around, Jill. I need to have you now. I've been a very patient man and have been waiting for you long enough."

His eyes flash feral and wild, alive with a masculine power that makes me want to be overtaken. My body aches to be under him, to be filled by him.

He swivels me around, backs me up to the bed. My knees hit the edge and I sink down. He grabs the bottom of my sweater and yanks it off, then reaches around to unhook my bra in seconds flat. He stares hungrily at my breasts, and my nipples harden from how he looks like he wants to taste and lick and touch every inch of me. Then his hands are on my breasts, kneading them, squeezing them. He feathers his hands down my stomach, unzipping my jeans quickly and tugging them off as I kick off my short boots.

He places one hand on my belly, and pushes me down on the bed, then shakes his head appreciatively. "You on my bed. I have wanted this since I met you."

"Really? Did you think about it when I first sang for you?" I scoot back and he climbs up, as if he's prowling his way toward me. I love the way he talks to me during sex, how he's always telling me what he wants to do, and I can't resist going fishing for more of his sexy, dirty mouth. Because it's yet another thing I'd never expect from him. And yet another thing I crave. Those filthy words from this classy man.

"No, back when I saw you in *Les Mis*, I imagined you completely naked in my bed and coming for me. Let's make that happen."

He tugs off my panties, and we're still in this same uneven zone where I'm undressed and he's only halfway there, but hell if I care as he presses his hands on the inside of my thighs, spreads my legs wide open, and brings his lips to where I'm aching for him. One kiss, one lick, and I am inside out with pleasure. I arch my back, lifting my hips to his face, desperate, terribly desperate for more of him as he caresses me with his talented tongue. His lips are so soft and his tongue draws the most delirious lines across me so that my vision goes blurry with the exquisite pleasure surging through my body. I moan and pant and grab hard at his hair, and I can hear him groaning too as he tastes me, licks me, tortures me with that tongue that I want to feel all over me.

His hands grip my ass, and he tugs me even closer to his mouth, like he can't get enough of me, and it's so intimate and intense the way he devours me. I don't need fingers this time, because with one more flick of his tongue against my throbbing center I am his, as the waves of pleasure ripple through me. I call out his name many times over, and I swear I dig my nails into his skull as I come hard and fast.

He layers kisses on my belly and my hips, and my legs are still trembling from the aftershocks. He travels up my body with his mouth, leaving a trail of kisses between my breasts and the hollow of my throat. He has the most satisfied look on his face. "You're like a drug to me. I'm not sure I'll ever be able to get enough of my fix. I'm going to need more and more hits, and even so, I'll only grow more addicted to you."

"Good. I'll be your enabler. I want you to be hooked." I love these words, love the reassurance.

Then he stands, and I push up on my elbows, watching as he unbuttons his jeans. My mouth is literally watering because I want him so badly. I want to see him in all his naked glory, and I watch him strip as if I have a front-row seat to the best show in the house as he takes off his jeans. He's wearing nothing but boxer briefs, and I crawl forward to the edge of the bed, kneel, and push them down.

His erection springs free, thick and hard and completely beautiful. Heat surges through me, and I run my teeth over my lips as I roam my eyes over him. Strong legs, smooth stomach, all those hard lines, leading to the V that draws me back down to what I want most. I take his cock in my hands, thrilled to be touching him without any limits now. He groans and grabs my hand, gripping me tighter around him, moving my palm up and down on his hard length.

"God, it feels so good to have you touching me," he says in a hot, hungry voice because he's held out for so long. His breathing shallows, and he closes his eyes as he rocks into my hand. I don't want to stop touching him, but the need to have him inside of me is immense.

"I want you," I whisper so I can have him between my legs. He inches me back on the bed, lowering himself onto me. I feel him hard against my thigh, and then his hand is on the back of my leg, opening me up, making room as he settles between my legs.

Holding his cock in one hand, he teases me with the head, rubbing himself against me, and I'm going to lose my mind if he doesn't slide inside of me now.

"Please. I want you now," I pant.

"Oh, you're going to have me. You're going to have all of me."

And then he sinks into me. I inhale sharply as he fills me, and he stills. "Does it hurt?" he asks gently.

I nod against him, my hands around his strong, solid shoulders. "I'm just not used to this," I admit.

"I know. I'll be gentle."

"You don't like to be gentle."

"I do with you. I'll be gentle, or I'll be rough. I'll do it however you want or need."

"I just need you."

Then I breathe again, and he brings a hand down to my leg, hitching up my thigh and holding me in place like that, opening me up as he pulls back, then strokes into me again. Slow, gentle, gliding strokes. Filling me up, stretching me, and when he's so far inside me he stops for a beat, brings his hand to my face, and cups my chin, so I'm looking at him, so I have to look deep into his beautiful blue eyes because that's what he wants. He wants to see all of me. To connect with me. To know me.

In all my fantasies, all my imaginary nights of pretending, I never really knew what I was missing. I never understood how out-of-sync my make-believe life was from this real-life, this phenomenally real moment with this man who makes me feel everything, who wants me to feel loved, and cherished, and desired.

"I know what you need right now," he says, and the moment is no longer suspended as he buries himself in me again, and my back bows, inviting him to take me further, to guide my body to wherever he wants it, because he alone has the keys.

"What do I need right now?"

"Wrap your legs around my back as tight as you can. I want to go deeper into you, and I'm going to kiss your neck the way you want me to. *Hard*."

I do as he says, opening myself even farther for him as he thrusts into me. I hook my ankles around him, surrendering to him in that position, to however he wants to fuck me, to make love to me, to bring me to the far edge of pleasure and back again. He bends his head to my neck, kissing me there as he drives inside me again and again, and the feeling of completeness is so astonishing, that I'm both here and lost in the waves of sensation that flood through my veins, as pleasure spins wildly inside me.

"I have wanted you for so long. For so fucking long, and now I have you, and you are completely and absolutely mine," he says with a low growl that somehow makes me hotter, and I didn't think it was possible to feel any more desire than I do right now. But then he thrusts into me again as he reaches his hands into my hair, fisting a handful and tugging, like he's always wanted to.

I arch into him, letting him know I want more.

He kisses me, hard and hungry, his teeth nearly piercing the flesh on my neck, and I cry out from the sensation. It's pleasure and just a touch of pain, but it's a good pain. It's a pain that surges through me, and reminds me I'm alive, I'm here, I'm living every moment. Davis never wanted just part of me. He wouldn't take the half of me I was willing to give anyone else. He wanted all of me, only all of me, and now he has it.

"You have me. You have all of me. You're the only one I want," I say as I thread my hands into his soft hair. I know he knows this. I know he feels it. But I have to voice it. I have to say all these things out loud that I feel for him, because I don't want to keep anything hidden anymore. I want the man I love to know he's the only one.

His body slides against mine, damp with perspiration, and I grab his shoulders, bringing him deeper, wanting all of him.

The world around us dissolves, and this is all there is, this closeness, this far edge of ecstasy. We are lost in each other, and there's nowhere we'd rather be.

I look at him, his eyes open and wild, his lips parted, his breath hard and fast and I'm there in an instant, I'm shattering beneath him once again, writhing and bucking my hips and pulling him deeper with an orgasm that tears through me, and it's all the more intense because he's coming apart with me.

At last.

34

DAVIS

We sleep well, but not much. I wake up in the middle of the night needing more of her, and I pull her against me, spooning her. She sighs sleepily at first, then wakes up, and brings my hand to her breasts and wriggles her backside against me.

"Let's go again," she says, and I am only too happy to oblige as I slide into her, her hot flesh surrounding me. We make love like that, slow and unhurried, and I have plenty of access to her breasts and her belly as she hooks her leg around my thigh, giving me more room to sink into her, in the dark of the night, all of Manhattan sleeping and we're the only ones awake. She moves languidly, wrapping her arm around my neck as I rock into her, and soon her voice is rising, and she's moaning and gasping and crying out, and I will never tire of making her come.

* * *

In the morning I make a quick breakfast of eggs and toast, and then we have to get ready because there are only four days left before opening night.

"I brought a change of clothes. I should probably go shower and get ready," she says.

I look at her as if that's the craziest idea in the world. "No. I don't think that will happen."

She tosses me a curious look. "I'm not allowed to shower here?"

"You're not allowed to shower without me."

I take her into the beige tiled bathroom, and there's room for two. As the steam fills the shower, I rinse the shampoo out of my hair. Then, I feel something absolutely fantastic as Jill's hands run down my chest, my legs, and then she's kneeling, taking me in her mouth, her beautiful lips surrounding me. I look down and groan because there is no hotter sight in the entire world than this. I watch her lips move, and I want to finish this. But I want her too, so I pull her off, grab her hips, and lift her up and against the shower wall, then bring her down on me hard and move inside her fast, furiously, as she grapples with my hair, my shoulders, my back until she comes apart, and I do the same.

Then, we go to work.

35

DAVIS

"This is awful. It's all terribly awful. It's the worst mess I've ever seen."

Alexis stomps her high-heeled foot dramatically down on the floorboards, decked out in Ava's costume for our final dress rehearsal.

"It's not," I assure her. "It's great. It will all be great," I tell her, doing everything I can to keep my cool as she throws her traditional dress rehearsal fit.

"No, it'll be a disaster," she whines, pursing her lips into a pout as if she's going to force herself to cry. "It'll close in eight days."

"Don't say that. Don't ever say that." I cajole her as if I'm talking to a petulant child, but one I need to encourage because that's the only way to end this sort of tantrum, since she's now flung herself dramatically onto the steps that lead to her dressing room. "It's going to be fantastic. Now, come on and let's do the final number."

Her head hangs between her legs in the most

woeful pose. I offer her a hand. "You can do this, Alexis."

She shakes her head and heaves her shoulders. "I need a minute alone."

She retreats up the stairs to her private dressing room, slams the door, and stalls the rehearsal for a full ten minutes as she's locked in there, the rest of the cast waiting for her to deign to return. Shannon gives me a wide-eyed look and taps her watch. *Tick tock.*

I sigh heavily, then march up the steps and knock on the door.

"Alexis, we need to finish up. I know you can do this. I have absolute faith in you."

She opens the door and peeks out, and in a meek voice she says, "You do?"

"Yes, you're Alexis fucking Carbone, for God's sake. Everyone loves you. Now let's finish the rehearsal." I offer her a hand, but instead she flings her arms around me, clasping me tight.

"Thank you. Thank you for believing in me, Davis."

She lets go and flashes me a smile, and as she does, I can smell whiskey on her breath. I roll my eyes when she looks away. She heads down the steps holding the railing, descending as if she's some southern belle at a debutante ball, waving to the cast on stage waiting for her. Then the heel of her shoe hooks into the metal on one of the steps, and in an instant, her leg is bent, and she's grabbing at the railing but missing as she tumbles in a wild mess down the stairs.

The entire theater turns starkly silent for one brief moment, then the quiet is broken with a deafening wail that rings through the house. I rush down the steps and Shannon races to Alexis as the star of the show clutches her knee, shrieking.

An hour later, Shannon calls me from the hospital to tell me Alexis has a torn ACL and will be on crutches for four to six weeks, and out of commission for even longer.

I find Jill in her dressing room, chatting with Shelby, and looking at photos on their phones. I don't smile, I don't laugh. I'm not glad that Alexis is hurt. But it feels a bit like payback, and a lot like karma for Alexis.

I rap my knuckles against the doorframe. Jill looks up. "It appears you'll be opening the show, and starring in it too, for the foreseeable future."

Her eyes go as wide as saucers, and she tries to hold back her glee with little success as I tell her what happened.

"Is she going to be okay?" she asks, and I'm proud of Jill for having the common decency to ask.

"She'll be fine in time. As for now, the show must go on."

36

JILL

I can barely eat the next day, I am so aflutter with nerves. But I force myself to finish off a piece of toast, and Kat brews me tea.

"I believe it's the drink of choice for all the superstar sopranos," Kat says as she hands me a mug.

I take a deep breath, and it's probably the fiftieth or the five hundredth I've had to stop and take today to quell the butterflies. I always knew it was a possibility that I might go on, but I figured it would be a night here, a night there. Not opening night. I drink the tea then grab my purse and head for the door.

"See you after the show? You'll come backstage, right?"

"Like I would miss it." She rolls her eyes. "Get out of here. And I'd tell you to break a leg, but somehow I don't think that's the right thing to say at the moment."

I reach for the door handle, then stop, and turn back. "Kat?"

"Yeah."

"I love you. I just wanted to say it."

"I know, silly. I love you too. I'll be in the third row, and I will be your biggest fan."

"Bye."

Then I leave and I take the subway, because I always imagined when I went to work in my first starring role that I'd take the subway, I'd emerge from the New York underground into the neon and lights and noise in Times Square, and I'd walk purposefully to the theater, head backstage, get into costume, and do a few quick warm-up vocals.

So that's what I do. As Shelby and I run through our exercises I am jittery, I am jumpy, but I am also confident. I've been ready for this since before we even started rehearsals. I know Ava, I know this show inside and out.

I don't take over Alexis's dressing room because that would seem a bit rude. I stay with my chorus girls, because I am still a chorus girl. I'm just the lucky one who gets to swoop in at the last minute.

At six forty-five, Davis comes by to tell us to break a leg. He is business-like and professional, and that's what I would expect.

"You're all going to be great," he says to the group of us, and then tips his forehead to me, then the hallway. I stand up and join him in the hall.

"Do you remember what I said the first night I rehearsed you? How I wanted you to be able to blow the audience away?"

I nod. "I remember everything about that night."

A smile plays on his lips. "Me too," he says in a sexy

voice then he returns to his directorial one. "I told you I wanted them to melt for you. To fall for you."

I nod, eager to hear what's next.

He leans into me, brushes his lips on my forehead. "You've got this, Jill. They will. They will fall for you."

"Thank you," I say, feeling warm and glowy from both the kiss and the praise.

"I'll see you after. We'll go celebrate."

"Of course. But you might have to come to the cast party because, you know," I say, teasing him, "I gotta hang with my actor peeps."

"I would be honored."

Then he heads down the hall on his way to find Patrick and give him a pep talk. A few minutes later Shannon knocks on the door to tell me my brother is here.

Even though I saw Chris a few days ago, I still jump into his arms.

"Hey, little sis."

"Hey, big pain in the ass."

Then I turn to meet McKenna, and she's so pretty and has the coolest dress on—a rockabilly number with dog prints on it. "I can't believe I'm finally meeting you. I've only seen you in your Instagram videos and you're prettier in person."

She blushes. "Stop that."

"No, seriously. I can't believe my brother snagged a fox. How did you trick her, Chris?" I ask, teasing him. Then I lower my voice and whisper to the woman he loves. "I'm so glad he found you. He's mad about you."

"The feeling is completely mutual," she says.

When they return to their seats, I head to the dressing room, where I touch up my makeup, making my mascara pop even more, and then applying lipstick and lip liner. Shelby smooths out my hair for the first scene, pulling it back into a simple ponytail and spraying it.

"I can't resist being the hairstylist," she says happily.

"I love it," I tell her.

Then all of the chorus girls in the dressing room do a few quick yoga stretches to loosen up. When we're done, Shelby grabs my arm as if she forgot something. "We need to go say hello to the ghost," Shelby says excitedly.

"You're right! We have to."

We rush down the red-carpeted hall, pop backstage and wave grandly to the pretend ghost of Hammerstein in the balcony, since he's only here on opening night. I peek at the audience members filing into the theater, thrilling at the sight of them taking their seats, opening their Playbills and seeing *my* name in the white slip of paper that was inserted into the programs tonight.

At tonight's performance, the role of Ava will be played by Jill McCormick.

I take my place in the wings. Shelby grabs my hand hard and squeezes it. "You're going to be great," she whispers.

I nod a quick thanks and when the overture fades, I make my entrance to the stage in front of the packed house at the St. James Theater for my first performance ever in a Broadway show.

It is electrifying.

I spend the next two and a half hours singing and acting and crying and fighting and kissing and falling in love with Paolo. Because that's who Patrick is to me. I leave myself behind, but this time it's as it should be. This is when I can forget who I am and become someone else. Because this kind of pretending is what feeds my heart and my soul as I become this broken-down character who somehow finds a way through her pain and loneliness to the other side.

When we sing the final lines in the final song, and then fall into each other's arms for a last staged kiss, I feel as if I am flying. This is the highest high, and the purest joy I've ever felt—performing and doing what I love with my whole heart.

The curtain falls, and Patrick grabs me for a bear hug. It is a friendly, affable embrace, and then he high-fives me. "I knew we would be great together on stage," he declares with a fist pump.

"It was amazing," I say with a grin as wide as the sky, and maybe that's how Patrick and I were meant to be together—as actors, playing parts, and making the audience believe. Perhaps, that was always what was in the cards for the two of us.

He rushes off to stage left, I head to stage right, and we wait in the wings. I am still riding on the adrenaline and I probably will be for years, as the audience starts cheering and clapping when the curtain rises again. The chorus members rush out to take their bows. Then the supporting actors and featured stars make their way, one by one, to the front of the stage.

The notes to our signature song flood the theater

and I beam at Patrick as we rush out and meet in the middle. He grasps my hand, and we head to the front of the stage and take our bows together.

In the audience, I see Chris and McKenna, Kat and Bryan, Reeve and Sutton, and I wave to them all. The cast links hands together for one more bow as the cheering grows even louder, and we gesture to the orchestra in the pit who played the beautiful score.

Finally, the curtain falls, and I am overcome with emotion. Fat tears slide down my cheeks, but they don't last long when Shelby jumps in my arms.

"You were absolutely amazing! You broke your Broadway cherry! And you did it in a big way!" she says, and I stop crying tears of happiness because now I am laughing. We return to our dressing room, and I'm still floating on this magic carpet ride of the most amazing night of my life as I change out of my costume, pull on jeans and a sweater, and sweep my hair into a loose ponytail.

My friends all stop by for congratulations, and then it's time to hang with the cast.

"Ready for Zane's?"

"Yeah, let me meet you there," I tell Shelby, then pop out of the dressing room to look for Davis. I head down the hallway, but I don't see him anywhere, and even when I peek at the empty stage he's nowhere to be found. I hunt around more, and finally, I leave the stage when I see a handful of people lingering in the now empty seats.

There's Davis's lawyer, Clay, as well as a man in a sharp suit and a woman in black slacks. They look cool and business-like, and Davis is holding court with them. He's leaning against one of the chairs in the front row, his long legs stretched out as they chat.

They must be the *Twelfth Night* producers, and there's a part of me that kind of likes watching him, unseen, as he conducts business and is wooed by the financiers of the theater world who want his talent, his vision, his eye. My lips curve into a grin—that's my man over there, and everyone wants a piece of him, but I get to have him.

A woman walks down the aisle, and I tense. The last time I saw her was at the gala. Only it's not Madeline. It's Joyelle Kristy, the actress who was interested in *Twelfth Night*. She joins the crew, and I tell myself not to be jealous because this is his job, and he will work with many beautiful people over the years, just like my job is sometimes to kiss men on stage and I did that tonight.

But she smiles at him, and it's so unlike the way Madeline looked at him. Madeline was all distance, but Joyelle has this happy, buoyant vibe around her that I can't quite put my finger on. Then, it hits me. She looks like *me* when I first learned I was cast. Like me, she's throwing her arms around Davis, gripping him in a huge hug, and he responds by hugging her back and smiling.

I step back, nearly stumbling. That's how he treated me outside Sardi's. He's interacting the exact same way, and seeing the two of them unleashes a new feeling in me, a foreign feeling. Something I haven't felt before because I haven't loved like this.

The *fear* of us unraveling.

He sees me in the corner of the theater, untangles himself from Joyelle, and gestures to them that he'll be right back.

"You were breathtaking," he says when he reaches me.

"Thank you. What's going on?"

"The *Twelfth Night* producers are here."

I nod a few times, trying to prepare myself for what I know is coming. Him leaving. "So you're taking the job in London?"

"Yeah, I am. But you knew I was leaning toward it."

"And Joyelle? Is she Viola?" I ask, my body flooding with worry that this most wonderful thing could fall apart when a new leading lady walks onto his stage.

"Hey," he says running his thumb along my jawline. "She's just happy she was cast."

"Right," I say with a nod. *Just happy she was cast.* Like I was, and I can see it all unfolding again. He'll be in London, away from me and working with her. She'll have late nights with him. She'll have private rehearsals with him.

"I better let you finish your meeting," I say, as my heart starts to race at a frantic pace, like it's trying to escape from my chest.

"I'll see you at Zane's."

"Yeah," I reply, but I feel completely unmoored as he walks away and rejoins the people he'll be working with next as he moves on from me.

All along, I thought I'd be the one to hurt someone. I'd avoided relationships for that reason. But Davis has my heart, I've given him my most valuable possession, and now he can hurt me too.

I grab my coat and leave the theater, the heavy stage door clanging shut behind me. I button my coat, and head out to Forty-Fourth Street, and am shocked when there are audience members waiting for me, asking me to sign their Playbills. It's thrilling, and I sign several and pose for a few photos too, but when I leave I am awash in stupid worry.

That doubt escalates as I flash back to all the days and nights we spent together. To all the things he said. To how he plays actors like instruments to get the performance he wants. From Patrick to Alexis to me, he knows all the right notes to hit, and he plucks them perfectly, creating the masterpiece he wants from the tools we give him. Ourselves.

I lean against the wall of a nearby apartment building and wrap my arms around myself, as if that can somehow protect me from all these images smashing into my brain and pricking at my heart. I can see him and Joyelle in London, alone in the theater after hours, rehearsing, running lines, digging deep for emotion, connection, passion. I know far too well how easy it is to get swept up. It happened to me. It happened to him.

It happened as he turned me into Ava. All along I never saw that my relationship with him mirrored Paolo's and Ava's. But he broke me down to get the best performance from me, as Paolo does to Ava.

I start walking again, but I'm wrung dry and worn out, and as I enter Zane's I want so desperately to recapture the way I felt many minutes ago on stage, as well as the way I felt all the days before. But it's hard to grasp onto what's real because now I'm sick with worry that the one real thing could slip from my fingers. That he could be far away from me and forget all that we shared.

Inside Zane's, I do what I've always done. What I'm used to. I shuck off the past. I ignore all the things that hurt, that don't make sense, that I don't know how to deal with, as I grab a beer and join Shelby and the others in round after round of endless opening night toasts. As the minutes turn into an hour and he still doesn't arrive, my heart is a brick inside my chest, and I wish I could rip it out, and replace it with a mechanical one, because I think I'd be better off that way.

Better off like I used to be.

Then, like I've been slapped stupid, I pick myself up. Because I wasn't better off. I was acting all the time. I was living a life of pretend. But then he came around, and with him there was never any faking, there was never any make-believe.

I rewind to the night in my bedroom when he listened to me, and he helped me, and he saw me through.

I flash back to the direction he gave me at our first private rehearsal: *"But then she transforms. Love changes her. Love without bounds. Love without reason. She becomes his, and that changes her."*

How I loved the sentiment, how I felt it ring true in every cell in my body, how I longed for it to take shape in my life. I can picture the next scene, I can hear the music swelling, the orchestra growing louder, because this is the moment in the show when the heroine has to face all her fears.

For better or for worse, I need to know.

I grab my coat, my purse, and leave Zane's. I won't sit here and mope, and I definitely won't walk away from this man without trying to protect what's mine with every ounce of my heart and soul.

37

DAVIS

The meeting is taking forever, and I'm antsy and eager to leave. But Clay has made it clear that the producers —Tamara and Carter Shey—like a casual, family atmosphere. They want a director to be involved, to chitchat, to engage in long, deep discussions about Shakespeare. So I hold my own, sharing some of my vision for *Twelfth Night*, and how I want to bring a new take to one of the Bard's most popular plays.

Joyelle is enrapt in my ideas, and at one point, she even bats her eyes and casts me a huge beaming grin that seems a bit too adoring at this point. Or really, at any point.

I look at my watch, and they realize it's nearing midnight.

"I'm so sorry we've kept you so long, but we're thrilled to have you onboard," Tamara says, and shakes my hand.

"There's one thing I'm going to need though to

make this final," I say, then nod to Clay. "He'll let you know what it is because I need to go."

I clap Clay on the back and leave it up to him to work out the most important detail of my contract. "You know what I need," I say as I pull him aside for a brief chat.

"Always do. I'll keep you posted."

"You're heading to San Francisco on the red-eye, right?"

"That's the plan. I've already been instructed by Jill's soon-to-be sister-in-law that I need to meet her sister Julia, who's a bartender there."

I raise an eyebrow. "Then be on your way and meet the bartender. Don't do anything I wouldn't do."

Clay laughs. "Doesn't limit me much, does it?"

I shake my head, say goodbye to the others, grab my jacket, and head down the alley. If I know Jill, she's already starting to worry. I'll have to work on that with her, to reassure her that things don't always unravel. That things can keep getting better.

But I don't have to go to Zane's, because she's walking toward me, marching right up to me. She has the most determined take-no-prisoners look on her face, and her blue eyes are fixed on me. She stops inches from me, reaches for the neck of my shirt, grabbing the fabric. It's not an angry gesture, but a pleading one, matched by her voice when she speaks. "Please tell me you're not going to fall for Joyelle," she says.

I laugh once, shake my head, and clasp my hand over hers, pulling her closer.

"Tell me," she says again, insisting.

"I'm not. That's not even remotely possible."

"Tell me why," she demands.

"Because of you," I say simply. The answer is patently clear to me.

"I need to know you're not going to fall for her. I need to know that if you work late with her, help her become a better Viola, you're only going to think of me," she says, and I can't help but grin.

She points at me, accusingly. "Why are you smiling?"

"Because I love your jealous, possessive side. It's completely endearing."

She narrows her eyes at me. "You haven't answered the question. Are you going to fall for your Viola?"

I shake my head and curve a hand around her neck. "It's impossible."

She leans into me, and her voice softens. "Tell me, Davis. Tell me why it's impossible."

I cup her cheek in my hand and look her in the eyes. "Because she might play Viola, but *you* are my Viola. You are my Ava. You are my Eponine. You are every part ever written, but most of all, you're my Jill, and you're the only woman I want," I tell her, and she closes her eyes briefly and sways toward me. But I'm not done. I have more to say. "I will work with other women and you will be on stage or screen and kiss other men, and we will come back to each other because nobody else can come between us."

Then she melts into me, pressing her body against mine on the streets of Manhattan, outside the St. James Theater, where I first told her on that cold evening that she was in my show. "Do you want to know why I took so long in there? What was so important to me that it kept me away from you on a night like this?"

"What?"

"I told them I would only do *Twelfth Night* if it was worked into my contract that I could come back once a week during rehearsals."

Her eyes widen and sparkle, as if she's filling with happiness. I love that she responds this way. "Really?"

I nod. "Yes. *Really*," I emphasize. "I want to see you. I want to have a future with you. I'm not going to jet off without a way to see you as much as I can."

She shakes her head, as if she's berating herself. "I'm an idiot for doubting you."

"No, you're human. But you've got to realize that even though I might be in London for two months, I'm not going anywhere."

"I love you," she says fiercely, grabbing my shirt again, and fisting the fabric. "I fucking love you so much it hurts. But it's a good hurt, because it makes me feel like I'm alive, and it's not pretend and it's not fake, and I want to keep loving you and trying not to hurt you, but sometimes doing it anyway, and then forgiving, and I want that with you. Only you."

"Good. Now, why don't we skip Zane's, because I think there are other things we should be doing right now."

"What could you possibly have in mind?" she asks playfully as she takes my hand and I hail a taxi.

"Come back to my place and find out," I say, then open the door and let her in first.

And I show her everything I have in mind all night long.

* * *

Later, after a few fantastic rounds in the bedroom, she wraps her arms around my waist in a tight embrace. "Davis, I love you so much. I can't imagine being without you either," she whispers, and I might be the happiest man alive right now.

"Good," I tell her. "Because you won't be."

After a quick bathroom break, I return to the kitchen, and she's made herself at home, perched on a black leather barstool at the counter. She's still wearing her sweater, but nothing on the bottom.

"That's a good look for you," I say. "It'll be even better if you take the top off."

"Consider it done," she says, and pulls off her sweater and bra, and crosses her legs. She looks so unbelievably sexy, all naked and blonde and just-been-fucked, sitting on my barstool, in my kitchen, in my home.

"I have something for you. For us," I say, then open the stainless-steel fridge and remove a bottle of champagne. "To celebrate your first Broadway show. Your first ever performance on the Great White Way."

I pop open the bottle, pour two glasses, and sit down next to her. I hold up a glass to toast. "To many, many more."

"To many more," she repeats, then takes a sip.

I tip my forehead to the stool. "You look good on

that stool. You look good in my home. You should make it yours."

She gives me a curious look, as a grin plays on her lips. "Are you asking me to move in?"

I shrug a shoulder playfully. "You said your room-mate's moving out soon. I figured why not."

"So I should move in since it's hard to find a place in New York?" she jokes.

"That. And because it makes it easier to fuck you, and make love to you, and kiss you, and hold you, and touch you, and be with you," I say, then I pause, taking a beat, so she knows I mean this from the heart. "And because I love you."

She hops off the stool, wraps her arms around me and kisses me wildly, so I take that as a yes.

EPILOGUE

Davis

Four Months Later

In the morning, I go for a run with Ryder. I've got energy to spare today, so we hit the path at dawn.

"Today's the day?" he asks as we pick up the pace.

"It is."

He whistles in appreciation. "Fucking awesome."

"I think so too." I glance over at him. "What about you? Have you still solemnly sworn off love?"

"Love kicked me in the balls once. No need for me to let it happen twice."

"There's really no one you'd even consider dating seriously again? I thought you mentioned a woman at work you had your baby blues on?"

He turns away for a second.

"Ah, so there is someone."

He huffs. "Of course not."

"Liar. Fucking liar."

"She's gorgeous and brilliant and plays a mean game of ping pong," he admits grudgingly.

"Do I get to tell you to be careful now? Or to have some fucking fun?"

He laughs as the sun rises. "That's the question now, isn't it?"

Jill

"You are the most beautiful bride I've ever seen," I say as I hand Kat a tulip bouquet, all in purple, her favorite color.

She whispers a thanks and takes a breath as if she's prepping herself for this momentous step.

"You're not nervous, are you?"

"I've never been more sure of anything in my life."

"Good," I say with a smile.

The string quartet begins Pachelbel's Canon, and that's my cue as the maid of honor to walk down the aisle, a white runner spread out across the lawn at Le Belle Vie, an inn in Mystic, Connecticut, where Kat grew up. It is June, and she and Bryan are getting married outside under the warm afternoon sun on a beautiful blue-sky Saturday, the ocean waves lapping the nearby shore.

When I reach the steps of the gazebo, I take my spot across from the groom and his best man. Bryan looks so handsome in his tux, and so happy as the wedding march begins and Kat walks down the aisle. He only has eyes for her, and she for him, as it should be.

She's radiant, with her hair pinned up in a gorgeous twist, in the perfect dress she found at the bridal shop in the West Village. She reaches the gazebo and stands across from Bryan, and the two of them are so ridiculously happy. I catch a glimpse of Davis in the third row, looking as classy as ever in a button-down shirt and tie that I want to unknot later.

For now, I keep my eyes on the bride and groom as the justice of the peace begins the proceedings.

"Dearly beloved, we are gathered here today to celebrate one of the greatest joys in life and witness the union of Bryan Leighton and Kat Harper in marriage, which is an institution ordained by the state and made honorable by the faithful keeping of good men and women," he says. "Marriage is founded upon sincerity, trust, and mutual love." Then he pauses, as if preparing for a quip. "As well as a mutual love of movies, coffee drinks, and Paris."

I beam, and so does Kat. We know it's true because that's how Kat and Bryan fell in love again.

"Kat and Bryan have a strong and solid foundation. They support each other, they care for each other and, as I understand it, Bryan is quite good at making her laugh."

Now it's Bryan's turn to smile proudly. He won Kat

back into his heart in many ways, but especially because he always made her laugh.

Then the justice of the peace grows more serious. "They are each other's true and forever loves, and today they take that pledge before God, family, and friends." He turns to Bryan. "Do you, Bryan, take Kat to be your lawful wedded wife?"

"I do."

"Will you love, respect, and honor her in all your years together?"

"I will."

Then he turns to Kat.

"Do you, Kat, take Bryan to be your lawful wedded husband?"

"I do," she says.

"Will you love, respect, and honor him in all your years together?"

"I will."

After they exchange rings, the justice of the peace says the words we've all come to hear. "By the power vested in me by the state of Connecticut, I now pronounce you husband and wife. You may kiss the bride."

Bryan steps forward and kisses his new wife, as a tear of happiness slides down my cheek, and I sneak a look at the beautiful man in the third row, who's already looking at me.

* * *

Later, the bride and groom dance as dusk falls, the rest

of us joining them on the dance floor in that kind of hazy, lingering after-the-cake-has-been eaten way as the wedding party winds down.

"I know the bride is supposed to be the most beautiful woman here, but you'll always hold that title for me," Davis says, as he takes me in his arms for a spin on the dance floor. Strings of lights twinkle from the canopy above us. I can smell the saltwater from the lazy ocean waves, rocking the shores gently after twilight.

"As it should be."

"And I suspect you'll be equally stunning tomorrow night on the red carpet," he says. "Have I told you how proud I am of you?"

"Only twenty million times," I say playfully, moving closer to him, because I am unable to stay away. He's been back from London for several weeks now, and I can't get enough of him. Even though I saw him once a week while he was gone, it wasn't nearly enough, and we've been making up for all that lost time. Tonight is my first Saturday evening off since I took over as Ava on opening night. But I have a good understudy in Shelby, and I'm sure she's kicking ass and taking names right now back in Manhattan. The theater will be dark tomorrow night, but Davis and I will be walking the red carpet into Avery Fisher Hall at Lincoln Center for the 68th Annual Tony Awards, since we were both nominated for *Crash the Moon*.

"And I'm proud of you. You're still my favorite director," I say as I play with his collar.

He laughs. "Your *only* director."

"Hey! Just because I'm still working my first job,

doesn't mean I can't have a favorite." Then my hands stray to the buttons on his shirt and I start to fiddle with the top one. As I do, I flash back to our first kiss in his office, to how I couldn't resist touching him then either.

The mood shifts between us as he grips my hand and tugs me tighter against him. His voice is rough and heated. "Jill, when you do that, it makes me want to undress you too."

A ribbon of heat runs through me. "Then we should get out of here because that's my favorite outfit to wear with you—nothing."

After we say our goodbyes, we duck into a town car that will take us all the way back into Manhattan and down to Tribeca where we live. Davis hits the button for the partition. "Such a long ride back to the city. Whatever will we do?" he muses as he fingers the short hem on my black and white dress.

"I have no idea how we could pass the time," I say, as he grabs my hips and shifts me on top of him so I'm straddling him in the car. He brushes his lips against my throat, trailing his tongue between my breasts as he hikes up my skirt.

"Take those off," he tells me, and I quickly shed my panties as he unzips the crisp gray slacks he wore to the wedding. I inch them down his hips, licking my lips reflexively as the boxer briefs slide down too.

Then he grabs me and brings me down on him, and I moan loudly at the delicious feeling of him inside me. I move on him, slowly, taking my time because it's a two-hour ride back to the city, but even so it doesn't take me long because he knows what to do to bring me over the edge. He always has, he always will, and we come together one more time.

Once we reach Manhattan, the car heads down Columbus Avenue and Davis leans forward and lowers the partition to talk to the driver. "Can you make a stop at Lincoln Center?"

"Yes, sir."

I give him a curious look.

"Getting a head start on tomorrow?"

"Perhaps," he says evasively.

When we stop, he opens the door and reaches for my hand. I'm not quite sure what the plan is, but I go along with it, as we head up the steps of the plaza outside Lincoln Center. The fountain shoots sprays of water high above us in a majestic pattern, lit brightly on a summer night. We are surrounded by the ballet, the theater, the orchestra, the opera, and Juilliard. This is the heartbeat of the arts in New York City, and it's always felt like a hamlet to me.

He stops at the fountain and pulls me in close. "I've always wanted to kiss you by the fountains at Lincoln Center. You don't mind, do you?"

"Not at all," I say, as he brushes his lips against mine, kissing me slowly at first, tenderly, then claiming my mouth with his in the way I love, the way that makes me feel like I'm his, because that's all I want to be.

When he breaks the kiss, I am still stunned. Because kisses from him only get better, and I can feel this one in my knees, in my toes, all the way in my fingertips. "You're such a romantic," I tell him.

"You don't know the half of it, Jill," he says with a note of mischief.

"What do you mean?"

"This is what I mean," he says, as he bends down on one knee, reaching for my hand. I gasp when I realize what he's doing. "I fall more madly in love with you every day and it's never going to stop. I want to be with you always, to laugh with you, and work with you, and love you more than any man has ever loved a woman. And when we come here tomorrow night, and walk that red carpet, I don't want to go in as the director and the actress. I want to go in there with you as the man you're going to spend the rest of your life with. Will you marry me?"

I fall to my knees too, wrapping my arms around his neck and kissing him between happy tears and my reply. "Yes, yes, yes," I say as I plant kisses all over his beautiful face. "I don't think I can stop kissing you right now."

"How about for ten seconds so you can let me put this ring on you, then?" he asks with a grin.

"I almost forgot about the ring," I say because I am overcome. I hold out my hand and he slides a gorgeous diamond onto my ring finger. I don't know anything about diamonds, and I can't tell the cut or carats, but I don't care because it's from him, and it's about us, and it's the most beautiful thing I've ever worn. "I love it so much. I love *you* so much. I love being yours."

"You are. Now, and always."

THE END

Interested in Ryder's story? Be sure to check out the smash hit THE KNOCKED UP PLAN! It's an office romance meets baby making story and it'll melt your heart and panties!

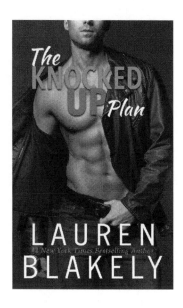

ACKNOWLEDGMENTS

If you see someone struggling with depression, there are resources to turn to. The American Foundation for Suicide Prevention offers a range of resources on risk factors and warning signs, as well as strategies if you are worried about a friend. You can also find resources there on grieving if you've lost someone to suicide, as well as survivor support programs. If you are feeling in crisis yourself, here is the hotline number: 1-800-273-TALK (8255).

On another note, readers often ask about the names of characters in her book and whether any are real. Michael Cerveris and Audra McDonald are indeed two Tony-Award winning performers. Many of the Broadway shows in the story are fictional, created for this story. Wicked, The Lion King, Chicago, Phantom, Les Mis, and Fiddler on the Roof, are, of course, real shows.

I am grateful for the support of so many amazing people. First and foremost, I am in mad love with all my readers. Thank you from the bottom of my heart for making this possible. Abiding thanks to Rosemary, Helen, Lynn, Karen, Virginia, and Janice.

I also owe a thanks to my parents, who introduced me to the theater long ago. Like Jill, the first show I saw was *Fiddler on the Roof* and I fell in love with the theater. I have no talent for the stage, but Broadway remains my first love as a spectator. The inspiration for Patrick's fictional two-day rehearsal for *Wicked* stemmed from Marcus Lovett, who learned the lead role in Carousel on Broadway in a similar time span back in 1994 when the star fell ill. I saw his performance in Carousel—he was magnificent.

Finally, thank you to my friends and family.

ALSO BY LAUREN BLAKELY

FULL PACKAGE, the #1 New York Times Bestselling romantic comedy!

BIG ROCK, the hit New York Times Bestselling standalone romantic comedy!

THE SEXY ONE, a New York Times Bestselling standalone romance!

THE KNOCKED UP PLAN, a multi-week USA Today and Amazon Charts Bestselling standalone romance!

MOST VALUABLE PLAYBOY, a sexy multi-week USA Today Bestselling sports romance! And its companion sports romance, MOST LIKELY TO SCORE!

WANDERLUST, a USA Today Bestselling contemporary romance!

COME AS YOU ARE, a Wall Street Journal and multi-week USA Today Bestselling contemporary romance!

PART-TIME LOVER, a multi-week USA Today Bestselling contemporary romance!

UNBREAK MY HEART, an emotional second chance USA Today Bestselling contemporary romance!

BEST LAID PLANS, a sexy friends-to-lovers USA Today Bestselling romance!

The Heartbreakers! The USA Today and WSJ Bestselling rock star series of standalone!

CONTACT

I love hearing from readers! You can find me on Twitter at LaurenBlakely3, Instagram at LaurenBlakelyBooks, Facebook at LaurenBlakelyBooks, or online at LaurenBlakely.com. You can also email me at laurenblakelybooks@gmail.com

Made in the USA
Columbia, SC
06 June 2020